I0576081

Erased

ANDERS EDWARDS

Echo
Press

Echo Press Publishing

First published by Echo Press Publishing 2025

First edition

ISBN (paperback): 979-8-9924911-1-1
ISBN (hardcover): 979-8-9924911-9-7

Cover art by Driss Chaoui

To my kids and wife who always encourage me to keep going.
This story is just as much yours as mine.

ANDERS EDWARDS

Erased

Echo
Press

Foreword

Dystopian stories are meant to challenge our worldview, to make us question the systems we have come to accept without hesitation. They force us to ask, "How could the world ever be like that?" But life is more of a slippery slope than we realize. Small shifts create a slow unraveling of freedoms until one day, we wake up in a world we no longer recognize.

This story takes place in the year 2123, in what is simply called *the city*. The specifics of government, geography, and nations are irrelevant—what matters is the society that has emerged. A place where progress is measured in optimization, and safety is valued above all else. A world where individual choice has been carefully molded into compliance, where certainty is preferred to freedom.

These values have reshaped life as we know it. Crime is a relic of the past, but so is privacy. Every movement, every transaction, every decision is tracked and analyzed, all under the guise of a better future.

But who defines "better"?

Technology is neither good nor evil; it is the hands that wield it that shape its impact. The people of the city were not forced into this reality overnight—it was a series of choices, small and seemingly rational, that led them here. And now, the question remains: when you live in a world where choice is an illusion, what does it mean to resist?

As you read this story, I encourage you to reflect. Not just on the world of 2123, but on the world we live in now. Progress is inevitable, but it is not always synonymous with freedom. We must always ask: at what cost?

I

Part One

1

Seph

Seph leaned against his desk, his eyes drifting to the large window next to him where the city's skyline loomed. He was sitting in one of his last classes at The Institute before graduating in a few weeks. The city outside seemed worlds away from the lecture on data structures happening in front of him.

"Seph! You've gotta check this out." Callum's voice cut through the haze.

Seph turned to see his friend grinning, holding out his halophone. The clear, glowing screen displayed a graph of biometric data, lines spiking and dipping like a living heartbeat.

Callum's excitement was palpable. "Look at this—my heart rate's been climbing for the past three minutes. I started thinking about our final exam, and the chip sent me a stress warning. Isn't that insane?"

Seph leaned closer, studying the screen. Callum had been one of the latest in their class to get the nano chip implanted. Now, he was still exploring its capabilities, marveling at every new feature. The chip tracked everything: heart rate, hormone levels, sleep patterns, and disease detection. Seph knew that NexTech—the company that made both the nano chip and the software that interpreted its data—was working on even more ways for the nano chip to improve everyday life and he couldn't wait to see what was coming next.

"That's incredible," Seph admitted, his voice tinged with both awe and envy.

The chip's functionality was undeniable, but it wasn't without its controversies. For years, his Aunt June had railed against it, leaving Seph caught in the middle, desperately wanting to fit in but knowing he wasn't able to. His jealousy rose as he watched Callum scroll through the intricate functions on his halophone, now enabled by the power of the nano chip.

"You're next," Callum teased, nudging Seph with his elbow. "You can't dodge it forever. Not in our field."

Seph smiled faintly, but the knot in his stomach grew. Callum wasn't wrong. Seph's future in computer science practically demanded he get the chip. How could he show up to a job interview without it? Companies like NexTech didn't just encourage the chip, they required it.

"I don't know," Seph said, shrugging. "My aunt would lose it if I came home with one of those things."

Callum laughed, scrolling through another set of biometrics. "Bet you'll have one within two months of graduation. You can't even apply to NexTech without it. My cousin said they scan your ID for chip compatibility just to let you into the building."

Seph's smile faded. He could practically hear June's voice arguing with him about the nano chip. But for Seph, who'd grown up dreaming of building the next big thing, it felt like a key—one he needed to unlock the future he wanted.

The classroom's bright lights blinked faintly as the lecture wore on. Mrs. Peterson's voice droned from the front of the room, but Seph's mind wandered. He loved technology, loved the endless possibilities it presented. The nano chip was undeniably the best invention of their time—seeing Callum's real-time biometric data only reinforced that. But the idea of defying June, of ignoring everything she'd taught him, felt like a betrayal.

Callum tapped his halophone, breaking Seph's focus. "You're gonna have to convince her, man. She's stuck in the Stone Age. This is the future. We're already living in it."

Seph didn't respond. He knew Callum was right, but the weight of the decision felt enormous. At nearly seventeen, Seph was on the cusp of graduating with a degree in computer science. In his aunt's day, kids had until college or even after to decide what they wanted to do with their lives, but those days were long gone. School had been compressed into eight years, with students choosing career tracks by the time they reached what was once high school. Most career programs took two to four years, meaning sixteen to eighteen-year-olds now entered the workforce.

It was efficient, practical, and effective … but it also left little room for error. Seph's career—his future—depended on his ability to navigate this transition seamlessly. And the nano chip? That was the next hurdle.

"Class is over," Mrs. Peterson announced, snapping Seph back to the present. Her tone was as flat as her expression.

"Don't forget that your final project is due one week from tomorrow. If you don't already have a rough draft, you're in trouble."

Chairs scraped against the floor as students gathered their things.

Callum slung his bag over his shoulder and grinned at Seph. "Think about it," he said, gesturing to the data still on his halophone. "You'll thank me later."

Seph watched him go, the screen of his own halophone reflecting his disappointment. The world outside the classroom was moving faster than ever, and he felt like he was barely keeping up. The future was here and it wasn't waiting for anyone—least of all him.

Seph quickly got up and dashed to get to the transpo so he could make it home before it got too crowded with the after-work congestion. The transpo was not just his only way to travel; it was the backbone of the city's transportation system, its speed and efficiency reducing the need for individual vehicles on the road. Now, the streets were dominated by sleek transpos, with only a handful of personal vehicles driven by those wealthy enough to afford them. With its aerodynamic design, smooth metallic curves, and whisper-quiet engine, the transpo glided effortlessly through the bustling city.

Inside, Seph was greeted by plush, ergonomic seats and large holographic panels that displayed routes, news, and entertainment. Soft, ambient lighting bathed the cabin, creating a serene and luxurious atmosphere that made every ride feel effortless.

Seph sat down in the first available seat and immediately felt the vibration pick up under his feet. He sensed the gentle rock as they lifted off the ground and zipped over traffic to the next stop. He stared out the window and watched as the transpos glided down the street in perfect synchronization, like skaters tracing effortless patterns on a frozen lake, each movement precise and unbroken. He watched as passengers moved towards the wall of the transpo and watched as the side panels changed to display a personalized experience for the nano chip it sensed. Seph looked around and noticed everyone else watching a video, catching up on messages, or reading news articles. Next to Seph it was blank, yet again, another symbol that reminded him he was missing out. It was moments like these that he felt like a foreigner in his own world.

Before he could dwell too long on his misfortune, he was already at his stop which was two blocks down from his apartment. He lived in an older part of the city, built in a past that had almost been completely replaced by new modular construction. His building looked dated and old, but he also felt at peace every time he saw it. When he retreated inside the walls of his home, there was no more comparing with others, there were no more obvious signs that he was different. He could breathe a sigh of relief and just be.

The sun shone brightly outside as he made his way from the bus stop to his apartment. Kids were playing soccer near the entrance of the building, and an unfamiliar neighbor was shooing away an aggressive salesman. This was about as bad as it got; whether it was day or night, it was easy to feel safe walking home.

Just as he stepped under the archway that covered the entrance of his building he felt a gust of wind over the top of his head as a medic drone whizzed by. Someone's nano chip must have triggered the emergency response drone system that now arrived within thirty seconds of detecting a medical emergency or criminal activity.

Seph headed up the stairs and flung open the door to his apartment, heading straight for the fridge. After he poured a glass of milk he turned around and saw his Aunt June sitting at the dining table, looking stunned.

"Are you okay?" Seph said, observing his aunt's stoic face. Her once-chestnut hair was littered with silver, giving a softness to her complexion.

"It's happening—what I have always feared," she said, her eyes fixed on the wall.

"June, what are you talking about?"

"President Walker gave a public address today… Didn't you see it?" June broke eye contact with the wall and finally looked at Seph. Seph stared at her blankly. She pulled open a video on her halophone. The phone emitted a bright light and projected the recorded image onto the wall in front of them.

"Today, I am proud to announce that eighty-six percent of the adult population has embraced the future by receiving the nano chip," the President began, his tone imbued with a sense of accomplishment. *"This technology has revolutionized our way of life, ensuring unparalleled safety and advancing our healthcare to unprecedented heights. Crime of all types is down to a level that is statistically unmeasurable."*

He paused. *"I understand that there are concerns among those who have yet to receive the chip. Let me be clear: the government will not mandate the nano chip. It remains elective."* President Walker's gaze seemed to reach through the screen, addressing Seph personally. *"However, choosing not to receive the chip means opting out of the safety and benefits it provides. Our banking and healthcare systems will no longer accept any other type of identification. If you choose this path, you must be prepared to live without those amenities.*

"We respect your free will and choice. The government has no intention of pursuing those who choose to live without the NexTech nano chip. Remember, it's a privilege to partake in the advancements we offer. The choice, as always, is yours. There is a two-week grace period for anyone who has yet to receive the nano chip but wants to remain connected to banking and healthcare. Please book your appointment online and that appointment confirmation will allow you to retain access until you have the chip implanted."

Seph pondered the implications of his words. "Why are they cutting off access to healthcare and banking if you don't have the nano chip?" he asked.

"This is what I have been saying for the past ten years... There is more to that nano chip than people realise. Yes, it has done some good things, but I don't trust it. There is something more going on, and I'm not going to subject myself to it," June said defiantly.

"But June, we can't buy groceries if we don't have access to our bank, no one accepts cash anymore. It will be absolutely impossible to live without," Seph replied, trying to reason with his aunt. He just wanted her to see the nano chip for the positives instead of always worrying about the 'what if's.

He'd heard countless lectures over the years about why he needed to resist it, about why they still lived in an old building that hadn't been adapted to the latest smart-home automations. His sympathy for her fears had run out years ago, but June was the only family Seph had. His parents had died when he was younger and June, his mom's sister, became his only caretaker. She was all he had. So as much as his

9

frustration grew with her opinions, he'd always chosen to continue following her rules.

"Seph, I have decided to move out of the city." June replied, her voice carrying a weight that instantly dispelled any doubt. "I'm joining Duke off-grid. I was really hoping it would never come to this, but I can't stay. I will never get the nano chip and be subject to government surveillance."

Duke was June's cousin and even more skeptical about the societal changes than June. He'd moved far out into the mountains several years earlier and a few other family friends had moved out to be near him. June and Seph had visited him but chose not to relocate, until now. June had fallen in love with the simple way of life that resisted technology, but Seph had made it very clear he did not like it. It was like stepping back in time, devoid of all the things he'd begun to love. His heart raced. "Leave? But I thought…"

June interrupted him gently, "I don't have much time. They're tightening their grip and I need to be ahead of it."

"You can't just go!" Seph's shock was turning into frustration. He wished she could just be normal like everyone else.

"I've already set up a decoy appointment for the chip to be installed next week to buy me a few days," June responded calmly. "But at this point, there are a lot of concerning signs that if I wait much longer, I won't be able to get out of the city."

"Why can't we just wait and see how this plays out?" Seph pleaded.

"Seph, I know this is all happening fast, and I should have prepared you ahead of time. But I am giving you a choice to come with me or stay here. If you stay here, you can finish up school and keep the apartment. I can prepay rent so you have time to get a job."

"Wait, so I would live here alone?" Seph was shocked again. He'd never thought of living alone before.

"Yes, but if you do stay, I am not sure how our communication will work. It will be very hard to make contact at least for the first while, but as soon as things settle, I will find a way."

The gravity of June's words sank in. This was it—she was leaving everything behind. She was leaving him behind. She knew he wouldn't agree to go and live with Duke, and perhaps that was why she had never mentioned this plan before. It was clear to Seph she'd been working on this plan for some time.

June stood up and embraced her nephew. Seph let out a big breath and sunk into her arms before watching as she grabbed a suitcase from the closet and started placing things in it.

As Seph glanced around the room, he noticed there were already other boxes packed. He walked into his room and sat down on the end of his bed, a memory flashing through his mind. It was his tenth birthday, celebrated in this very room, where he was surrounded by laughter and love. It felt like a lifetime ago.

"Seph," June called from the living room, her voice breaking his focus. "I need to know if you are coming. If you are, you really need to begin putting your things together."

He nodded, swallowing the lump in his throat. This was more than just leaving; it was abandoning a life they could no longer have. He sat still on his bed until he heard a knock and voices at the front door.

A few minutes later, Duke entered Seph's room. He was a tall, rugged man with a gentle demeanor. "Hey, kid," he said with a warm, albeit sad, smile. "Feels like ages since we last saw you."

"Yeah," Seph replied, forcing a smile. "Been busy with the program, you know."

Riley, Duke's son, walked up behind Duke and gave him a big embrace. Riley was a year younger but somehow looked much older than Seph now. They hadn't seen each other for two years.

Duke clapped Seph on the shoulder. "June doesn't think you want to come with us. But I want you to know, if you change your mind later, we will find a way to come back for you."

Seph looked around his room. "I just … my whole life is here… I want to finish the program. I know you guys are nervous about what may come next with the nano chip, but it's made a lot of things so much better. I want to finish school and see what is next for me here." He looked down, worried they were going to argue with his resistance.

Duke's expression softened. "You'll find your path, Seph. You're one of the smartest guys I know. I don't doubt there are great things ahead for you, and I hope you are right. I hope our fears never come true."

In the living room, June was meticulously checking each bag. She looked up as Seph and Duke entered, her eyes scanning the room, deciding what else needed to be packed.

Seph picked up a small photo frame—the last picture he had of his parents.

June noticed and gave a small nod of approval. "Keep that," she said softly. "You're not coming with us, are you?"

Seph shook his head. It was hard to look her in the eyes, but he also knew he needed to stand by this decision as a man. He couldn't hide behind her anymore. Whether he was right or wrong about everything, this was a defining moment for him. He'd read books when he was younger about teenagers who went off to college, leaving their parents' homes to live in apartments or dorm rooms. He longed for the kind of freedom that came with that coming-of-age transition, but he found himself facing a similar experience with absolutely no preparation. As shocked as he was, he did his best to put on a brave face, one that displayed the confidence he wished he felt, giving his aunt comfort that he was going to be okay on his own.

"I am going to prepay the next nine months of rent. I know you will land a job quickly and if you budget carefully, you can afford this place on your own. Don't move into one of those new buildings, it would be way too invasive. This is one of the few buildings where you still have total privacy inside. No one is tracking you in here and this apartment will be the safest way for us to communicate when we can. Especially if you need help."

Duke pulled something out of his pocket and handed it to Seph. It looked like an old calculator that he'd seen in a museum once. His hand wrapped around the black plastic and he felt its warmth, from being safely held in Duke's pocket. He let his index finger softly run over the buttons and looked up at Duke with a question in his eyes.

"It's an old relic that we have retrofitted for communication purposes," Duke explained. "You won't be able to contact us with it, but if we need to get a message to you, this is how we'll do it. If anyone else stumbles upon it, they will assume it's an old calculator passed down generationally. Keep it in your apartment. IF we need to use it, we will."

"So when do you leave?" Seph asked.

"Now," June said.

Seph blinked, disoriented. The reality of his situation crashing down on him. He was hoping they'd have a few more days, or at least a few more hours. He stood and watched June, Duke, and Riley carry out the rest of June's things to the truck outside. They moved through the apartment like shadows, their movements swift but careful—a choreographed dance of escape.

After they'd gone, Seph stood in the eerie quiet of the apartment, frozen in the moment of their abrupt departure. Dishes lay on the rack, a half-read book on the sofa. A life interrupted.

2

Seph

Since June left, Seph had been living in a fog. He'd sequestered himself to his room for several days to finish his final project. It was the only safe space where he didn't ache from her absence. But now, standing outside the apartment having turned in his project, he was faced with reality: he was now completely on his own. He hesitated, key in hand, before turning the lock. The door creaked open, revealing a space that was familiar yet hauntingly foreign. The air was stale, thick with the silence of June's sudden departure.

Seph's eyes moved across the room, taking in the stillness. Although the furniture was still there and he could still see the space his clutter took, June's things were gone. It was as if someone had selected her belongings, hit the delete button, and she had been erased.

Determined to shake off the unsettling feeling, Seph set to work. He opened the windows, welcoming the rush of city air and its distant murmurs. His movements were methodical and precise as he began to dust, rearrange, and cleanse the space. Each action transformed the apartment from the home he once shared with June into his strategic base for a solitary life ahead.

As he methodically sorted and organized, Seph's thoughts were fixated on the monumental task that lay before him:, graduating and beginning a career. It had all felt important before, but now things were different. As the night wore on and his cleaning was making visual progress, his mind felt clearer. For the first time, his life began to feel purposeful. He didn't think it was a coincidence that he was graduating from The Institute as one of the top of his class with the exact skillset to get a job at NexTech. He'd heard the speeches for years about NexTech looking for top talent and what it took to get hired. He'd never put his name in the mix for those opportunities because they weren't the type of jobs he wanted. But now, that had changed.

As he wiped down the counters of the kitchen, he mentally laid forth his plan. He was going to graduate, acquire the nano chip, get hired at NexTech and find out what was really going on. Not just for June and Duke—he needed to know for himself if the conspiracy theories were true. What was NexTech really doing with the data it collected from each nano chip?

Aside from June and Duke, it seemed that everyone Seph talked to was all for the latest inventions that technology could bring. They felt like all NexTech did was make life better. Could they all really have been blinded by a sinister plan, as June feared? If Seph was going to live in this world of high-tech luxury and keep a relationship with June, he had to find a way to uncover the truth of what was going on. If there was something malicious coming with President Walker's changes, he needed to find out what it was. And with graduation just days away, he had the perfect opportunity to do just that. With his plan cemented in his mind, Seph stepped outside to get food.

Kim Henderson, a kind older neighbor stopped Seph on his way out. "Seph, dear. We were starting to worry about you!" she exclaimed, her expression a mix of relief and concern.

He realized he'd been a hermit over the last few days. "I'm so sorry, Mrs. Henderson. I've been consumed with my final project the past few days. Graduation is next week! June is staying with a relative who needs extra help at home." Seph offered a weak but convincing smile. He knew June didn't want anyone to know why she'd left, but they never had time to discuss her cover story.

"Oh, you poor thing! Well, I'm glad to see you," Kim said, her tone motherly. "Take care of yourself and tell June hello when you talk to her next, okay?"

"Will do, Mrs. Henderson. Thanks," Seph replied, feeling a twinge of guilt for the deception. But he also knew that Mrs. Henderson was the queen of the nosey neighbor club—telling her was just as effective as hanging up a sign. At least this way, no one else would ask him about June's whereabouts. By morning, the whole block would know she was out of town.

Back inside the apartment, Seph turned to his computer. He composed an email to The Institute's career center, explaining his desire to get an application to the NexTech graduate program. He knew the deadline had passed months ago, but was hoping there was still a way in. It was the most competitive job for anyone in the Computer Science program and Seph hadn't been interested until now. He was planning on finding a small startup company where he could really make an impact on something unexplored.

He hit send and the beat of his heart instantly sped up. Every action, every word was now a calculated step in a much larger game—one in which the stakes were higher than they had ever been.

As he settled into the evening, Seph felt a sense of resolve solidifying within him. He was no longer an uncertain young man. In preparing for the days ahead, he had a purpose, a mission, and he was ready to face whatever challenges confronted him in his quest for the truth.

* * *

Seph attended his last formal class before his final exam and graduation. The next day, he would receive the nano chip, a step that felt like both a betrayal to June but a necessary step for his future. In class, Seph pretended to be engrossed in a conversation with his friends, but his tangled mind was elsewhere.

"Man, I am so ready to finally be done with school!" Callum exclaimed.

"Don't get too excited, you still have to pass the final exam," Grace said. "And then the real work begins—getting an actual job."

"Don't suck the joy out of today, Grace. We all can't study twenty hours a day, right, Seph?" Callum teased back.

"Seph doesn't need to study. He always aces everything," Grace said.

"Wait, what?" Seph interjected, finally hearing his name.

"Dude, where is your mind today?" Callum smacked his friend on the back.

"Oh sorry, the pressure of getting a job is starting to get to me."

"You, out of everyone, should have nothing to worry about," Callum said.

"Yeah," Grace said, pointing at Callum, "it is you, that should be worried. No one is going to take into account your hours logged in VRGamer."

Seph forced a laugh. He was used to this banter between Callum and Grace. Callum always used jokes to mask his insecurity and Grace put Callum down, trying to somehow motivate him to work harder. But despite the comfort of their goofing off, Seph was screaming inside, yearning to share his burden. He'd never been one to keep secrets, and for the first time he was realizing how isolating secrets were.

"I'm getting my nano chip next week," he overhead a classmate announce with excitement. "It's going to make things so much easier, right? No more wallets, keys, or forgetting passwords." The group nodded in agreement.

Seph managed a weak smile. "Yeah, it's amazing how far technology has come." He'd been begging for the nano chip for years, but now that he was finally getting it, an uneasy feeling was growing inside him. He tried to shake off the doubts that had been implanted within him by June for so long.

As the day wore on, Seph's sense of isolation deepened. He aced his exams with a mechanical efficiency, his mind barely registering the questions before him.

After class, Seph found a secluded spot on campus. He sat there, alone, trying to process what was going on. He was on the brink of graduation, a milestone that should have been a cause for celebration. Instead, it felt like he was walking towards a precipice. He thought of June, Riley, Duke—and even his parents. He thought of the mission, the need to uncover the truth about NexTech Systems and the nano chip. It was a burden he had chosen to bear, but that didn't make it any easier.

Seph got up, his steps heavy, his heart heavier. Tomorrow, he would be chipped. Tomorrow, he would enter the next phase of his life. He was excited to finally get to experience the nano chip technology that his friends have been bragging about for years. But in the back of his mind was June's voice of concern. Was he wrong to have stayed?

Tonight, he was still just Seph. There was no nano chip in his arm tracking his biometrics, just Seph, alone with his thoughts, fears, and an overwhelming sense of a life divided.

The next morning, Seph sat at his desk, his heart pounding with a mix of anticipation and dread. He turned on his halopad, his fingers hovering over the digital keyboard. His eyes flickered to the clock; it was almost time for his nano chip appointment. But first, he needed to check his email—one last connection to his normal life before crossing the irreversible threshold.

His inbox refreshed, revealing a new message that caught his attention immediately. It was from NexTech, the subject line reading, "*NexTech Interview Confirmation*". Seph's breath hitched. This was it, the opportunity he had been preparing for—the door to the inner workings of the company he wanted to infiltrate. He hadn't realized that one email would move this process along so quickly.

He clicked on the email, his eyes scanning the words. The

appointment was scheduled for the day after graduation, a formal full-day interview to evaluate his candidacy within NexTech's development team.

He quickly responded to the email with confirmation of his attendance and with a deep sigh, Seph closed his laptop. It was time to get the nano chip. He stood up, feeling as though he was stepping out of one life and into another.

Seph entered the clinic, his steps echoing in the silent hallway. It was sterile and impersonal, its walls a stark white. The receptionist greeted him with a practiced smile, leading him to the waiting area.

"Seph Thompson? We're ready for you!" a nurse called out, her voice disrupted the quiet waiting room.

Seph followed her down a narrow corridor to a small room, where a modern chair and an array of medical equipment awaited him. The room was cold, clinical, the air tinged with the scent of antiseptic.

The nurse explained the procedure in a calm, detached tone: "The nano chip implantation is quick and painless. You'll feel a slight pressure, but no pain. The chip will be inserted into your forearm, right here." She pointed to a spot halfway between his wrist and the inside of his elbow.

Seph nodded, his heart racing. He watched as she prepared the injection device, a sleek, metallic instrument about six inches long and two inches wide. Its smooth, silver surface reflected the sterile glow of the clinic lights, appearing as a single, unbroken piece of metal. It looked seamless—until the technician pressed a button on the top. With a faint click, a thick needle slid silently from the tip, its cold, clinical precision sending a wave of nerves up Seph's spine. The reality of what was about to happen hit him. He was about to be permanently marked by the very technology that he both loved and was beginning to question.

"Ready?" the nurse asked, her professional smile unwavering.

Seph took a deep breath, trying to steady his nerves. "Ready," he replied, though his voice betrayed a hint of apprehension.

The nurse pressed the device against his skin. Seph felt a slight pinch followed by a weird sensation of something expanding under his skin. He watched, fascinated and horrified, as the nano chip, no larger than a grain of rice, disappeared into his forearm.

"There, all done," the nurse announced cheerfully.

Seph rubbed his forearm, feeling the tiny bump where the chip now resided. He was surprised it didn't hurt or feel out of place. It was surreal, knowing he was now connected to a vast, unseen network, his movements, his data, all subject to NexTech's artificial-intelligence programs.

"If you have any issues, make sure you get it checked out at a processing center, trying to adjust the chip yourself is dangerous," the nurse said.

"Oh, are issues common?" Seph asked nervously.

"Very rare, but we have to remind everyone because the nano chip is fused to your main artery, the only way to adjust or remove it safely is with special equipment. If you try to remove it yourself, a drone will locate you and take you to a hospital for medical attention, so you don't accidentally bleed out."

"I had no idea," Seph said, still staring at his arm.

"You are now officially part of the NexTech network. All your halophone and personal data is connected to your nano chip and it will function at full capacity immediately. You will get notifications over the next few days, walking you through how to use the digital features … if you don't already know them that is," the nurse concluded with a smile.

Outside of the clinic, everything looked the same, but for Seph, everything had changed. He hopped back onto the transpo and found the first vacant spot next to a display panel. Immediately, for the first time, the wall next to him populated with entertainment personalized to his unique interests. He saw options to find a route to a nearby restaurant, to check his emails, or select from a variety of entertainment sites and blogs he frequented on his halophone.

As the transpo picked up speed, a countdown began next to him that read, *"4 minutes until you are home"*.

Seph spent the rest of the day fixated on every nano chip function and feature he could learn. He was absolutely amazed at all this grain-sized chip could do.

* * *

In the morning, Seph woke up with adrenaline already pumping. It was the morning of his last exam at The Institute. It was a comprehensive evaluation providing a score that would be used when he applied to any computer science job in the future.

The examination hall was a cavernous room lined with rows of computers, each a portal to a test that would determine so much more than just his academic performance. Seph found his assigned station and logged in, his eyes scanning the long list of complex questions that awaited him. The test was a rigorous assessment of his technical and analytical skills, demanding complete focus and precision.

The hours ticked by and the intensity of the exam began to take its toll. Seph's mind started to drift, fatigue clouding his thoughts. He leaned back, rubbing his temples, trying to shake off exhaustion, knowing he should have gone to bed earlier. His anxiety started to spike as he worried what might happen if he failed, if he couldn't get a job, and then couldn't afford rent.

A notification popped up on the exam window reminding him to breathe. His nano chip was obviously integrated into the exam software and sharing data. As he paused to breathe, he let his eyes wander off the screen and it was then that he noticed the raised, red spot on his arm where the nano chip had been implanted. It was the exact reminder that he needed; this wasn't just about getting a good job, this was about getting THE job that would allow him access to the information he needed. This wasn't just about passing a test; it was about securing his place at NexTech Systems, getting one step closer to uncovering the truth.

With renewed determination, Seph bent over his keyboard, his fingers flying over the keys as he tackled each question with renewed vigor.

As soon as Seph finished the last question, a screen popped up saying, *"Exam Complete, please exit the room."* Seph felt an initial sense of relief. This was quickly followed up with an overwhelming sense of concern. Had he done well enough? Was he too distracted? Too tired? What if he didn't score high enough to get into NexTech?

Exiting the exam hall, Seph encountered some of his classmates, fellow test-takers discussing their own experiences.

"How do you think you did?" Callum asked, clapping him on the back.

"It was tough … and longer than I expected. Some of those questions were really out there," Seph said. "What about you?"

"I didn't have to guess on everything, so I'll take that as a win," Callum said, always finding a way to see the positive in every situation. He wasn't known for being the smartest in class.

"Yeah, I had to guess a couple of times," another classmate, Vera, chimed in, shaking her head. "Hope it doesn't hurt my score too much."

Their words were a comfort to Seph. They all shared the same blend of hope and uncertainty, but for him, the stakes felt much higher. This wasn't just about passing or failing; it was about gaining access he desperately needed.

As he walked away from the group, Seph tried to quiet his doubt and focus on what came next: the job interview. It was another hurdle to clear, another test of his ability to navigate. He knew they probably already had his exam score, and unless they cancelled his interview, he was going to remain hopeful that he'd passed it with a high enough score.

He rubbed the spot on his arm where the nano chip had been implanted, a physical reminder of the path he was choosing. The chip was a symbol of his commitment, a constant prod to keep fighting, keep pushing, despite the uncertainty.

3

James

The clock turned over to 10:00am as James Kent leaned back in his office chair, the morning sun filtering through the floor-to-ceiling windows. Outside, the city hummed with life, a sprawling testament to his achievements. From this vantage point on the 67th floor, James could see the parks, schools, and quiet streets—a utopia built on the foundation of his invention: the nano chip.

The office itself was a monument to his success. Shelves lined with leather-bound volumes of scientific journals stood alongside awards encased in glass. A polished desk, free of clutter, held only his halopad, a mug of coffee, and a framed photograph of his late parents. Yet despite the tranquil surroundings, James's mind was a storm of equations and projections. He'd been vocal at the last board meeting, making clear his concerns about requiring the nano chip for identification access to banking and healthcare. But ultimately, he had lost when it was put to a vote.

President Walker had made it clear that if NexTech could help implement a universal ID solution, they could reduce the financial crime and insurance fraud that had become a blight on society. He understood the advances that could come, but it went against his core belief that technology was supposed to improve life, not impede it. He felt it was still too soon to force it on someone who wasn't ready.

James clicked on the latest crime report on his halopad. The numbers glowing on his tablet were staggering. Violent crime had plummeted to levels once thought impossible. Personal theft was nearly nonexistent. Assaults were so rare that they no longer dominated headlines. These were the results of the nano chip's sophisticated tracking and deterrent systems, which had turned society on its head.

James had originally invented the nano chip to revolutionize healthcare by tracking biometric readings with unparalleled accuracy. Designed to monitor vitals such as heart rate, oxygen levels, and cortisol production, the chip was intended to provide real-time data that could transform patient care. After clinical trials showed a staggering ninety-nine percent accuracy, he formed NexTech, an organization developing advanced artificial intelligence programs that were capable of analyzing the immense volume of data the chip provided. NexTech unlocked the ability to detect diseases days, and sometimes even years, before symptoms typically appeared. This preventative approach marked a groundbreaking revolution in healthcare, saving countless lives and billions of dollars in treatment costs.

The nano chip had been widely adopted and its potential applications expanded rapidly. An ambitious board of directors saw the opportunity to secure a lucrative partnership with the government. With government funding, NexTech broadened the chip's capabilities beyond healthcare, venturing into public safety. The focus shifted to reducing crime, a move that would cement the nano chip as an essential tool for societal stability. Through this partnership, NexTech implemented a sophisticated tracking system that cross-referenced individual nano chip data with an expansive network of emergency-response drones. These drones could detect incidents and arrive at the scene of a crime within seconds.

Since NexTech retained access to vast stores of user data, the organization developed an advanced algorithm capable of predicting and identifying likely perpetrators based on behavioral patterns, location history, and biometric fluctuations. At first, the system was rough and riddled with inaccuracies. False accusations and errors almost sparked a public outcry, and NexTech faced scrutiny. However, the board's relentless pursuit of refinement and their unyielding belief in the AI's potential gradually smoothed the system's rough edges. Over time, the public embraced NexTech and the nano chip, celebrating how safe the world had become along with the prevention of most disease. Some felt they were living in a utopia compared to the world they once knew.

"Almost unreal," James murmured to himself, scrolling through the data. His satisfaction was immediate, but it came with a lingering unease. He scribbled a quick note on his halopad: *"Lives saved: incalculable. Cost?"* His handwriting faltered, and he erased the last word with a swipe. Now wasn't the time for doubt.

As if on cue, his phone buzzed with an incoming call. The screen displayed an unknown number. Frowning, James hesitated before swiping to answer.

"Dr. Kent, this is Helene Moreau from the Nobel Prize Committee," said a crisp voice with a faint European accent. *"I am pleased to inform you that you've been selected to receive the Nobel Peace Prize for your contributions to The City's safety."*

James froze, his pen hovering above the notepad. He cleared his throat, trying to sound composed. "Thank you, Ms. Moreau. I wasn't expecting to win again." James had won five years before.

"You deserve it," she replied. *"The chip has revolutionized public health and safety. Few inventions have had such a profound impact on society."*

As the call ended, James set the phone down, his hand trembling slightly. The Nobel Prize was a lifetime achievement for any scientist. Yet instead of elation, he felt a gnawing weight in his chest.

Before he could dwell further, his office door swung open. Claire Sanders, the head of NexTech's Public Relations department, strode in. Her tailored suit and sleek haircut exuded professionalism, but her warm smile added an approachable edge.

"Congratulations, James," she said, extending a hand. "A second Nobel Prize is well deserved."

James shook her hand, his mind still racing. "Thank you, Claire. But let's be honest—this one is much more about NexTech's success than about mine this time."

"Exactly," Claire said, taking a seat across from him. "And that's why I'm here. The board wants to transition you from the lab to the public eye. You're the face of this technology now. People need to see the man behind the miracle."

James stiffened. "Claire, I'm not a marketing guy. I'm a

scientist. My work speaks for itself."

"True," she said, leaning forward, "but the world has questions. The technology is perfect, but the brand? That's fragile. There's always been skepticism about the government's involvement, some still are concerned about privacy. You can bridge that gap. You're genuine, James. People trust authenticity."

"I trust equations, not cameras," he replied flatly.

Claire's smile softened. "You won't be doing this alone. We're bringing in a media-relations expert to help. You'll have the tools and the team. All I'm asking is that you consider it—for the good of what is coming next."

James turned his chair to face the window, staring at the city below. The streets were calm, children played in the parks, and not a single emergency siren wailed in the distance. He'd created this peace. But at what cost? He did understand the small resistance against the nano chip. Not everyone wanted to know when a deadly disease was brewing. And some wanted to know but didn't want their personal information stored on a NexTech server. They'd spent a lot of time ensuring the technology was secure and all databases were encrypted, but still, some feared the worst. He'd spent his entire career building the nano chip's technology; now the board wanted him to sell it.

"Fine," he said finally. "I'll do the interviews. But I'll need some time to continue working with the engineering teams."

Claire beamed. "That's all I ask."

She left him alone, and James turned back to his tablet. A notification blinked—a new report from the Ethics division. With a swipe, he opened it, scanning the updates. Everything was on track: public adoption was nearing ninety percent, the government's expansion plans were moving forward, and development on next-gen chips was well underway.

Yet a single line caught his eye: *"New emotional data collection algorithms in beta."*

He frowned, tapping on the phrase to read more, but the file was restricted. *Emotional data?* That wasn't part of any plan he'd read before.

Before he could investigate further, his assistant, Sarah, knocked on the door.

"Dr. Kent? The board meeting starts in five minutes," she said, poking her head in.

James sighed, closing the report. "Of course. Thank you, Sarah."

As he gathered his notes and headed to the meeting room, James couldn't shake the feeling that something was shifting—not just in the world he had helped shape, but within himself.

In the sleek, glass-walled conference room, the board members greeted James with enthusiasm. These were the men and women who had supported his vision from the beginning, funding NexTech's growth and ensuring the chip's implementation.

"Dr. Kent," said Thomas Greaves, the chairman, "congratulations on the Nobel Prize. This is a win for all of us."

James nodded politely, taking a seat at the head of the table. "Thank you. I'm honored, but the credit belongs to everyone who contributed to the nano chip's success."

Greaves chuckled. "Always modest. But let's get to business. Phase Two."

James's fists clenched under the table. "Phase Two?"

"Public integration," Myles Fitz chimed in, his tone brisk. "The chip isn't just about safety anymore. We need to think about what's next, how to ensure that the nano chip and NexTech stay indispensable."

James looked down and glanced at the Phase Two proposal. He could see that the next step was to put measures in place to ensure virtually everyone was connected to the NexTech system through the adoption of the nano chip. His nano chip.

James raised an eyebrow. "Indispensable? That's not what this was about. The chip was meant to protect people, not control their lives."

"Control?" Thomas echoed, laughing lightly. "No one's controlling anything, James. This is about improving lives, streamlining society. Think of the possibilities: we have the tools to eliminate divorce and unemployment. The chip is the ultimate tool for empowerment. And this document is just a draft, you are here just like the rest of us, to make your voice known and help shape Phase Two."

James leaned back, his mind racing. Nothing on paper seemed terrible. But was he naïve to think it would stop there?

As the meeting progressed, James's unease grew. The board's enthusiasm for expansion was palpable, but so were the blind spots in their vision. They saw the chip as a product, a means to an end. James saw it as something far more delicate—a technology that could either uplift humanity or strip it of its essence.

Back in his office, James sat at his desk, staring at the city once more. He thought of his late parents—how they had always believed in his potential, even when he doubted himself. His mother, a teacher, had instilled in him a love for learning. His father, an engineer, had sparked his fascination with building things that mattered.

"You'd be proud of what I've done," he whispered, though a part of him wasn't sure if that was true.

His phone buzzed again. Another unknown number. This time, it was the President's office, requesting a meeting to discuss the chip's future applications.

James sighed, rubbing his temples. Everyone wanted so much from him. The chip had made him a hero, but heroes didn't get to rest.

4

Seph

Graduation day passed quickly. Seph had gone through the motions. He declined the invitation from his friends to celebrate afterwards, in part to stay rested for his interview, but in part because he couldn't wait to download the NexTech app onto his halopad. He spent hours devouring the data and was shocked at how much information it had already gathered about him. He'd been given diet recommendations and mindfulness exercises to reduce his stress.

The next morning, Seph sat in the stark, modern waiting room of NexTech Systems, his mind a whirlwind of anticipation and nerves. Around two dozen candidates sat in a similar state of tense expectation, their expressions a mixture of hope and anxiety. He recognized only a few from The Institute, which meant the rest of the candidates were coming from other jobs or computer science programs. The room was silent except for the soft hum of the air-conditioning and the occasional shuffle of feet.

Suddenly, the door opened and a NexTech employee stepped in. She was a young woman, dressed in the sleek, professional attire that seemed standard for NexTech staff. Her badge identified her as *'Lena—HR, New Hire Representative'*.

"Good morning, everyone," Lena began, her voice clear and confident. "I want to thank you all for being here today. You represent some of the brightest minds and talents, and we're excited to see what you can bring to NexTech Systems." She clicked her remote at a large screen on the wall, and a video started to play. The room darkened slightly as futuristic images and graphics illuminated the screen, showcasing NexTech's latest technological advancements.

Seph watched, fascinated and slightly awed, as the video displayed innovations he'd never seen before. There were glimpses of advanced AI algorithms, next-generation nano chips capable of incredible processing power, and even experimental fields that NexTech was pioneering.

Seph felt a surge of excitement despite himself. The technology was groundbreaking, the kind of work any tech enthusiast would dream of being a part of. Yet underneath that excitement, his mission for truth simmered.

"As you all know, today's process involves a series of interviews and assessments," Lena continued after the video concluded. "You'll meet with various team representatives and participate in a few practical experiments. These assessments are designed to evaluate not just your technical skills but also how you fit into the NexTech culture and ethos."

She paused, letting her gaze sweep over the room. "Remember, this is highly competitive. We select only about one out of every five hundred candidates who go through this process. So, give it your best, but also keep in mind the level of competition you're up against."

The room was thick with newfound tension following Lena's words. Seph could feel the collective anxiety rise, the air charged with a silent, competitive energy.

Candidates were then called one by one for the first round of interviews. Seph watched as each person left the room, returning later with expressions that ranged from hopeful to despondent.

Finally, his name was called. Seph stood up, steadying his breath, and followed another NexTech employee down a sterile hallway. The first interview was with Brock, a project manager from the AI development team.

"Seph, review the code on this screen. What is it programmed to do?" Brock asked.

Seph studied the code, consciously aware that each moment he took to review was being analyzed. He tried to scan, recognizing several functions quickly.

"It looks like it's a large language model that has been programed to analyze data based on certain keywords. When it hears one of these words listed here, it logs the next several sentences, then another algorithm is triggered to review all the logs for anything concerning," Seph answered, watching Brock's reaction.

"Good, what do you think the purpose of this is?" Brock followed up.

Seph looked back at the code.

"The answer won't be there," Brock said.

Seph pulled his focus back from the code and instead

thought for a moment. What did Brock want to hear?

After a few more seconds he said, "Well considering the vast amount of data that the NexTech system is receiving at all times, I am guessing this is an algorithm designed to cut through all the noise and pick out the areas it needs to focus on."

"Right, so our systems are receiving constant data from thirteen million nano chips every second. Plus they receive data from other systems like cellular towers and anything posted online. So how would NexTech strategically use a program like this?" Brock asked.

Seph felt like Brock was asking for something more, something deeper. "This program would do two things. First, it would streamline the data and allow the program to work in the most efficient manner, not wasting its time on unnecessary data. Second, it would flag threats pre-emptively. The triggers could be set to indicators that something is about to happen, not just identifying things that have already taken place." Seph hoped this was what Brock was looking for.

"Exactly! The code you just looked at was the first beta program we launched that led to the steep decline in crime. We were able to identify different keywords or themes that would appear in someone's data before they did something criminal. The system would flag threats and pass those along to another system that would then put a surveillance bot on that person, watching them in depth. Over time, we learned to stop the crime from even happening."

"That's incredible," Seph said.

"It is. This is one of many of the amazing projects we get to work on here at NexTech," Brock said with pride.

* * *

As the day progressed, Seph found himself in various rooms, facing different interviewers, each bringing a new challenge. One memorable session involved a collaborative task with other candidates, where they had to solve a complex problem under observation. Seph focused on balancing his need to stand out with the necessity of not appearing overly ambitious and making a careless mistake.

The practical experiments were the most intriguing. In one, he was given a piece of code with hidden flaws and asked to debug it under time pressure. In another, he participated in a group discussion on the ethical implications of AI, a conversation that resonated deeply with Seph's own internal conflicts.

"So what valid arguments do you think exist against getting the nano chip?" the interviewer asked the group of candidates.

Seph felt caught offguard. He didn't want to give away any of his own suspicions regarding NexTech's operations.

"Privacy!" said a girl quickly, a few seats over from Seph.

"Unknown long-term health impact," said the boy next to Seph.

Seph watched as the interviewer nodded her head as others chimed in. Her eyes met Seph's, waiting for his answer.

"Well, I can understand the valid concern for privacy." Seph paused. "But that is why it is valuable that the nano chip remains elective. Each person gets to weigh the pros and cons and decide to get it, or not."

The interviewer nodded and the conversation carried on. Seph hoped his hesitation hadn't counted against him.

Throughout the day, Seph remained acutely aware of the

nano chip in his arm, a silent observer to his every move.

As the final skills test concluded, Seph returned to the waiting area, his mind a mix of exhaustion and cautious optimism. He'd done everything he could; he'd displayed his skills and adaptability, but whether they were enough remained to be seen.

Seph looked around at his fellow candidates, wondering about their stories, their motivations. Were any of them like him, with secrets and missions hidden beneath a veneer of ambition?

Mental fatigue had set in. Seph's eyes felt like they weren't as sharp as he struggled to read the fine print on the snacks in the candidate waiting room. He was half listening to a conversation between two other candidates next to him—it felt like every sentence required a few extra seconds for him to process what they were saying.

Finally, Lena re-entered the room. "Candidates, thank you for your patience and for giving your best today. We will now announce those who have made it to the final interview which will happen in fifteen minutes. Those not selected will be asked to leave."

Seph braced himself, ready for whatever came next. This was the moment of truth.

A few seconds passed and Lena clicked a button on her remote, the screen behind her flashed a list of three names. "*Seph Thompson*" was listed.

He sat there frozen as the room became disruptive with movement, as people full of disappointment filtered out. One of his fellow classmates, Grace, caught his eye. She nodded a look of congratulations as she remained seated as well. Seph looked up and saw her name was also on the screen. A third,

"*Alexander Rivera*", was unknown to him, but he saw a boy who looked much younger than Seph and Grace sitting alone.

After a minute, the room was quiet again.

"You three should feel proud for making it this far," Lena said. "It's rare for us to select three for a final interview in one week, let alone one day. We know it has been a long day. Please grab a water and snack while you wait. You will each be called back in about twelve minutes to speak with the supervisor who is going to make the final decision on whether you will join their team. They are reviewing all your results right now."

Seph felt a sense of calm knowing that this was almost over. He drank a bottle of water but couldn't stomach any food as his hunger had been pushed down with nerves. "I didn't realize you were here today," he said, turning to Grace.

"I didn't realize you had even applied," Grace replied.

"I'm keeping the mystery alive. But seriously, congratulations. I don't doubt you will get an offer." Seph genuinely expected Grace would go far with her high test scores and even higher work ethic.

"Same to you." Grace smiled.

When he was called back, Seph was taken to a modern conference room. Across from him sat Marlene Hughes, the Senior Director of the Emotional Data Analysis Division. Seph had never heard of Emotional Data Analysis. Marlene's demeanor was sharp, her eyes keenly observant.

"Mr. Thompson," she began, her voice even but probing, "your performance today was impressive, but there's something we need to address. During the group test, it was evident that you held back. You have the skills to outshine your peers, yet at times you chose to blend in. Can you explain why?"

Seph felt a knot form in his stomach. He was momentarily at a loss for words, his mind racing to find an answer that wouldn't betray his intentions. Drawing on his personal history, Seph decided to tell a version of the truth: "My parents were killed when I was young, and the attention I received during that time was overwhelming. I learned to avoid standing out, and to fit in instead. It wasn't a conscious strategy for today, just a part of who I am. I didn't realize this could be observed, and I didn't realize it was impacting my performance."

Marlene listened intently, nodding slightly. "Thank you for your honesty. Your technical prowess was evident from your exam scores at The Institute. We had high expectations for you even before you arrived. However, what truly intrigued us is your mental flexibility, something we observed during the group tasks today."

Seph's mind whirred at her words. Mental flexibility? How had they measured that?

Marlene leaned forward, her eyes locking with Seph's. "It is rare to find a candidate that is comfortable in the tension of competing viewpoints. Human nature encourages us to pick a binary choice. It is comfortable to see the world in black and white. What we observed in you is the ability to see the complexity in issues. That something that appears black and white on the surface may actually be more complex and nuanced. This quality we believe is invaluable to solve issues others can't."

She continued "One of the core functionalities of our nano chip is to collect emotional data from its host."

The term 'host' struck Seph. It seemed so impersonal to describe a person as one. He was also taken aback by the idea of emotional data collection.

"The chip can accurately detect the core five emotions—happiness, sadness, anger, fear, and disgust—with ninety-nine percent accuracy," Marlene continued. "This data, combined with tracking information, has been pivotal in our crime-reduction efforts, allowing us to understand and predict human behavior in ways we never thought possible."

Seph's mind raced. The scope of the nano chip's capabilities was far beyond what he had imagined, far beyond what they were sharing publicly. Collecting emotional data? It was both fascinating and frightening. The feeling that June was right started to flood Seph. He knew his nano chip was reflecting that tension right now. *Could Marlene tell? Was she reading his data right as he sat there? Was this part of this test?* He refocused on Marlene's words and simultaneously gave an effort at slowing his breathing.

"But emotions are complex, more nuanced than just these five categories," Marlene said. "Our next goal is to understand and detect more subtle emotions, like betrayal, which is quite distinct from anger—although our current AI algorithms struggle to differentiate them. Once we can accurately detect these emotions, we can start to further diagnose things like intent to betray, or dishonesty."

She paused, giving Seph a moment to absorb the information. "This is where you come in. We believe your unique blend of technical expertise, strategic thinking, and mental flexibility makes you the ideal candidate to join our team. We need someone who can help us refine our technology to understand these complex emotional states. Help us understand what we have been missing over the past few years, help us take this to the next level. We can't release a software algorithm that detects emotions at a seventy-five percent level of accuracy. Even ninety-percent accuracy would create too many levels of error."

Marlene softened as she went on to explain that this team has not been able to successfully achieve its goal. It was clear that Marlene believed in the work. Seph could sense behind her tough demeanor that she was kind, but she was under a pressure that was forcing her to conceal that warmth. He also realized this wasn't actually a final interview. She had already decided to offer him the position before he sat down. For some reason, she needed him. Despite his ambivalence, there was something valuable she felt he could offer.

Marlene handed Seph a piece of paper. "So I want you to read over this job offer. I'm sure you read on our careers page that we make offers in person and you have to accept or reject it today. We have a fast-paced environment here and unfortunately, we just don't have the bandwidth to wait around for candidates to consider other possibilities. I'll also shoot straight with you: this is my last opening and I don't have any wiggle room in my budget to increase the salary. But if you contribute significantly, we can look at an increase during performance reviews next spring."

Seph looked down and saw a salary figure of $290,000. He was hoping to hit six figures but in no way had he imagined a starting salary of almost $300,000. He sat with a mix of emotions churning within him. He was being offered a position that went to the heart of what he'd come to uncover. Yet the implications of what he was hearing were extremely alarming. June and Duke had no idea this was going on, or if they did, they'd never discussed this with him. He'd always assumed their concerns were based on theories, not facts. A creeping sense of dread filled him for the first time. If this revelation was easily uncovered in a final interview, what else was yet to be revealed? Seph had spent hours learning about the nano chip and NexTech in school, as well as reading articles and blogs—he knew the public had no hint of what they were really accepting when they took the nano chip. He wondered if the government realized themselves. Evan Walker seemed like a good president, but was he in on this too? Was the government really aware of what was being built?

Seph signed an NDA that morning, and was briefed with all the new hires on not sharing anything about the interview process with anyone outside of NexTech.

"You will be a key part of the team working on advancing the nano chip's emotional-detection capabilities," Marlene concluded. "We believe your insights could be invaluable."

Part of Seph wanted to reject the offer and find a way to contact Duke and figure out how deep the rabbit hole really was. He spent another minute staring at the offer letter, and although he felt like a double agent, he picked up the pen on the table and signed his name at the bottom of the page. Formally accepting the position, the salary, and the reality that things were not what they seemed.

As Seph left the interview room, his mind was a whirlpool of thoughts. He'd achieved his first objective: he was in. But the revelation about the nano chip's capabilities was a stark reminder of the immense responsibility he carried. He was now on the inside, a spy in the heart of an organization that was pushing the boundaries of technology and ethics. He was so busy thinking about this he didn't even see Lena waiting for him in the hall.

"Congratulations, Mr. Thompson," Lena said with a smile, holding out an envelope. Seph took it, his hands slightly trembling.

"Thank you," he managed to say, his voice a mixture of relief and apprehension.

Inside the envelope, he found a sleek badge bearing the NexTech logo and his name. Below it was a small card with his start date and time.

"You'll start next Monday at 8:00am," Lena said, her voice barely reaching Seph as he examined the contents of the envelope. "Your badge will grant you access to the building and your designated work area. Be punctual and ready to begin your journey with NexTech."

Seph clutched the badge, feeling its weight. It was a symbol of his new identity, a key to the world he needed to infiltrate. He was officially part of NexTech Systems now, on the brink of uncovering what lay beneath the surface of its groundbreaking technology.

5

Seph

The sun had barely risen when Seph arrived at NexTech Systems. The towering glass building caught the first light, reflecting a spectrum of colors. He felt a mix of anticipation and apprehension as he entered the lobby, aware of the significance of this day.

The morning was a whirlwind of orientation activities. Along with a small group of new hires, he was guided through the sprawling campus. Their tour began with its state-of-the-art laboratories, the heart of NexTech's technological advancements. The labs were a maze of high-tech equipment and technicians in white lab coats moving with precision as the operated equipment Seph had never seen before. Seph didn't realize the group had already moved down the hall as he watched a tech assemble a component, placed it under a microscope and the magnified image was displayed on the wall next to him. He was in awe as he analyzed the digital screens displaying real-time data and complex analytics.

Seph looked up and realized he was standing alone. He hurried down the hall just as the group was watching a robotic arm skillfully assemble tiny components that appeared to be the device used to implant the nano chips.

Next on their itinerary was the employee wellness center, a modern facility designed to cater to the physical and mental wellbeing of the staff. It boasted an array of amenities, including a fully equipped gym with personal trainers, yoga studios, and a serene meditation area. The center also offered wellness workshops and personal counseling services, underscoring NexTech's commitment to its employees' holistic health. The tranquil ambiance of the wellness center, with its soft lighting and calming music, provided a stark contrast to the high-energy atmosphere of the labs.

Finally, the group was taken to the expansive cafeteria. This vast space was filled with a variety of dining options, from healthy organic meals to international cuisine, catering to diverse tastes and dietary needs. The cafeteria was designed not just as a place to eat but also as a social hub where employees could interact and relax. Large windows offered panoramic views of the campus, and the decor was bright.

In a small conference room, Seph received his work computer and went through the process of gaining access to NexTech's systems. He spent a considerable amount of time signing a stack of paperwork, each document outlining various policies and nondisclosure agreements. The weight of the commitment he was making to NexTech, and conversely, to his secret purpose, settled heavily upon him.

Lunchtime found Seph navigating the packed cafeteria, the hum of overlapping conversations filling the air. The room was filled with an organized chaos—employees clustered at tables, trays clattering, and the faint aroma of roasted vegetables with the sharp tang of freshly brewed coffee hanging in the air.

As Seph scanned the room, he caught sight of Grace sitting at a small table near one of the windows, her short curls catching the sunlight. She waved him over, her expression warm and inviting. Balancing his tray—a bowl of vegetable soup and a small sandwich—he made his way through the maze of tables and dropped into the chair opposite her.

"Figured you'd already made a new circle of friends," Grace teased, nudging her tray aside to make room for his.

Seph chuckled, shaking his head. "Not quite. It's been a lot to take in."

"Tell me about it," Grace replied, unwrapping a granola bar. "So, how's the first day treating you?"

Seph hesitated, searching for the right words. "It's … a bit overwhelming. I haven't met my team yet, but just seeing all that happens here goes way beyond what I imagined."

Grace raised an eyebrow, chewing thoughtfully. "Did you not do a lot of research before the interview process?"

Seph nodded. "No, it was actually a last-minute change in direction for me. So, I didn't go to any of the preview days. But what about you? What team did you land on?"

Grace leaned forward, her voice dropping slightly as if sharing a secret. "I am on the Troubleshooting Team. It's exactly what it sounds like. When a nano chip malfunctions, we're the ones who step in to figure out why. It's not common, but when it does happen, the results can be … let's just say, unexpected."

Seph tilted his head, curiosity piqued. "Unexpected how?"

Grace toyed with the edge of her granola bar wrapper, her gaze distant for a moment before meeting his. "Well, the chip isn't just monitoring vitals—it's integrated into so many systems. Malfunctions can lead to weird glitches, like people receiving health warnings that don't match their actual condition. There was this case recently where a guy's chip flagged a heart attack while he was sitting calmly at his desk."

Seph's brows shot up. "That's ... unsettling. Did they figure out what caused it?"

Grace sighed. "Sort of. Turns out, his chip had some faulty programming, cross-referencing his elevated caffeine levels with heart-rate variability. It triggered an alert because the system couldn't differentiate between natural fluctuations and actual distress."

Seph leaned back, letting the information sink in. "So, even with all this precision, there's still room for error?"

Grace nodded. "That's why we're here. The stakes are too high to leave room for mistakes. And it's not just health glitches; the chip is connected to everything now. A single error could ripple across someone's entire life."

A shiver ran down Seph's spine. He stirred his soup absentmindedly, glancing at Grace.

"Doesn't that scare you? I mean, how much control does the nano chip really have over someone's life?"

Grace shrugged, her expression thoughtful. "It's not about control—it's about integration. The chip isn't deciding anything; it's just ... facilitating. At least, that's the official line."

Seph nodded slowly, filing away her words. This was the first sign Grace had any distrust towards NexTech. He chose not to press her on it now and took a sip of his soup, its warmth contrasting with the chill that Grace's revelations had left behind.

"So, what made you join NexTech?" Grace asked, steering the conversation. "You've always seemed like someone who marches to the beat of their own drum."

Seph hesitated, his spoon hovering above his bowl. "It's complicated," he admitted, choosing his words carefully. "I've always been fascinated by technology—the way it can solve problems, make life easier. But I guess I'm also trying to understand it better. Especially something as transformative as the nano chip. Originally, I was looking at joining a small startup where I could really dig into an unsolved problem and find a solution. But to be honest, I had some changes at home that forced me to prioritize stability. It's not that I don't want to be part of a large corporation like this, I just never necessarily saw myself here. But the job offer is more than I could imagine, and I am hopeful that I'll like what my team is working on. I honestly didn't realize some of what NexTech was working on until the day of the interview."

Grace studied him for a moment, her sharp eyes scanning his face. "Fair answer. I think a lot of us feel that way—wanting to make a difference. Startups are fun and scrappy but a large organization like this has the power to really get things done."

Their conversation lapsed into a comfortable silence, the background noise of the cafeteria filling the gaps. Seph found himself relaxing slightly, grateful for the moment of camaraderie in a day that had been anything but ordinary.

After lunch, Seph was directed to the department where he would be working. The atmosphere in the office was one of focused energy, with small groups engaged in deep discussions or working intently at their stations. As he looked closer to each of the workstations it appeared that each indicated a different emotion.

He was introduced to his cohort, a close-knit group that had been working together for months. They welcomed him, though there was an unmistakable team bond that Seph knew he was an outsider to, at least for now. The team lead, Martin, briefed Seph on their progress.

The workspace had a red symbol on it. The team had been assigned anger and were working on differentiating the emotions within anger, such as betrayal, rage, envy, and frustration. Martin shared sample data they'd gathered and what they'd done in the past with little result.

"This is the team," Martin said pointing at three others. "Collin and I were the first to start about a year ago, Franky joined eight months ago, and then Emma."

"Welcome to the team, Seph. We're excited to have you on board," Emma said, pushing back her long brown hair and extending a friendly hand to Seph.

Their connection was instant. Emma's brown eyes were soft, kind, and made Seph feel instantly at ease, a feeling he hadn't expected in this environment.

"Thanks, I am excited to be here." Seph smiled back, having a hard time looking away from her eyes.

"You must have made an impression with Marlene," Franky said.

"Yeah, the position has been vacant for almost six months," Collin added.

"I didn't realize this was such a hard position to fill," Seph said.

"Well, since we haven't been able to solve it, they kept

trying to perfect the candidate profile that would be the right addition to the team," Martin explained confidently.

"So, you must fit the bill," Franky added.

Seph felt accepted by the new team immediately. He could tell they all enjoyed what they did. "So do you all work together or is a lot of it independent work?" he asked.

"It's a bit of both," Collin said. "We have team meetings to discuss our current priorities and divide up work. We also share ideas and brainstorm with each other. Then we go off and work independently and report back any major findings."

"You'll get used to it pretty quickly," Emma added, encouraging him. "I know it's a lot to join a new team and figure out how you fit in. I was the new one—until you, that is."

"Emma, why don't you show Seph his workstation?" Martin suggested. She nodded and the others went back to their desks.

"Alright so this is your desk," Emma said, gesturing at a white desk that had two half walls on the side. It wasn't completely open to the others, but had some privacy that would allow him to work without distraction. On top of the desk there was a sealed box with the words *"Welcome Seph"* printed on it.

"Wow, I hadn't really thought about having my own workstation," Seph said. It was much nicer than the setup he had at The Institute.

"Oh yeah, the accommodations here are the absolute best. That box should have your equipment in it." She paused. "If you want, I can help you set it up."

"That would be great." Seph started to open the box. Inside he found a NexTech hoodie, a polo shirt, a mug, a few pens, a VR headset, halodock, keyboard, and mouse.

"So you have two main options to work. You can either

wear the VR headset and work immersive, or you can just click this button here to have the halodock connect to the screen on your desk."

Seph watched as Emma clicked the button on his halodock and the back wall connected to his workstation flashed, filling with the login screen.

"That whole wall is a screen?" Seph asked.

"Oh yeah, you would be surprised what isn't capable of projecting your work in this building." Emma laughed.

"So how long have you worked at NexTech?" Seph asked.

"I've been on the team for six months. But I did an internship during my last year at Prep," Emma replied.

University Prep was an elite school for kids of government employees. They got the best teachers and best career opportunities as long as they passed their final exam.

As they talked, Seph found himself genuinely smiling for the first time since June left. Emma didn't discuss the tasks at hand, but instead made Seph feel welcome and comfortable.

The rest of Seph's afternoon was spent getting acquainted with his equipment and reviewing the open projects the team was working on. The depth and scope of their work were both impressive and daunting. Seph knew he had to tread carefully, learn quickly, and find a way to fit in while keeping his eyes and ears open for any information that could help him understand more about NexTech's true intentions.

As the day drew to a close, Seph left the NexTech building with a full mind. He had successfully gotten one of the best jobs The Institute advertised, but the real work, the dangerous and delicate task of uncovering the secrets hidden within the organization, was just beginning.

That night, Seph went to bed for the first time not stewing

about NexTech, June, or the complexity of his life. He fell asleep with his mind fully fixed on one thing: Emma.

* * *

Seph's second day at NexTech Systems began with a deep dive into the past work of his new team. Seated at his workstation, surrounded by monitors filled with lines of code and experiment logs, he felt a familiar thrill—the joy of unraveling technological puzzles. As he sifted through lines of code, Seph could see the intricate layers of programming that went into analyzing the data the nano chip was collecting. He noted areas where the code could be streamlined or made more efficient. Occasionally, he stumbled upon snippets that hinted at more complex, perhaps even hidden functionalities. His mind raced with the implications of these discoveries, but he kept his observations to himself, worried about drawing too much focus to a suspicious direction.

Seph had begun to mentally construct an understanding of the system's architecture, focusing on how the nano chips interacted within the broader network when he noticed someone walking back from the breakroom.

"Hey man, how are you getting settled?" Franky asked.

"Good, I think, just trying to learn as much as I can," Seph responded with a smile.

"Well, don't work too hard without snacking on some freebies." Franky chuckled as he held up his coffee and muffin.

"I'm on my way there now!" Emma said. "Want to come?"

Seph hopped up without hesitation and followed Emma to the breakroom. It was a large room with several couches and tables. The back wall had three large refrigerators filled with every drink he could imagine and a large table in the middle was filled with fresh pastry items and a yogurt bar.

"Is this just for our department?" Seph asked.

"No this breakroom serves two other departments that are on this floor too," Emma said, scanning the refrigerator for something to drink.

Seph laughed. "It's going to take me a while to get used to all the amenities here."

"NexTech does almost too good of a job making it comfortable here. With less of a reason to leave the office, the more you work," said Emma.

"I didn't think about that. It all comes back to efficiency," Seph said, grabbing a cold coffee and a bagel.

"Well, I have a to get to a meeting, but swing by my workstation anytime if you have questions." Emma gave Seph one last smile before heading out.

Seph munched on his snack as he dove back into his work. At the heart of this intricate system was a massive database at NexTech, where the collected data was meticulously stored and categorized. It was organized not only by each individual host, but also by geographical locations. One of the key functions of this system was its role in crime reduction. The servers dedicated to this task analyzed the data on a location basis, cross-referencing the information from all nano chips present in a particular area. This allowed for a comprehensive and dynamic understanding of any given locale.

However, Seph was most intrigued by the individual *host* files. These files contained long-term data on every person with a nano chip. Seph realized that understanding these files was crucial. They were more than just a collection of data; they held insights into the daily lives and behaviors of people.

Despite his keen interest, Seph faced a significant hurdle: his access to the system was limited. As part of his team, he was only privy to a fragment of the overall code. His current project was to delve into the emotional data collected by the chips, with a specific focus on distinguishing the nuanced emotions related to anger. While this was a critical aspect of the chip's functionality, Seph knew it was just a small piece of a much larger puzzle.

As he pondered over the limited access he had, Seph understood that to truly grasp the scope and implications of the nano chip's capabilities, he would need to find a way to access more of the system. The challenge was not just technical, it was also a matter of navigating the complex hierarchy and security measures of NexTech Systems.

Seph attended his first department meeting where various team leads were sharing updates on their recent projects. Martin, his team leader, known for his concise and direct communication style, began his presentation with a focused intensity.

"We've been encountering a challenge in our recent experiment," Martin reported. His tone was matter-of-fact, yet the content of his update was anything but mundane. "Our latest data shows only an eighty-five percent accuracy rate in distinguishing complex emotions that manifest as anger. This is below our target threshold. We need to refine our algorithms to improve the accuracy."

Seph absorbed every word, recognizing the significance of this challenge. The nano chip's ability to accurately interpret human emotions was a crucial aspect of its functionality, especially in the context of monitoring and potentially predicting behavior. An eighty-five percent accuracy rate, while impressive, was not sufficient for the precision NexTech aimed for.

Martin continued, "The team is currently analyzing the discrepancies in the data. We suspect the issue lies in the algorithm's inability to effectively differentiate between anger and other high-arousal emotions like frustration or anxiety."

Seph found this particularly interesting. The complexity of human emotions was vast, and the task of digitally quantifying them was fraught with challenges. The nuances between different forms of anger and similar emotional states posed a significant hurdle for the team.

As the meeting progressed, Seph thought about the implications of this work. The ability to accurately interpret emotional data could have far-reaching consequences, not just for individual privacy but also for how such data could be used or misused in the wrong hands.

He realized that gaining a deeper understanding of this aspect of the nano chip's functionality was crucial. It would provide valuable insight into the company's broader goals and potentially reveal vulnerabilities or ethical dilemmas inherent in the technology. This knowledge was not just important for his immediate project, but it was also vital for the wider mission he was secretly undertaking.

Lunchtime provided a welcome break, and Seph found himself sitting with Emma in the cafeteria. The two had crossed paths briefly that morning, exchanging polite smiles, but this was their first chance to actually talk.

The cafeteria was alive with the familiar sound of conversations and the occasional clatter of dishes. Seph carried a plate of pasta and a side salad as he watched Emma sit down.

"Mind if I join you?" Seph asked, gesturing to the seat across from Emma.

She looked up, her warm brown eyes lighting up. "Of course, Seph. I was starting to think everyone here eats in their own bubble."

Seph chuckled, sliding into the chair. "Yeah, it does feel a bit isolating. I guess people here are just really focused."

Emma nodded, tearing off a piece of her bread. "Focused is an understatement. I've worked here for six months, and some weeks Martin and Collin barely say two words unless it's about work. Not that I mind—I like my peace—but it's nice to have a normal conversation once in a while."

"Well, I'll do my best to keep this normal," Seph joked, earning a laugh from Emma. Her laugh was easy and genuine, a sound that seemed to cut through all the analysis Seph's mind was so entrenched in.

"So," Emma said, leaning forward slightly, "what do you think of NexTech so far? Overwhelmed yet?"

Seph took a bite of his pasta, chewing thoughtfully before answering. "It's … a lot. The technology is incredible, but I'm still wrapping my head around everything. It's fascinating but definitely complex."

Emma nodded. "It's tough. Emotions aren't exactly binary. Even within anger, you've got so many layers—it's like untangling a web. I mean most people have a hard time identifying what they're feeling. So now we are tasked with programming a computer to detect it with near perfect accuracy? It is kind of crazy."

Seph nodded. "Exactly. Teaching the system to recognize those layers almost seems impossible. What aspect have you been working on so far?"

"Endless amounts of data," Emma replied with a small smile.

"I look at trends over time: heart rate, cortisol levels, neural activity. It's like putting together a mosaic. Each piece on its own doesn't say much, but when you step back, you start to see the bigger picture."

Seph leaned forward, his curiosity piqued. "Does it feel invasive? Knowing you're dealing with such personal information?"

Emma hesitated, her gaze drifting toward the window. "Sometimes, yeah. But I try to focus on the good it can do. If we get this right, it could revolutionize mental health. Imagine being able to detect a panic attack before it happens or prevent someone from spiraling into depression."

Her passion was evident, and Seph couldn't help but admire it. "You really believe in this, don't you?" he asked, his tone softer.

Emma met his eyes, her expression earnest. "I do. I know the technology has its flaws, but I think the potential outweighs the risks." Emma brightened, changing the subject. "So, Seph, where did you grow up?"

"I grew up in Old Town," he replied sheepishly. He was grateful for the lighter topic, but growing up in Old Town was also a clear sign that he was more of a "has not" than a "has". But Emma didn't show any sign of judgement. "What about you?"

"I grew up out in the country actually," she said, her eyes sparkling with a hint of nostalgia. "We moved here when I was five."

"Ah so you were part of the great migration." Seph remembered when all the kids from the country moved into the city to be close to NexTech in first and second grade. That was when the technology utopia was first created. The new kids stuck out like sore thumbs for a few years until they assimilated into city life. "What was that like?"

"Nothing like this place. I grew up surrounded by mountains and wide-open spaces. Coming here was a bit of a culture shock, but I've gotten used to it."

"Do you miss it?"

"All the time," Emma admitted with a small laugh, "but my mom has struggled with major depression her whole life so my dad jumped on the bandwagon of the nano chip hoping it would provide a cure. I loved the mountains, but it feels like home here too."

"I'm so sorry to hear about your mom," said Seph solemnly.

"It's okay. It hasn't been easy to watch someone I love suffer, but it also gives me purpose behind what we do here. What about you? What was it like growing up with your aunt?"

"All things considered, it was good." Seph paused, this was normally where he stopped with any personal information, but he felt comfortable in Emma's presence so he decided to open up to her. "I don't remember a lot about my parents. I was only seven when they … when the accident happened. But what I do remember feels more like a series of snapshots than memories: my mom's laugh, my dad's hands on the steering wheel during long drives. Little things…"

Seph took a deep breath and met Emma's eyes. "My aunt, she did her best. She really did. But she wasn't them, you know? She didn't know how to handle a kid who … who just didn't want to exist in the world anymore. I spent a lot of years angry, and a lot of years numb. She'd try to make Christmas special or throw me birthday parties, but it all just felt … empty. It wasn't all bad, though. She taught me how to stand up for myself. She made sure I had the opportunity to go to The Institute. And … she gave me stability. But growing up without my parents? It's like there's this hole inside you that never quite fills. You learn to live around it, but it's always there."

"I can't imagine what that was like for you. Seven seems so young to experience that kind of grief," Emma responded softly.

"As painful as it was—and is—it also has made me who I am. It's a reminder of how short life is and has helped me not sweat the small stuff." Seph shifted in his seat as he let the muscles in his shoulders relax.

"That reminds me of a quote I read once: *'Sometimes you have to walk through fire to see the light'.* It stuck out with me when I read it. But I'll be honest, I've never experienced that like you have, Seph."

They sat in silence for a few moments reflecting on each other's stories. Seph felt a rare sense of ease around Emma and he was grateful she hadn't experienced the kind of pain he had.

6

Seph

Seph's third day at NexTech Systems started out just like the day before, entrenched in the data of his team's past experiments. After an hour he got up, stretched, and headed to a nearby breakroom to grab a boost of caffeine.

The breakroom smelled of coffee with the faint hint of something burnt—probably the toaster someone had abandoned. Seph stood by the counter, stirring creamer into his mug, when Emma walked in, carrying a stainless-steel travel cup. She looked up and grinned.

"Taking a break from saving the world one sensor at a time?"

Seph chuckled. "Something like that. Figured I'd step away before my brain fried from staring at code."

She grabbed a seat at the small table by the window, motioning for Seph to join her. He hesitated a moment but then sat down across from her, his coffee steaming gently.

"Late night working?" Seph asked.

Emma shook her head. "Not last night, thankfully. Actually, I spent most of it cooking."

"Cooking?" Seph raised an eyebrow. "You actually have energy for that after work?"

Emma laughed, a bright, genuine sound. "I love cooking—it helps me unwind. I made chicken piccata. Have you ever had it?"

"Chicken what?" Seph asked, narrowing his eyes.

"Piccata. It's chicken cooked in a lemony butter sauce with capers and white wine. Super simple, but it tastes amazing." She gestured animatedly as she described it, her enthusiasm infectious.

Seph stared at her, a mix of curiosity and disbelief. "I've definitely never had that."

Emma blinked, surprised. "Wait, what?! You've never had chicken piccata?"

Seph shrugged, suddenly self-conscious. "I don't really cook much. Actually, I don't cook at all. My Aunt June used to make meals when she lived with me, but she moved a few months ago to stay with a relative. Since then, it's been all frozen dinners and boxed mac and cheese. That's kind of my level."

Emma frowned, not in judgment but in genuine concern. "So, you're telling me you live on processed food?"

"Well … yeah. It's easy, you know? And it doesn't taste that bad," he said defensively, though even he wasn't convinced.

Emma shook her head, looking almost offended on behalf of good food everywhere. "That's tragic."

"Tragic?" Seph laughed. "I think it's efficient."

"No, it's tragic," Emma insisted. "You're missing out on real food. Food that doesn't taste like preservatives."

Seph shrugged again, sipping his coffee. "I mean, I wouldn't know. It's not like I've had much else."

Emma set her travel cup down with a determined look. "Okay, that's it. You're coming to my place for dinner tomorrow. No arguments."

Seph blinked at her, caught off guard. "What?"

"You heard me," Emma said, her tone leaving no room for debate. "You need to experience a proper home-cooked meal. It's practically a moral obligation at this point."

"Are you serious?" Seph asked, laughing nervously.

"Completely serious," Emma said, crossing her arms. "To-morrow night. My place. I'll make something good—maybe not chicken piccata again, but we'll see."

Seph hesitated, feeling both flattered and a little out of his depth. "I mean … I don't want to impose."

Emma waved him off. "You're not imposing. I'd feel worse knowing you're out there eating freezer-burned burritos for dinner. Besides," she added with a sly grin, "I'm curious to see if you actually know how to hold a fork properly."

Seph rolled his eyes, laughing. "Okay, fine. You've con-vinced me. But I'm warning you—my bar for food is pretty low."

"Perfect," Emma said with a smirk. "That just means I'll impress you even more."

As they parted ways, Seph couldn't help but feel a flicker of anticipation. He wasn't just looking forward to the meal—he was curious to see Emma in her element, outside the clinical walls of their office. Something in him hoped tomorrow night might be more than just dinner.

* * *

Later that day, Seph had a meeting with the biotech health department, a standard procedure for all new NexTech employees. He was ushered into a sleek, modern office where he met with a nurse who began to explain the results of a diagnostic test he had unknowingly taken during his interview.

"The scan you underwent is part of our initiative to ensure the optimal health of our employees," the nurse explained, displaying a series of complex images and data on a screen. "We've detected an early onset of a cancer gene in your system. With our advanced biotechnology, we can identify problematic cells long before they form a mass."

Seph was stunned. The revelation was both alarming and a relief. He couldn't help but wonder what his fate would have been had he not received the nano chip and joined NexTech.

"The good news is, we have a treatment ready for you," the nurse continued. "It's a quick, ten-minute procedure, and as a NexTech employee, it's completely covered. Normally, this would cost around a million dollars out of pocket. As soon as we knew you were hired, we started the approval process for treatment."

The implications of this technology and the company's healthcare benefits were not lost on Seph. He felt a complex mix of gratitude, unease, and a growing awareness of the divide between those with access to such advanced medical care and those that chose to go without.

"Are there any side effects from the treatment? Can I return to work after this?" Seph asked.

The nurse responded, "We are catching it while it's still in the cell form, there are really no side effects noted. Occasionally someone reports they felt tired or a bit of a headache, but nine out of ten times they don't report any symptoms. I honestly think the fatigue and headaches are just a placebo effect." She paused. "Okay, let's have you change into this robe and then you will lay in the treatment bed behind you. The system already has the frequency set to the detected cancer cells, so it will kill those, while leaving all your healthy cells unharmed."

Seph turned around and noticed a machine that didn't look like a bed at all. As the nurse moved behind him, she waved her hand over it. It started to split in two and revealed a flat surface where he understood he was to lie.

"If you are nervous we can give you a sedative, but it may make you groggy for the afternoon," she said as she noticed his hesitation.

"No, I think I will be okay. I am just still absorbing everything about this place."

Seph motioned to open the robe she'd given him and she turned around while he quickly slipped his clothes off and covered himself in the provided green robe. He stepped inside the machine, and noticed it was surprisingly warm despite its cold appearance.

"Okay, I am going to close it now, but if you need anything I will be right here," the nurse said. "It will start in a few minutes and really it just takes about ten minutes."

The bed began to close with Seph inside. He noticed a halopad turn on above his head. It listed out three choices: music, recaps, and news. He selected recaps and saw several options for recent popular TV shows—ten-minute shortened clips of the latest episodes. People were often too busy to watch a full hour of TV, but they could watch recaps and still keep up with what was going on in their favorite shows. They even had them for movies now.

Seph didn't see any options that caught his eye so instead he turned on some music. He picked a pop mix and closed his eyes. He didn't feel anything unusual and before he knew it, the machine beeped, opened up, and he was done. And presumably, now cancer-free.

* * *

The next evening, Seph found himself in a self-driving car with Emma, heading to her house for dinner. Seph was used to the transpo and had never been in a car before. The ride was smooth and automated, giving Seph a glimpse into technological advancements that were still new to him. Not only had Aunt June rejected new inventions, she'd had her career in public education and wasn't ever cash flush for a purchase like that.

Arriving at Emma's home, Seph was immediately struck by the level of technological integration. The house was not just a living space; it was a hub of cutting-edge tech. From automated lighting and temperature-control systems, to interactive surfaces responding to touch, it was like stepping into the future.

Dinner was an eye-opening experience. The "home cooking" Emma had mentioned was actually partially prepared by a state-of-the-art kitchen robot. She could press a few buttons and instruct it on what to prepare. Fresh bread or pasta was just a few clicks away.

Seph watched, fascinated, as the robot expertly prepared fresh fettucine noodles while Emma whipped up a sauce on the stove. The robot's mechanical precision and efficiency was a stark contrast to the human touch he associated with cooking.

As they sat down to eat, just the two of them, Seph shared his amazement. "I've never seen anything like this," he admitted. "I'm used to cooking being much more ... of a manual process."

Emma laughed. "This is pretty standard for us. The convenience allows us to have all fresh ingredients and not rely on processed food."

Seph nodded, his mind racing with thoughts about the disparities in access to technology. Here, in Emma's world, technology seamlessly catered to every need, while in his own life, such luxuries were unheard of.

"Who is 'us'?" Seph asked.

"Ah, yes, this big house is not just for me. My parents are at a work dinner for my dad. He's a congressman. And my little brother, Tucker, is staying at a friend's house while they are away. He's fourteen so he could definitely be here alone, but he doesn't like to be. Even though he would have all he needed right here, he feels lonely in the house when my mom isn't here."

Seph could tell by the way Emma spoke that she had a lot of affection for her family.

The evening passed with more conversation, laughter, and an exchange of perspectives. Seph found himself increasingly intrigued by Emma's worldview, so shaped by technology and privilege, yet he was attracted most to her openness and warmth. He was drawn to Emma in a way he had never felt before. He wanted to continue getting to know her and see the world as she did.

As he left Emma's home that night, Seph couldn't help but feel he was straddling two very different worlds. He had one foot in the technological utopia with Emma, and the other in a reality where such advancements were still the stuff of dreams. The divide was stark, and Seph found himself more determined than ever to understand the full implications of NexTech's work, not just for those like Emma, but for everyone.

* * *

The following Monday, Lena, the HR representative at Nex-Tech, called Seph in for his one-week check-in. It was a standard part of the new hire process, but Seph felt slightly uneasy as he made his way to her office. He couldn't help but wonder what this meeting would entail.

As he entered Lena's office, he noticed the array of screens displaying various employee metrics. Lena greeted him with a professional smile.

"Seph, thanks for coming in. Please, have a seat. Tell me, how are you adjusting here?"

Seph settled into the chair across from Lena's desk, trying to read her expression. "So far, it's been great. I'm getting up to speed with our team's progress. I know my way around all the systems and this huge campus. So I would say it's going well," he said, attempting to sound casual.

Lena glanced at her tablet, then back at Seph. "Your performance has been outstanding, Seph. You've integrated well into the team already. However, there's something else we need to discuss."

Seph felt his heart rate quicken slightly. "Oh? What's that?"

Lena shifted her gaze to a graph on her screen. "It's about your interactions with Emma. We've noticed you've been spending a significant amount of one-on-one time with her, more so than anyone else in your department."

Seph's mind raced. He knew NexTech had a sophisticated employee monitoring system, but he hadn't expected his personal interactions to be under scrutiny.

Lena continued, "Another team at NexTech has been working on a compatibility scoring system, part of our initiative to foster a positive workplace environment. And, well, you and Emma have a ninety-two percent compatibility rate."

Seph was taken aback. "Compatibility rate? I wasn't aware such a thing existed here."

Lena nodded, "Yes, it's a new system we're piloting. A score above eighty-five percent is considered very high, indicating strong potential for a successful marriage. We automatically approve such cases for official romantic relationships as per HR policy."

Still processing this information, Seph asked, "And what if the score was lower?"

Lena leaned back in her chair. "Currently, we're handling lower scores on a case-by-case basis. The idea is to prevent any potential workplace issues, especially when both individuals are on the same team. In some cases, it might mean a team transfer for one of the individuals. But with your high score, you don't need to worry about that."

Seph's mind was swirling with thoughts. "So, what happens now?"

Lena smiled, "For now, nothing. It's just something for you to be aware of. If, and when your relationship with Emma becomes official, just let us know. We'll take care of the necessary paperwork. We would look at your relationship very positively and love to use it as sample case for the pilot program we're running."

Seph let curiosity get the best of him, "Is this program just for internal employees of NexTech or is it going to be used … outside of NexTech too?"

Lena smiled. "Right now, we are piloting here as a way to assist our HR team that handles romantic relationships. That's always been a tricky place for companies to manage. We don't want to be overbearing but we also have to protect the culture and dynamic of teams. As soon as you work with a couple that breaks up, you'll understand the complication. Well, I hope you never have to, now that we have relationship scores. But long term, this whole project's premise is to reduce the divorce rate, similarly to how we reduced crime. As crime has declined and economic growth risen, we have still an alarmingly high divorce rate. At NexTech we have dozens of departments working to solve these complex problems we face, and after successful pilot programs, we work with our partners to roll them out on a larger scale."

Seph left Lena's office unable to shake off a feeling of intrusion. The idea that his personal life, his potential relationship with Emma, was being quantified and analyzed by NexTech was unsettling. He wondered what other aspects of his life were under the microscope.

7

James

J ames Kent sat in his dimly lit office, the blue glow of his tablet illuminating his face. He adjusted his glasses and leaned back in his chair, rereading the email he'd just opened. Attached to it was a confidential document titled *"Phase Two Final Implementation Plan."* The weight of those words sat heavily on his chest, and he couldn't ignore the feeling that things were shifting in ways he hadn't fully anticipated when he first created the nano chip.

He tapped on the screen, opening the document. The introduction began innocuously enough—an overview of the success of Phase One, highlighting how crime rates had dropped dramatically, healthcare costs were down, and the public's response to the chip had been overwhelmingly positive. But as he scrolled further, his brow furrowed.

Phase Two wasn't just about public safety and making things better for the world. The chip would now integrate into systems far beyond personal-health monitoring or criminal apprehension. The plan detailed how it would serve as a universal identifier, replacing driver's licenses, passports, and bank accounts. Citizens would use it to vote, to access social services, and even to pay for groceries. The idea was marketed as a step toward efficiency and convenience, but James couldn't shake the unease creeping up his spine. Underneath those enticing perks, was something James worried about. He had been voicing his concern for weeks now, but as he read the final plan it was clear it had fallen on deaf ears.

He knew the Innovation team was busy at work at NexTech. It had already pushed some projects past his comfort level but every time he raised concerns, Myles Fitz, the head of Innovation, always confirmed that any pilot program was only happening internally with those who consented.

Myles had been handpicked by the board about four years ago and he'd never seen eye-to-eye with James. It was now clear to James that Myles had been selected for this innovation push. He already knew that the pilot programs he'd been spearheading would one day get released into the production environment and start gathering data on everyone with a NexTech nano chip without their consent. And this data would give NexTech and Evan Walker all the power they need to make very drastic policy changes. The chip would know where everyone was at any time. It would know what they bought, who they interacted with, and even what they said. There were even teams working on emotional collection and thought patterns.

What if they started arresting people for having an intrusive thought about killing a spouse in a fight, even though they would never act on that thought? James could read between the lines and foresee a future where the police arrested people pre-emptively. What would happen to free will?

James set the tablet down and ran his hands through his hair. He'd always believed in the potential for technology to improve lives, but this—this was something else. This was a runaway train hurtling toward a cliff, and no one could see the danger ahead.

He picked up his halophone and dialed Claire, the person he liaised with the most at NexTech when he needed to influence the board of directors. "Claire, can you come by my office?" he asked when she answered.

"Of course," she replied, her tone professional but warm.

Ten minutes later, Claire arrived, a folder tucked under her arm. "You wanted to see me?"

James gestured to the chair across from his desk. "Close the door first."

Claire obliged and sat down, her expression calm but curious.

"I just went through the Phase Two plan," James began, folding his hands on the desk in front of him. "I need to understand what my role in this is supposed to be. It seems … much bigger than what I expected from the last board meeting."

Claire gave a small smile, though it didn't reach her eyes. "I had a feeling you'd say that. Here." She slid the folder across the desk.

"What's this?"

"Your new schedule," she said. "Starting next week."

James opened the folder and scanned the pages. His usual five-day workweek in the lab had been replaced with a packed itinerary that left him in the lab only on Fridays. The rest of his time would be spent in meetings with CEOs of major corporations, coordinating with government officials, and participating in public relations campaigns to support the rollout of Phase Two.

"This can't be right," James said, looking up at Claire. "We talked about helping out a little, but I said I needed to keep time to work with the engineers."

Claire leaned forward. "James, you're the face of this technology. People trust you. They see you as the brilliant scientist who created something to make their lives better. That trust is crucial for Phase Two to succeed."

James stared at the schedule, feeling his stomach churn. "And what about my real work? I need to be around to help influence how Phase Two rolls out. So much to—"

"Our teams can handle the day-to-day," Claire interrupted gently. "Your focus needs to shift now. This is bigger than just the technology. It's about integrating it into society, building partnerships, and ensuring public support. President Walker and the board believe you're an important piece of doing that effectively."

James leaned back in his chair, the weight of the folder in his hands feeling heavier than it should. "And what if I say no? I am not a hundred percent on board with what I just read about in Phase Two."

Claire's expression didn't change, but her silence was telling.

He sighed, closing the folder. "Ask Sarah to set up a meeting with President Walker, I need to really understand what the end goal is here. I am not sure what part I want to play." His tone was resigned but firm.

Claire looked at him for a few moments longer than usual. Finally, she spoke: "James, can I offer you some advice?" He nodded, analyzing her. "We've worked together for over ten years. I have watched you tirelessly pour your heart into NexTech. And everything that has been accomplished couldn't have been done without you. But your vision for the nano chip was improving healthcare. You never envisioned reducing crime. That vision came from the collaboration with government leaders and a board who saw how this technology you created could be applied to do even more. You are the inventor, but you are not the visionary. And I don't say that with disrespect. I say that because I really believe the good that will come from this goes beyond what you think. And I am sure it feels uncomfortable to step into a new role, but, it's what the company needs from you."

James looked out the window. Not sure how much he could reveal to Claire about his concerns. "It's not just the discomfort of a new role. I realize I am getting older. I know most people in my position would have stepped aside long ago. I just…" He looked back at her and they studied each other. "I need to feel confident this is a direction I can support both publicly and privately. There needs to be guardrails put in place."

Claire nodded. "I'll make sure you speak with President Walker as soon as possible."

* * *

Two days later, James found himself staring at the President's Office from his halopad, sitting across from Evan Walker. The room was grand, but its opulence only added to James's sense of unease.

Walker was a charismatic man, his sharp features softened

by a practiced smile. He leaned forward, resting his elbows on the desk as he spoke. "James, it's good to see you. I trust the board has brought you up to speed on what's next for Phase Two."

"They have," James replied, keeping his tone neutral.

Walker's smile widened. "Good. I know this is a big shift for you, but I need you to understand just how important your role is. What you've created isn't just a technological marvel—it's a tool for building a better world. Safer, more efficient, more unified."

James nodded slowly. "I understand, Mr. President. But I have to admit, some of the plans for Phase Two caught me off guard. The level of integration … it's a lot to take in. There are things in here, that concern me, they could be used in … unhealthy ways … with the wrong intentions."

Walker's expression softened, and he leaned back in his chair. "James, let me ask you something. When you created the nano chip, what was your goal?"

"To improve healthcare," James said without hesitation, "to make it more accessible and personalized, and preventative."

"And you did that," Walker said. "But along the way, you also gave us a tool to reduce crime, to save lives, to bring people closer together. That's what this is about—taking your invention to its full potential. Imagine a world where no one has to worry about identity theft, where voting is secure and instantaneous, where everyone has equal access to resources. That's the world we're building."

James hesitated, choosing his words carefully. "I can see the benefits, but I'm also concerned about the risks. The level of oversight this system would provide … it's unprecedented. How do we ensure it's used responsibly?"

Walker's smile didn't falter, but his tone became firmer: "James, this is why we need you on board. People trust you. They need to see that you believe in this. That trust is what will keep this system in check. We have good people working on this. We want what you want. We want more preventative healthcare. People in jobs that are a perfect fit for their aptitude. Couples marrying that won't end in divorce, families growing when the time is right."

James nodded again, though his unease hadn't lessened. He'd realized during this conversation that the application of the nano chip he'd feared was already underway. President Walker was thrilled at the prospect of bringing control and manipulation to the very freedom that James felt was everyone's God-given birthright. "I'll do my part," he said carefully.

"I know you will," Walker said "You're not just doing this for the The City, James, you're doing it for the future."

The call ended, the halopad went dark and the President was gone. James sat alone, staring out the window at the city skyline. He thought about the promise of the nano chip, the potential it held to improve lives, but now it felt like that promise was being twisted into something else entirely.

He picked up the folder Claire had given him and flipped through the pages again. His face was on nearly every page—press releases, campaign strategies, news interviews. He was the face of Phase Two, whether he wanted to be or not.

The only reason he would go ahead with the plan was to remain in the know. If this was Phase Two, what would they be planning for Phase Three? James knew that if he played the part for now, it bought him time to figure out how to derail the train before it crashed.

8

Seph

Weeks had passed since Seph joined NexTech Systems, and he had settled into the rhythm of his new job. He spent most of his days deeply immersed in code, unraveling the intricacies of the nano chip's software. The more he learned, the more he realized the importance of contributing to the team's efforts, even though it meant working on technology he had reservations about.

During a routine team meeting, Seph decided it was time to voice some of his ideas for optimizing the code. He presented his suggestions with a mix of nervous excitement and technical confidence. "I believe we can streamline the data processing sequence here," he explained, pointing to a highlighted section of code on the shared screen. "It could enhance the system's efficiency without compromising its functionality."

Martin, the team leader, leaned forward, his chin resting on his hand. "Interesting. Walk me through how you arrived at this."

Seph clicked through a few lines of the code, his voice steady despite the adrenaline coursing through him. "Right now, the process loops back unnecessarily to verify emotional categorization. By reordering these functions, we eliminate redundancy and cut processing time by roughly twenty percent."

Collin, a senior developer who often had a skeptical air, furrowed his brow. "Won't that introduce new dependencies? If one of those functions fails, it could disrupt the entire flow."

"Not necessarily," Seph replied, anticipating the concern. He pulled up another section of the code. "By isolating the categorization process here, any failure would be contained without affecting downstream processes. It's a modular fix."

Emma, seated at the far end of the table with her arms crossed, chimed in: "That's clever. But have you thought about how this might impact the real-time analysis? Faster isn't always better if we're sacrificing precision."

Seph nodded, appreciating her input. "I've considered that. I've run a simulation to check the integrity of the outputs, and the results showed no loss in accuracy. I'm happy to share the data if you'd like to see."

Emma raised an eyebrow, her expression softening. "You ran simulations on this already?"

"Yeah," Seph said, feeling a bit more confident. "I wanted to make sure it was worth bringing up before wasting everyone's time."

Martin leaned back in his chair, a small smile playing at the corners of his mouth. "Your observations are spot on, Seph. It's an elegant solution. Let's implement it and see how it performs."

Collin's skeptical look shifted to reluctant approval. "Well, it's not every day someone improves on the existing framework this quickly. I'll give you that."

"Thanks," Seph said, keeping his tone measured despite the satisfaction swelling inside him.

Emma tapped her pen against the table, a thoughtful expression on her face. "What about scalability? If we're adding more data streams down the line, will this approach hold up?"

"Good question," Seph said, turning to her. "I've accounted for scalability by decoupling the logic here." He highlighted another part of the code. "This way, even as we scale, the performance impact should remain minimal. But I'll admit, we'll need to monitor it closely."

Emma nodded, a hint of a smile tugging at her lips. "Fair enough. Looks like you've done your homework."

Martin clasped his hands together. "Alright, team. Let's move forward with Seph's suggestion. Emma, can you oversee the integration and testing? Collin, provide support where needed."

"Got it," Emma said, giving Seph an approving glance. "I'll start with the initial implementation and keep you updated."

"Sure thing," Collin said, still sounding a bit begrudging but clearly on board.

The conversation shifted to other updates, but Seph couldn't help feeling a mix of relief and pride. He'd moved from observation to active participation, earning the trust and respect of his colleagues. Yet, as the meeting wrapped up, that familiar pang of unease returned. Each line of code he improved or wrote was another brick in the foundation of a technology that he wasn't sure he could support in the long run.

As the team packed up to leave the conference room, Emma lingered. She caught Seph's eye and walked over. "Hey, good work in there," she said, her tone kind. "It's nice to have someone shake things up a bit."

"Thanks," Seph said, surprised by her compliment. "It means a lot, coming from you."

"Don't let it go to your head," she teased. "But seriously, keep bringing ideas like that. We need fresh perspectives."

"I'll do my best," Seph said with a small smile.

* * *

Later that week, Seph found himself out again with Emma. They decided to visit one of the city's newest attractions, a futuristic virtual-reality park where visitors could experience different worlds and scenarios. Seph had never splurged on this type of activity before. He had heard about them from friends but never had enough money to justify it. Now, with his new salary coming in, he could afford this type of outing.

As they entered the park, they were greeted by a dazzling array of lights and sounds. The lobby buzzed with energy, a kaleidoscope of neon signs advertising adventures like *Dinosaur Kingdom*, *Deep Sea Explorer*, and *Galactic Odyssey*. Emma's eyes lit up as she scanned the options.

"I've been wanting to try the 'Galactic Odyssey' experience. It's like exploring a whole new galaxy!" she exclaimed.

Seph smiled, caught up in her enthusiasm. "Sounds amazing. Let's do it."

As they approached the Galactic Odyssey station, a park

attendant handed them sleek VR headsets and motion con-
trollers.

"First time?" the attendant asked.

Emma nodded eagerly. "Yep, can't wait."

The attendant grinned. "You're going to love it. Just follow
the prompts inside, and remember—you're the pilot, so keep
your wits about you."

Seph adjusted his headset and glanced at Emma. "Ready to
save the galaxy?"

"Born ready," she replied with a laugh.

The moment they put on the headsets, the bustling park
disappeared. They were instantly transported to the cockpit
of a futuristic spaceship. The galaxy stretched out before them
in stunning detail, a mesmerizing tapestry of stars, planets,
and swirling nebulae.

Emma let out a gasp. "Wow, this is incredible."

Seph took in the view, nodding. "It's like we're actually
here."

Their mission began with simple navigation, steering the
ship through asteroid fields and scanning distant planets for
resources. Seph manned the controls, while Emma handled
the scanner, her excitement palpable.

"Incoming asteroid at three o'clock," Emma warned, pointing out a massive rock hurtling toward them.

"Got it," Seph replied, gripping the joystick and veering the
ship just in time. The asteroid grazed past them, its surface
detailed enough to feel real.

"Nice move," Emma said, flashing him a grin. "I'd say we
make a pretty good team."

"Not bad for our first intergalactic flight," Seph quipped, his
voice light.

They continued exploring, discovering alien landscapes and mysterious ruins on far-off planets. Emma's awe at the virtual universe was infectious, and Seph found himself laughing more than he had in weeks. When the session ended, they removed their headsets, still glowing from the experience.

"That was amazing," Emma said as they stepped back into the real world. "I don't think I'll ever look at the night sky the same way again."

"Agreed," Seph said. "Although now I feel like I should add 'spaceship pilot' to my resume."

Emma laughed. "Let's see if NexTech has a division for that."

They decided to explore the park further and found themselves in the digital garden, a serene landscape filled with exotic, luminescent plants and interactive light displays. The air seemed to vibrate softly, and glowing firefly-like drones flitted around them.

Emma ran her fingers through the light trails left by the drones, her expression calm. "This place is so peaceful. It's like stepping into a dream."

Seph watched her for a moment before speaking: "It's a nice change of pace from work."

Emma nodded, her expression soft and contemplative, as she turned around, her hand brushed the back of Seph's shoulder. The touch was light, almost accidental, but it lingered just enough to send a ripple of sensation through him. Her fingers trailed down his arm in what felt like slow motion.

Seph froze, his breath hitching as the hair on his arms stood on end, a visceral reaction to the sudden warmth flooding his senses. His heart stumbled over itself, hammering in a way that made him feel both alive and off balance, as though the ground beneath him had shifted.

For a moment, time seemed to pause. He could still feel the ghost of her touch, lingering like an imprint, more real than anything else in the park.

"Thanks for today," Emma said, looking at him. "I needed this."

"Me too," Seph replied honestly. "It's nice to step away and just ... be." Just as he started to consider if he should lean in for a kiss or reach for her hand an announcement interrupted them.

"Galaxy Park is closing in ten minutes, please make your way to the exit."

She smiled. "Well, I'll see you at work tomorrow. Don't let the galaxy-saving skills go to your head."

"No promises," he said with a grin.

Seph watched her go, and let the feeling of missing June resurface, wondering what his aunt was doing, and what she would think of Emma.

9

Seph

Seph's halophone buzzed on his desk, the soft glow illuminating the corner of his office space as he sifted through lines of code on his work monitor. Distracted, he glanced at the screen to see a message from Callum:

"Are you alive? Haven't heard from you in weeks. Starting to think you've been kidnapped by NexTech."

Seph let out a laugh, shaking his head. He leaned back in his chair, grabbing the halophone and typing a quick reply: *"Still alive, just buried under work. How's life on your end?"*

The response came almost immediately: *"Life? You mean my endless job hunt? Yeah, it's a thrill. Turns out no one's impressed by a guy who spent his last year of school playing Call of Duty instead of networking."*

Seph smirked. *"Hey, maybe you can pitch that as strategic-planning experience: 'Led a team to victory in high-stakes simulations.'"*

"Ha, hilarious. Meanwhile, you've probably landed the coolest gig in the city and forgotten all about us regular folks."

Seph hesitated for a moment, unsure how much to share. Finally, he decided to keep it light: *"It's been busy, that's for sure. Work's intense, but it's also ... interesting. Plus, I've been getting to know this girl on my team, Emma."*

"Emma, huh? So that's why you went radio silent. Forget work—spill the details. Who is she?"

Seph shook his head, grinning at Callum's predictable response. He propped his feet up on the desk and typed back: *"She's smart, driven, and definitely the kind of person who'd be annoyed at how much you procrastinated in school."*

"Sounds like a keeper. How'd you meet her?"

"She's on my team at NexTech. We've been working on this big project together, and, well, we've kind of clicked. She's different from anyone I've met before."

"Dude, is she the reason you're suddenly so into this job? Be honest."

"Let's just say she's a bonus. The job itself is ... a lot to get used to. But yeah, it's been nice having someone there who makes it easier."

"So, what you're saying is you've got a killer job, a smart girl, and you've completely forgotten your broke, unemployed best friend?"

"Not forgotten. Just ... preoccupied. We should catch up soon, though. How about I buy you lunch? My treat."

"You'd better. I'll pick the most expensive place I can find."

"Deal. But only if you promise not to ask me for Emma's number."

"No promises."

Seph laughed, setting the halophone down and feeling a rare sense of normalcy amidst the whirlwind of his new life. Callum might not have his act together, but he had a way of reminding Seph not to take things too seriously.

As the screen dimmed, Seph turned back to his work, his mood noticeably lighter. He slipped on the virtual-reality headset that had become an essential tool in his daily routine. The headset provided him with three massive virtual screens, each displaying a different aspect of his current project. On one screen, he watched footage from a past experiment where participants were viewing emotionally charged movies. Their reactions, ranging from tears to laughter, played out in vivid detail. The second screen displayed real-time data being collected from the nano chips implanted in the participants. The graphs and numbers fluctuated, indicating the hosts' emotional responses to the movies. The third screen was dedicated to the code that interpreted this data: a complex maze of algorithms and commands. Seph's eyes moved deftly between the screens, analyzing the interplay between the visual stimuli, the emotional responses, and the code's interpretation.

As Seph worked, a sudden pang of hunger interrupted his focus. He realized he hadn't eaten anything since breakfast. Just as the thought crossed his mind, a pop-up notification appeared on his VR screen, almost as if the system could read his thoughts. The notification presented him with a choice of three snacks: a protein bar, a small bag of mixed nuts, or a piece of fruit. Seph, intrigued and slightly amused by this unexpected convenience, selected the protein bar. He barely had time to wonder how the snack would arrive when he heard a soft whirring sound approaching. An indoor drone, sleek and efficient, hovered into his workspace, gently dropping off the protein bar at his desk.

Seph removed his headset and looked at the drone in

fascination. It was a small, quadcopter design, equipped with a precise delivery mechanism. The drone waited for a moment, as if ensuring the delivery was successful, then buzzed away, disappearing as quickly as it had arrived. As Seph unwrapped the protein bar, he couldn't help but wonder how far the surveillance went. Could it read his thoughts, or had it just analyzed his low blood sugar?

As the day drew to a close, the hum of NexTech's sprawling office space began to subside. Seph sat at his desk, his fingers poised over the keyboard as he reviewed his notes from the day. The VR headset lay neatly to one side, a reminder of the hours he'd spent immersed in testing and analyzing code. He leaned back in his chair, rubbing his temples, when a familiar voice broke through his thoughts.

"Burning the midnight oil?"

He turned to see Emma standing a few feet away, her bag slung over one shoulder and her jacket draped over her arm. She smiled, her expression softening the exhaustion that lingered in her eyes.

"Something like that," Seph replied, leaning back in his chair. "Just trying to make sense of the algorithm's emotional misreads. It's … a lot."

Emma nodded, stepping closer. "Tell me about it. I've spent the past three hours combing through the emotional-response data."

"Right?" Seph said, his tone animated. "I mean, the program's good at identifying the obvious stuff—but anything nuanced, and it's like it throws up its hands and guesses."

Emma chuckled, perching on the edge of his desk. "'Guess-work' should not be part of the pitch for the most advanced emotional tracking system in the world."

Seph smirked. "Maybe we should add that to the marketing materials. 'Ninety percent accurate, ten percent psychic.'"

"Don't give the marketing team ideas," Emma said, laughing. "They'd probably run with it."

For a moment, they both sat in companionable silence, the quiet of the office filling the space between them. Emma glanced at Seph's screen, where lines of code scrolled past.

"You've really been diving in, haven't you?" she asked.

"It's kind of my thing," Seph admitted with a shrug. "Once I get started, it's hard to stop. It's hard for me to a leave a problem unsolved."

Emma tilted her head. "Do you ever stop? Like, do you even know what 'free time' is?"

Seph smiled sheepishly. "Not often. But I've been trying to … balance things out more. You know, make time for stuff outside of work."

"And how's that going?" she asked, her tone teasing but kind.

"Better," he said, meeting her eyes. "Hanging with you helps."

Emma blinked, then gave him a small smile. "Well, I'm glad I could contribute to your work-life balance."

Seph hesitated, then asked, "What about you? What's your escape from all this?" He gestured vaguely around the office.

Emma's smile grew. "Cooking, as you know... I also like to spend time with friends and family, talking to people outside of work... It helps remind me there is more to life than what we are doing here."

Seph thought of his short conversation with Callum earlier and remember how good that had felt. "You're right," he said, nodding. "And you know, sometimes the best way to solve a problem is to stop looking at it so closely. I probably need to take a step back to see things from a clearer perspective."

"That's tragic. Here you go talking about work again!" Emma said, mock-serious. "We need to fix that. We should implement some sort of rule where we can't talk about work unless we are actually in a formal meeting to talk about work."

"Are you saying you want to spend more time with me away from work?" Seph asked, a hint of a smile playing on his lips.

"Maybe," Emma said with a shrug, though her eyes sparkled. "Since you've seen my house, it's only fair I see yours. I need to see how the other side lives."

"As I've told you numerous times, you'll be horrified at how tech-inept it is," Seph admitted. "But honestly, I'd be happy to have you over. It's been a bit lonely there since my aunt left. But today is not the day, I need time to actually clean before you come over."

Emma laughed. "Challenge accepted. You pick the date and I'll be there. But for now, you should call it a day. It's late, and you look like you've been staring at that screen for hours."

Seph glanced at the clock and realized she was right. The office was nearly empty, and his neck ached from sitting in the same position for so long. "Thanks for the reminder," he said, standing and stretching.

Emma gave him a playful salute. "Anytime. Have a good night, Seph."

"You too, Emma," he said, watching as she walked away, her footsteps echoing softly in the quiet office.

For all the chaos and uncertainty of his job, moments like this reminded him that there were still good things to hold onto.

10

Seph

Seph was diving deeper into the project at work. He'd been working on a few ideas that the team hadn't considered before, and amid his uncertainty, he'd stumbled upon the answer. Seph recognized that the key lay in the program's approach to analyzing emotional data. The current system was designed for speed, capturing the initial surge of vital signs associated with strong emotions like anger. However, this approach failed to account for the complex, layered nature of human feelings. Anger, Seph realized, was often just the surface expression of deeper, more nuanced feelings such as pain. Like many humans, the program was reacting to the initial wave of emotion without understanding the underlying cause. It was interpreting data at the peak of emotional intensity, where anger overshadowed the true feelings beneath.

The solution, Seph theorized, was to reconfigure the program to treat the initial spike in vital signs not as a definitive answer, but as a starting point. Instead of rushing to conclusions, the program needed to wait, to allow the person's emotional response to evolve and stabilize. As the vital signs began to normalize, the secondary data would reveal the host's true emotional state. This approach mirrored the human process of emotional regulation, where the cooling-down period often brought clarity and understanding. By applying this principle to the program, Seph was confident that it would more accurately identify the subtler, underlying emotions.

His certainty in this solution was unshakeable. It wasn't just a hypothesis; it felt like an undeniable truth waiting to be proven. The key to unlocking the program's potential lay in patience and understanding, in recognizing the complexity of human emotions and mirroring the natural process of emotional realization.

The breakthrough was exhilarating. But it also presented him with a moral dilemma. By improving this aspect of the software, he would be enhancing a system he fundamentally disagreed with, that could potentially manipulate people's emotions and decisions. Was he ready to contribute to a technology that could further erode the concept of free will?

Seph wrestled with this decision, torn between professional joy in solving a complex technical challenge and ethical concerns about the implications of his work. But not improving the algorithm meant passing up the opportunity to showcase his skills and solidify his position at NexTech—a position he needed to maintain to gather vital information on the future plans for this technology.

Enveloped by the glow of his computer screen, Seph faced a pivotal decision. It wasn't about career progression or personal recognition at NexTech; it was far more profound. This was about a deep-rooted allegiance to his own moral compass. Contributing to the program would undoubtedly earn him trust and recognition within NexTech, potentially granting him deeper insights into the company's workings. But would solving this problem do more harm than good? Enhancing the program's ability to interpret emotions was a significant leap in technology, and if the program hit the ninety-eight percent accuracy threshold that they were aiming for, how would this get deployed? Every improvement he made was a step towards perfecting a tool that could be used to manipulate and control the very essence of human decision-making. This wasn't just about choosing sides; it was about defining his role in a battle where the lines between right and wrong were blurred.

Seph decided he needed someone to process this with, someone who might understand the complexity of his situation. He thought of Callum and almost immediately dismissed the idea. Then he thought of Emma, she'd grown up in a house that had unwavering belief in NexTech, always seeing its positives, but she also had compassion and kindness that he thought might help him. He needed her perspective, and, he admitted to himself, her support.

He knew telling Emma was risking not just his relationship with her, but his job as well. She could turn him in and his access to NexTech would be gone. He trusted Emma, but he knew he needed to choose his words carefully. She'd become the closest person to him, they had a bond he didn't think could be broken easily.

Seph picked up his halophone and sent Emma a message: *"Hey, want to finally come over and see my apartment tonight?"* It was 3pm. He figured he could leave a little early and quickly clean up his apartment.

A few seconds later his halophone lit up with a response from Emma: *"Yes! Send me your address, I can be there at 6!"*

* * *

Seph zoomed around his apartment, his nerves threatening to unravel as he cleaned up.

When Emma arrived, there was a tension in the air, a sense that something significant was about to unfold.

She stepped into the room, her coat still on, her eyes scanning his face for some hint of what this impromptu meeting was about. "You okay?" she asked, her tone light but laced with concern.

"Yeah," Seph said quickly, then corrected himself. "No. I mean, I will be. Come in, sit down."

Emma hesitated for a moment, then walked over to the couch and sat, placing her bag at her feet. "You're being a little dramatic, you know that?" she said with a faint smile, trying to ease the tension.

"Fair point," Seph admitted, sitting across from her in the armchair. He leaned forward, his elbows resting on his knees. "But I—I need to tell you something, and I'm not sure how to start."

Emma raised an eyebrow, her curiosity piqued. "Well, starting somewhere is better than nowhere. What's going on?"

Seph took a deep breath, steeling himself. "It's about why I'm really at NexTech. Why I took the job in the first place."

Her expression shifted to one of quiet focus, and she nodded, encouraging him to continue.

"I've been holding back because it's … complicated," Seph began. "But I trust you. And I need you to know the truth."

He told her about his Aunt June, about where she actually went, and about his true purpose at NexTech. His voice wavered at times, but the words kept coming, tumbling out in a mix of confession and explanation. He spoke of his inner battle, the struggle between his role as an employee at the forefront of technological innovation and his deep-seated concerns about the implications of their work. He described the growing unease he felt with every breakthrough, every algorithm refined.

Emma listened intently, her expression a mix of shock and understanding. She didn't interrupt, letting him lay everything bare. When he finally paused, her voice was soft but steady. "So, you're saying you're at NexTech to … expose them? Or to fix something from the inside?"

Seph hesitated. "I don't know if it's that clear-cut. I just know that what they're doing—what we're doing—has the *potential* to change everything. And not all of it for the better."

Emma leaned back, running a hand through her hair. "This is … a lot. I mean, I've had my doubts about some of the things we're working on, but I never thought…" She trailed off, searching for the right words.

"I'm sorry to drop this on you," Seph said. "But you're one of the few people I feel like I can talk to about it. And after everything we've been working on together, I thought you deserved to know."

Emma's eyes softened, and she gave him a small nod. "I appreciate that, I do. But Seph, this is huge. If you're right about … all of this, what can you do?"

"That's the thing," Seph admitted. "I don't have a plan. Not yet. But I think I am close to a breakthrough with our emotional-analysis problem at work. But I am not sure I should actually do anything to improve the program. Not without knowing how it will be used."

Emma's brow furrowed. "So, you're trying to figure out what to do?"

"Yeah," Seph said. "I don't know if I should contribute, or just skate by and keep digging for more information."

Emma stared at him for a long moment, her mind clearly racing. Finally, she said, "You're walking a fine line, Seph. What you're talking about could get you in serious trouble. But at the same time ... I get it. I see why you feel like you have to try and find out."

He nodded, a flicker of relief crossing his face. "I don't expect you to agree with me. I just... I needed someone to know, someone I trust."

Emma's lips curved into a faint smile. "You're not in this alone, you know. If you need someone to bounce ideas off, or just someone to remind you to eat and sleep, I'm here."

Seph chuckled, the tension in his shoulders easing slightly. "I'll hold you to that."

As the night wore on, their conversation delved deeper into the complexities of NexTech's work, the ethical dilemmas, and the risks Seph faced.

Emma questioned, challenged, and empathized, her mind working to reconcile the conflicting worlds Seph presented. She didn't have the same immediate skepticisms that June had instilled in him. Emma wasn't convinced there was anything malicious going on, but she did understand Seph's perspective the more he shared the narrative he'd grown up with. "So there is always a chance that something bad could be happening. We obviously don't know everything. But what if there is nothing wrong? What if NexTech really is just trying to do good, and what if your breakthrough helps us find a cure for anxiety disorders?"

"But do I have a responsibility to find out the intent of this new tech before I implement the solution?" Seph shot back.

"Seph, you're not James Kent." Emma tilted her head at him.

"I know, but where does my responsibility end?"

"I think you have a responsibility to do the job you were hired to do, unless you have real solid evidence that this job is going against a moral code you can't support." She paused. "And then you would have to decide what to do about that. But you're kinda spinning your wheels before you have all the information."

"So you think I should tell Martin the solution?" Seph asked, analyzing Emma's facial expression.

She met his gaze and thought for a few moments. "You shouldn't do anything you're not comfortable doing. But if I was in your shoes, I would. Because the only way to get to the bottom of a pool is to jump in. Right now, you're dipping your toes in the water hoping to get wet, and that will never work." She paused. "If you're not willing to fully walk away from this life, then give it a chance and actually jump in. You won't know what is at the bottom until you finally do."

When Emma finally left, there was a new understanding between them, a bond forged in the complexity of their shared experience. Seph watched her go, feeling a mix of apprehension and determination. He knew what he had to do next—he needed to go all in.

11

Seph

Seph arrived at NexTech with a newfound determination, his mind clear and his purpose renewed. He walked briskly through the halls, the activity around him barely registering. His thoughts were laser-focused on one thing: the breakthrough he'd discovered. As he approached Martin's office, his solution to the emotional algorithm burned bright in his thoughts. He knocked lightly on the door, and Martin looked up from his desk.

"Hey Seph. Come in."

Seph entered, shutting the door behind him. "Martin, I've figured it out," he began, his voice steady with confidence. Without waiting for an invitation, he pulled up the diagrams and code snippets he'd prepared on his halopad and set it on the desk.

Martin leaned forward, his brows furrowing as he studied the display. "Alright, walk me through what you've got," he said, folding his hands together.

Seph launched into his explanation: "The problem is in how we've been interpreting the emotional data in real time. Each of the core emotions our teams are working on are such dominant emotional responses that they're overwhelming the subtler signals that come after. But if we delay the analysis and wait for the vital signs to start normalizing, we can pick up on those underlying emotions. Think of it like the ripples in a pond. The initial splash is anger, but the ripples are the emotions that tell us what's really going on: grief, guilt, even fear. We're missing those because we're too quick to analyze the data."

Martin sat back in his chair, rubbing his chin. "So, speed has actually been the downfall in our analysis," he mused. "We need to let the emotions breathe before we can accurately decipher them."

"Exactly," Seph said, his eyes lighting up. "I've already run simulations using historical data. The results are promising— our accuracy rate improves drastically. I am not sure if it will get us to ninety-eight percent but I think it will be close. We will have to put it into practice to know for sure."

Martin's lips curled into a smile, his initial doubt giving way to intrigue. "This is impressive, Seph. We need to share this at the department meeting this afternoon."

The timing was perfect. Seph had hoped Martin would jump on board and that his idea might get passed up the chain, but he wasn't sure how quickly it would happen. Martin's reaction had exceeded his expectations.

Martin immediately called Emma, Franky, and Collin into his office. The two arrived minutes later, curiosity evident on their faces.

"What's going on?" Emma asked, glancing between Martin and Seph.

Martin gestured toward Seph. "Seph has come up with a significant improvement to our emotional-analysis algorithm, and I want us to prepare a presentation for the department meeting this afternoon."

Collin raised an eyebrow, his skepticism evident. "That's a pretty quick turnaround. What exactly are we working on?"

Seph took a breath and launched into his explanation again, breaking it down step by step. As he spoke, Emma leaned forward, her expression shifting from interest to excitement. Collin's initial doubt gave way to cautious optimism.

"So you're saying we've been analyzing emotions too early," Emma said, summarizing. "If we delay, we can capture the more nuanced feelings underneath more accurately."

"Exactly," Seph said. "It's like waiting for the storm to pass before assessing the damage. The initial wave of anger clouds everything else."

"I'll admit, that makes sense," Collin said. "But we're going to need solid visuals and data to back this up if we're presenting it to the whole department."

"That's where you two come in," Martin said. "We have a few hours. Let's divide and conquer."

They quickly settled into roles. Seph focused on refining the technical explanation and pulling key data points from his simulations. Emma volunteered to create the presentation slides, weaving Seph's findings into a compelling narrative. Collin and Franky began analyzing potential questions or pushback they might face during the meeting and drafted responses to address them.

The energy in the room was electric as they worked. Seph

shared his screen with Emma so she could integrate his diagrams into the slides. "Make sure this one comes after the explanation of delayed analysis," Seph said, pointing to a graph. "It'll reinforce the point."

"Got it," Emma said, typing rapidly. "Do you have any visuals for the comparison between traditional and delayed methods?"

Seph pulled up another file. "Here. This chart shows how the accuracy rate shifts when we adjust the timing."

Franky glanced over. "That'll help. If anyone questions the validity, we've got the numbers to back it up."

As the clock ticked closer to noon, a drone arrived with their lunch—a selection of sandwiches and salads. Martin insisted they keep working while they ate. "This is turning into one of the most productive mornings we've had in a year," he said with a grin, biting into his sandwich.

"No pressure or anything," Seph joked, though he felt a surge of pride.

Emma looked up from her laptop. "Seph, how do you want to handle the presentation? Are you comfortable leading, or should Martin take the reins?"

Seph hesitated. "I think it's better if Martin starts, but I'm happy to jump in for the technical parts. You've all been at NexTech longer than I have. Your voices carry more weight."

"Fair enough," Martin said. "But don't undersell yourself, Seph. This is your breakthrough. People need to hear it from you. I think we should co-present it."

By the time the presentation was finalized, the team felt a shared sense of accomplishment. Emma clicked through the finished slides, nodding in approval. "This is solid. We're ready."

That afternoon, the department meeting was alive with anticipation. Marlene Hughes took the floor with an air of excitement, her usual measured demeanor replaced by palpable enthusiasm. Martin had sent her a message earlier that morning that his team would be presenting a breakthrough. After she'd gone through some standard updates and initiatives happening at NexTech, she invited Martin and his team up.

Seph sat on the first row eager to see how people would respond. The other teams representing the other core emotions were all there. He'd interacted with them in passing but didn't really know them beyond that.

Martin began, gesturing to the screen behind him, "We have a significant breakthrough to discuss, thanks to Seph."

All eyes turned to Seph, who shifted slightly in his seat, feeling both nerves and the uncomfortable weight of the spotlight. Martin launched into an explanation of his discovery, detailing how delayed emotional data analysis could revolutionize their work. The room was silent at first, the weight of the concept sinking in. Then, a ripple of murmurs spread through the teams.

"Wait," one of the senior developers, Ava, said, raising her hand. "You're saying we've been missing secondary emotions this whole time?"

Martin nodded. "Precisely. Seph's approach allows us to see past the dominant initial response and uncover the full emotional spectrum."

"That' s… brilliant," Ava said, glancing at Seph. "Why didn't we think of this before?"

Seph shrugged, trying to stay humble. "Sometimes it's just about looking at the data from a different angle."

As the implications sank in, the teams broke into applause. Seph felt a surge of excitement, mixed with a surreal sense of disbelief. His idea, born out of inner turmoil and sleepless nights, was now being heralded as a turning point.

After the meeting, the director, Marlene Hughes, approached Seph with a smile. "Seph, I have some news for you," she said. "I've recommended you for a mentorship session with James Kent. HR will send you the details."

Seph blinked, taken aback. "James Kent? As in, *the* James Kent?"

"The one and only," Marlene replied. "It's a rare opportunity. Every year each department director gets to nominate someone that is showing to be exceptional. I am using my spot for you."

"Thank you, Mrs. Hughes. I'm honored," Seph managed to say, though his mind was already racing.

Back at his desk, Seph couldn't shake the weight of what Marlene had told him. A session with James Kent was a defining moment where he would be face to face with the person who knew what was really going on in NexTech. This was the man who had invented the nano chip, whose work had reshaped society in ways both miraculous and potentially troubling.

Emma appeared at his desk, a coffee in hand. "I heard about your mentor session," she said, her tone soft. "Congratulations. Way to jump in."

"Thanks," Seph said, offering a small smile. "It's been a whirlwind day."

Emma studied him for a moment. "I think this might be the meeting you've been waiting for. You might finally see the bottom of the pool."

"I know. That's exactly what I was thinking." Seph smirked.

Later that evening, as the office cleared out, Seph found himself unable to leave for a while. The glow of his display cast shadows on the walls as he revisited his notes. The opportunity to probe deeper into the intentions behind NexTech's work was incredible and he wanted to make sure he didn't blow it.

A knock at his cubicle broke his concentration. It was Martin, holding a folder and looking unusually relaxed. "Still here?" he asked.

"Couldn't let it go," Seph admitted. "Just trying to make sure everything's airtight."

Martin nodded approvingly. "That's the kind of dedication that got you this far. Listen, about James—he's a visionary, but he's also a realist. Don't be afraid to ask hard questions. He respects that."

Seph raised an eyebrow. "Hard questions, huh? I'll keep that in mind."

12

James

J ames sat alone in his dimly lit living room, the noise of the city softly filtered through the thick glass of his apartment windows. The haloprojector on the wall flickered to life, casting a glow across the furniture. A lifesize image of President Evan Walker appeared, standing confidently on the steps of the Capitol. With the advanced haloprojector technology, it felt and appeared that the President was standing right there in James's living room.

James leaned back in his chair, a glass of whiskey resting on the table beside him. He swirled the amber liquid absently, his eyes fixed on the projection.

"Today, I am proud to announce that ninety-five percent of our population has embraced the future by receiving the nano chip," Walker began, his voice resonant and measured.

James tilted his head, studying Walker's every inflection, the practiced pauses, the subtle movements of his hands that punctuated his words. He was a well-rehearsed salesman. The announcement was no surprise to James. He'd been briefed on the speech earlier that week, but hearing it delivered with such charisma stirred a mix of emotions. What once had been a point of pride for his invention had slowly been giving way to guilt.

Walker's tone softened as he addressed the holdouts: *"I understand that there are concerns among those who have yet to receive the chip. Let me be clear: the government will not mandate the nano chip. It remains elective."*

James took a slow sip of his whiskey, the sharp warmth spreading down his throat. *Elective*, he thought, repeating the word in his mind—a choice that came with consequences so steep it was hardly a choice at all.

His gaze flicked to the small halopad resting on the armrest of his chair. It displayed a live feed of social-media reactions, updated in real time.

"Because of the widespread adoption of the nano chip, we have finally come to a place where we can subsidize the cost of most of our modern-day amenities. Over the next thirty days we are rolling out several programs that are fully subsidized by the government and free to all who embrace the nano chip.

"The first will be universal ID, this will replace your driver's license, passport, birth certificate, and all identifying documentation. Your chip already stores this data, and now with a simple swipe on UID receivers, that information can be shared instantly. Of course, this means the nano chip will be the only identification method accepted at stores, airports, banks, and medical offices.

"The second is universal healthcare, this had been made possible because of the brilliant work NexTech has done by leveraging health data; diagnosing and preventing disease before treatment

becomes costly. If you have the nano chip, you will be notified and alerted when medical attention is needed to treat the early signs of disease. If the nano chip detects a standard illness like the flu, it will alert you to stay home until symptoms pass. If we can get up to ninety-eight percent participation in the chip, our AI models predict certain illnesses will be completely eradicated.

"The public transpo and all educational institutions will also become free to all with the nano chip. We can better assess and predict the likelihood of career success for individuals so there will be no more wasted degrees. More exciting programs like this are in the works with NexTech Systems and I am very excited to see how we can continue to make life better for all.

"However," Walker continued, his gaze steely, *"I want to be clear that choosing not to receive the chip means opting out of the safety and benefits it provides. This includes access to banking, our advanced healthcare system, the public transpo, and all educational institutions. If you choose this path, you must be prepared to live off the city grid, in self-sustenance."*

James's jaw clenched as he heard the words spoken aloud. They'd been carefully crafted in committee meetings, but their delivery struck with a finality he hadn't anticipated.

He set his glass down and picked up the halopad, scrolling through the flood of comments:

"Incredible progress! Thank you, President Walker!"

"Finally, a leader with vision. The nano chip is the future."

"If people don't want the chip, let them live in the woods. Good riddance."

James frowned. The overwhelming positivity didn't comfort him. He knew better than anyone how easily public opinion could be shaped, how the promise of convenience and security could blind people to the erosion of their autonomy.

Walker's address concluded with a message that toed the line between unity and warning: *"We respect your free will and choice. The government has no intention of pursuing those who choose to live without the nano chip. But it is my duty to lead us into the future and protect those who want a better tomorrow from those who prefer to live without these advancements. Remember, it's a privilege to partake in the benefits we are offering. The choice, as always, is yours."*

As the image faded and the room dimmed once more, James exhaled slowly. The speech had been masterful, as expected. But it left him with a gnawing sense of unease. He set the halopad aside and walked to the large windows that overlooked the city. The sprawling metropolis glittered below, a testament to the advancements that had been made possible by the very technology he'd created.

He pulled out his own halophone, navigating to a private forum where dissenting voices still lingered, though they were fewer and quieter than they had been in years past. Most threads were barren, their participants either chipped or driven underground.

One post caught his eye: *"Walker's speech—another polished ultimatum."*

James clicked on it, skimming the comments. They were articulate, concerned, but ultimately resigned. *"What choice do we have?"* one read. *"Living off-grid isn't realistic for most people. They know that,"* said another.

He closed the forum, feeling the weight of his creation pressing down on him. The nano chip had started as a tool to save lives. Now it was the cornerstone of a society that teetered on the edge of something darker.

He returned to his chair, staring at the empty space where

Walker had stood moments earlier. *"The choice, as always, is yours"* rang in James's mind. He read between the lines. Today's assurance could easily become tomorrow's threat.

The soft chime of a notification interrupted his thoughts. It was from Claire, his second-in-command: *"James, thoughts on the address? Call me if you want to discuss."*

James tapped out a quick reply: *"Well executed. Let's connect tomorrow."*

He set the halophone aside and rubbed his temples. His mind drifted back to the early days of the nano chip, the excitement of the first trials, the lives they'd saved. For now, though, James's role was to stay the course, to be the face of progress, even as he questioned its cost. He picked up his glass of whiskey, drained the last of it, and sat in silence, the weight of his decisions settling in around him.

* * *

The next day James sat in his lab. What once was a safe haven for him to innovate without boundaries and push the world he loved forward, had become a dim reality of the consequences he saw playing out. His Friday lab sessions had become an opportunity for him to piece together the broader picture of NexTech's current projects. Today, as he delved deeper into the data and reports brought to him by the developer team leads, a chilling realization dawned upon him. He'd spent six weeks piecing together what he could from the resources available to him without drawing attention, but now he finally had enough of the pieces to see the plan.

The company he'd founded to enhance safety and improve lives was on a path that threatened the very essence of human autonomy. NexTech's plans, if brought to fruition, would mark the end of free will as society knew it. The systems they were developing would dictate career paths, not based on individual choice or passion, but cold, hard data. Marriages would be authorized not by personal connections, but by algorithmic compatibility. And the most personal of all decisions, medical treatments, would be determined not by patients and doctors, but by calculated cost-benefit analyses. The thought of a world where personal choice was obsolete, where lives were dictated by an impersonal system, filled James with a profound sense of grief and despair.

James left the office that evening with a heavy heart. The realization of what his creation had become was crushing. He'd envisioned a world made safer by technology, but instead, he'd inadvertently laid the groundwork for a system that could strip away the very core of human identity and choice.

As he drove home, the streets and lights of the city seemed distant, as if part of another world—a world where freedom and personal agency still mattered. Arriving home, James found no solace in the walls of his house. The rooms felt cavernous and empty, echoing his own sense of hollowness. He managed to make it to his bedroom before the full magnitude of his despair overwhelmed him.

The weekend passed in a blur of grief and guilt. James lay in bed, unable to muster the will to eat or drink. He was haunted by visions of a future where individuality was sacrificed at the altar of efficiency, where every human emotion, desire, and dream was reduced to data points in an algorithm. He thought of the people whose lives would be irrevocably changed, of the dreams that would be unfulfilled, and of the unique paths that would never be taken. The room felt stifling, suffocating, as if the air itself was thick with the weight of his regret.

In those dark hours, James confronted the reality of what he'd unleashed upon the world. The tool he'd created to protect and serve humanity was being twisted into a mechanism of control, a way to subdue the very spirit of human freedom.

Lying there in a state of desolation, James knew he could not remain passive. He had to act, to do whatever he could to steer the course away from this dystopian future. But for now, gripped by a paralyzing sorrow, he remained in bed, a broken man grappling with the consequences of his life's work.

13

Seph

Seph arrived at Emma's house for dinner, a small bouquet of flowers in hand.

Emma greeted him at the door, her usual bright smile glowing. "Thanks for coming," she said, taking the flowers and giving him a quick hug. "Dinner's almost ready."

Seph followed her into the kitchen, where the smell of roasted garlic filled the air. Emma turned back to the stove as she added some spices to her dish.

"Wow it smells great! What did you make?" Seph asked, leaning against the counter.

Emma hesitated before answering. "It's a potato hash and chicken cooked the way my grandma used to make it. One of my brother's favorite meals. I told Tucker I would make it to celebrate his career assessment today."

Seph nodded, recalling the conversation they'd had a few days earlier. The career assessments were the Department of Education's latest initiative, a partnership with NexTech to identify and direct children into careers based on their aptitudes. Every child turning fourteen within the last six months was required to undergo the evaluation.

"How's he feeling about it?" Seph asked cautiously.

"He was nervous this morning. Tucker's always been a dreamer. He's wanted to be an architect since he was nine. He even draws these elaborate designs in his sketchbooks. So, I honestly don't see how he could get selected for anything else," Emma said enthusiastically.

"You're a really good sister, you know?" Seph smiled.

"I won't argue with you on that." Emma laughed.

"So have you had Collin and Franky over for dinner?" Seph asked.

"Nope, you're the first from work to come over."

They were interrupted by the sound of the front door opening. Tucker walked in, his shoulders slumped and his steps dragging. When he entered the kitchen, both Seph and Emma froze. His eyes were bloodshot, and dark circles had formed under his swollen eyelids. He clutched a piece of paper in his hand, crumpled and damp with sweat.

Emma gasped. "Tuck, what happened?"

Tucker didn't answer. He just shook his head and walked past them, disappearing down the hallway to his room. A moment later, they heard the door slam shut.

Seph turned to Emma, his heart sinking. "I think I should go. He needs space, and I don't think he wants an observer."

Emma hesitated, then nodded. "You're probably right. I'll call you later, okay?"

As Seph was leaving, he heard Emma's parents coming through the back door. Her father's voice carried through the hall.

"I know he's upset now, but this is saving him years of heartache later," Mr. Miller said firmly. "It might seem harsh, but it will more quickly get him to the direction he needs to go. It will ensure that he finds a position where his intellect can be used for maximum impact."

"But—" Emma's mother started, her tone pleading.

Seph slipped out before he could hear the rest. He knew better than to get caught in what was clearly a brewing family argument.

Emma called a few hours later. Her voice was tight with emotion. "I'm sorry about earlier. It's... It's been a lot."

"What happened?" Seph asked, settling onto his couch.

"Tucker didn't do well on the assessment," Emma said. "The results came back, and he's been assigned to a technical maintenance track. Basically, he'll be fixing drones and mechanical equipment."

Seph winced. "That's ... not architecture."

"No, it's not," Emma said bitterly. "And the worst part is, the system doesn't care about what he wants. Tucker's dyslexia really hurt his scores. He's caught up a lot, but reading speed and comprehension are still challenges for him. The assessment couldn't look past that."

Seph listened quietly as Emma continued. "He's been drawing house designs since he was a kid. He wants to create housing structures for growing populations. But the assessment basically said he's not smart enough."

"That's not fair," Seph said, his voice firm. "Passion and determination count for a lot. More than test results."

"Try telling that to my dad," Emma replied. "He's convinced this is for the best. He thinks the assessment is saving Tucker from chasing an impossible dream."

"And your mom?" Seph asked.

"She's on Tucker's side," Emma said. "She and I both think he could overcome his challenges if he's given the chance. But Dad ... he's all about efficiency and maximizing potential. He sees the test as infallible."

There was a pause before Emma added, "It's like the system doesn't care about people. It's just ... cold. Numbers and algorithms deciding your entire future."

"I'm really starting to believe my Aunt June was right about everything, about how they might use our data to control us," Seph admitted. "The technology is incredible, but it's also limiting. It ignores the human element—aspiration, perseverance, creativity."

"Me too," Emma said, her voice rising with emotion. "And now I'm watching my little brother have his dreams crushed because some AI decided he wasn't good enough."

Seph's mind flashed back to his own interview at NexTech, the grueling battery of tests and simulations. He'd appreciated the rigor at the time, but now he wondered how many people had been rejected—not because they lacked potential, but because the system couldn't see it.

"What happens now?" Seph asked gently.

"Tucker's locked himself in his room. Mom's trying to comfort him, but he's not talking to anyone. Dad's pacing the house, insisting that this is for the best. And I... I don't know what to do."

"Maybe just be there for him," Seph suggested. "Let him know you believe in him, even if the system doesn't."

Emma sniffled. "Yeah. I'll try. And maybe when you meet with James, you'll get a clearer picture of NexTech's intent with this new program."

"I sure hope so," Seph said, remembering that meeting was tomorrow. "Let me know if you need anything, okay?"

"I will," Emma said. "Goodnight, Seph."

"Goodnight."

Seph woke up to the sound of the transpo outside his window, his alarm softly blinking on the ceiling. He stared at it for a moment, his chest tight with anticipation. Today was the day: the mentorship session with James Kent, the legendary founder of NexTech, was only a few hours away.

Seph's thoughts spiraled as he dressed and grabbed a quick breakfast, barely tasting his toast as he replayed potential conversation scenarios in his head. He glanced at his halophone and saw a message from Callum:

"Big day, huh? Meeting the guy who basically created the world we live in. No pressure."

Seph rolled his eyes but couldn't suppress a grin. He typed back quickly: *"Thanks for the reminder. I was totally calm until now."*

"You'll be fine. Just don't fanboy too hard. Remember, he's just a guy."

"A guy who revolutionized humanity. No big deal."

Callum's next message was a video of someone hyperventilating into a paper bag. Seph chuckled, his anxiety easing slightly as he pocketed his halophone and headed for the transpo. He was so used to Callum being by his side every day at The Institute that he missed his laid-back humor. It always eased his tension.

The transpo was already crammed with early commuters. Seph found himself scanning the faces of his fellow passengers, seeking familiarity. His nerves were on edge, and a distraction would be welcome.

Spotting Ava, a senior developer from his department, he waved and made his way over to her. She looked up from her tablet and smiled.

"Morning, Seph," she said.

He slid into the seat next to her. "How are you?" he asked.

"Not bad," Ava replied, setting her halopad aside. "I was just reading about this new exhibit at the Art Sphere downtown. It's supposed to be some kind of interactive digital installation. Ever been?"

Seph shook his head. "No, but it sounds cool. What's it about?"

"It's called '*Echoes of Humanity*,'" Ava explained, her eyes lighting up. "Apparently, it's this massive space where your movements and voice create these abstract visuals and sounds in real time. They say it's meant to reflect your emotional state."

Seph raised an eyebrow. "That's either really profound or really creepy. Not sure which."

Ava laughed. "A little of both, probably. I've always been into stuff like that, though. The idea of technology-enabled art is beautiful."

"Sounds like it could get intense," Seph said. "What if someone's having a bad day? Do they just get a wall of red?"

"Maybe," Ava said with a grin. "Or maybe the tech will surprise them. Reflect something they didn't realize they were needing."

Seph nodded thoughtfully. "I could see that. Could be a good way to process stuff, I guess. Might even be therapeutic."

"Exactly," Ava said. "I'm planning to check it out this weekend."

"What did you think of President Walker's announcements the other day?" Seph asked.

"Absolutely incredible," Ava said. "It's so exciting to work at NexTech and know that the things we are working on are making a real difference. It is so much safer now, I couldn't imagine having children twenty years ago and fearing for their life every day at school. What we do really matters."

"True," Seph said, a small smile tugging at his lips. "The nano chip has really done incredible things. Did you always want to work at NexTech?"

"Ha, not really," Ava admitted. "But I was the top of my class, and they made me an offer I couldn't turn down. Once I started working there, I learned of all the ways our technology was making things better and felt confident in my decision. What's got you so antsy this morning?"

"How could you tell?" he asked, his sheepish grin betraying him. "I have a mentor session with James Kent today."

"You've been fidgeting since you got on," she replied, laughing lightly. "Relax. James Kent's intimidating, sure, but he's also human. Just show him why they picked you for the session. I am actually surprised they picked you. I haven't heard of anyone with less than five years at NexTech meeting James one-on-one. So you are pretty lucky. Not to add any more pressure…"

"Easier said than done," Seph muttered, though her encouragement helped.

Ava adjusted her glasses and leaned closer. "If it helps, I heard from people who have been here for years say he's really easy going and isn't pompous at all, like you might expect. I think he'll appreciate your authenticity too."

Seph let out a big breath, "Thanks, Ava. That actually helps."

"You'll do great," she said, patting his arm as the transpo slowed to their stop. "Now go knock his socks off."

Seph swiped his ID badge and stepped into the NexTech atrium. The usual activity felt amplified today, every employee was a reminder of the sheer scope of the company's influence. He grabbed a coffee from the kiosk, hoping the warmth would steady his nerves. As he took a sip, he realized his hands were trembling.

He glanced at the clock. It was only 8:30am. The meeting wasn't until 11am. He tried to focus on his tasks for the morning, but his thoughts kept drifting back to James: *What would the legendary founder think of his work? Would he be impressed or dismissive? Would he share any insights into NexTech's true intentions?*

By 10:15am, Seph's efforts to concentrate had completely failed. He decided to take a short walk to clear his head. The hallways were quieter than usual, with most of the team buried in their projects. Seph passed by Emma's workstation and paused.

"Hey," she said, looking up from her screen. "Big day, right?"

"Huge," Seph admitted, leaning against the doorway. "I'm trying not to overthink it, but that's easier said than done."

Emma smirked. "Yeah, no pressure. Are you going to mention the announcement from President Walker?"

"I don't think so, like you said I should build some trust first. What I am hoping to do is use this meeting to ensure there is another."

"You'll do great," Emma said, her tone softening. "Just remember why you're here. You have a unique perspective, and that's exactly what he wants to see."

"Thanks," Seph said, feeling a little more grounded. "I'll let

SEPH

you know how it goes."

Time crawled. By 10:45, Seph could no longer sit still. He stood and stretched, taking a moment to collect himself. Just then, his workstation screen lit up with a notification:

"Mentorship Session—James Kent: Please proceed."

121

14

Seph

A glowing path appeared on the floor, illuminating a route through the labyrinth of the building. Seph was constantly amazed by the technology in the NexTech building. He'd worked there for several months and there were still new functions to learn about every week.

Seph followed the glow on the floor, his heart pounding. The light guided him past secured checkpoints, opening automatically at his approach. He was entering a part of the building he hadn't seen before. This section had more closed offices and less collaborative workspaces. He wondered what was behind some of the doors, and who was working in them. He felt a mix of awe and trepidation as he ascended to the executive floor, an area he'd only heard about.

At last, the path ended at a set of heavy oak doors. They swung open silently, revealing James Kent's office. The room was vast yet minimal, dominated by floor-to-ceiling windows offering a breathtaking view of the city. Unexpectedly, there were several full bookshelves —almost everyone read digitally now.

James sat at a sleek desk, his hands steepled as he studied Seph.

"Mr. Kent," Seph said, stepping forward. His voice wavered slightly, but he held his ground. "It's an honor to meet you."

James gestured to the chair across from him. "Seph, isn't it? Have a seat."

Seph sat, feeling the weight of James's gaze. The man looked tired. He always appeared so composed and energetic in videos. He wondered if that was a trick of the camera or if James wasn't feeling well today. Still, there was a gravity about him that filled the room.

"I've read about your work on the emotional algorithm," James began, his tone even. "Impressive. Tell me more about what led you to that breakthrough."

Seph launched into an explanation, detailing the challenges the team had faced and the moment of clarity that had led to his solution. As he spoke, James nodded occasionally, though his expression remained inscrutable.

When Seph finished, James leaned back, his eyes narrowing slightly. "You've done well," he said. "But tell me—do you ever think about the broader implications of your work?"

The question caught Seph off guard. "Of course," he said carefully. "The technology has the potential to do incredible good, but it also comes with risks. That's something I think about a lot."

James's lips twitched, almost forming a smile. "Good. It's important to question. To challenge. Technology isn't inherently good or bad—it's what we choose to do with it that

123

matters."

Seph nodded, his earlier nervousness fading. "That's what drives me," he said. "I want to make sure the work we're doing serves people, not the other way around."

For a moment, James seemed lost in thought. Then he spoke, his voice softer: "Sometimes, what we intend for good can be turned into something far worse."

Seph froze, the weight of James's words sinking in. They echoed sentiments he'd heard from June. Did James share her doubts? Was he, too, wrestling with the implications of NexTech's work? Or was this a test to see if Seph was loyal to NexTech?

The conversation moved back to Seph's code, other areas he could explore and James even suggested looking at work from other departments to challenge him and give him a more complete picture.

"I don't think I have access to any other department than the Emotional Data Analysis group," Seph said, in response to James's suggestion.

James smiled. "Well, the nice thing about a mentor session with me is ... I can change that."

Seph watched as James turned on his halopad and quickly scanned through several screens. After just a few moments he said, "Done."

As the session wound down, Seph felt a sense of connection with James, though it was tinged with unease. "Thank you for your time, Mr. Kent," he said as he stood to leave. "This has been ... illuminating."

James studied him for a moment, then nodded. "I hope we meet again, Seph. I think there is more for us to discuss. And call me James."

Seph hesitated at the door. "I think I have something you'll want to hear," he said.

James raised an eyebrow, intrigued. "Next week, then. I'll reach out directly with a time."

Seph walked back to his floor, his mind racing. The man he'd expected to be an unyielding advocate of NexTech's agenda had been something entirely different than his public persona. James Kent wasn't the infallible figure Seph had imagined—he was human, conflicted, and perhaps even an ally. For the first time in weeks, Seph felt a glimmer of hope. He had a plan—one that could change everything—but it hinged on James. Without his help, Seph couldn't pull it off.

When Seph got back to his desk he thought of Emma. He opened his halophone and typed out a quick message: *"How's Tucker doing today? Any better?"*

Emma's reply came quickly: *"Still upset, but Mom managed to get him to eat breakfast. He's talking a little now, which is progress."*

Then a quick second message: *"Thanks for being there for me. Your friendship means a lot."*

Seph paused, unsure what to say. Friendship… He'd been hoping this relationship had moved past the line of friendship. But did Emma not see that too? He also wasn't fully sure if they should be messaging about concerns with NexTech. He was almost positive their messages could be intercepted.

"You mean a lot to me Emma."

"So spill, how was James?"

"Want to come over later? Too much to type."

* * *

Emma arrived at Seph's apartment only a few minutes after he got home from work himself. He'd stopped to pick up some food that would be more appealing than the stack of frozen dinners he had stored away.

Emma walked inside and sat on his couch. Seph noticed the afternoon sunlight streaming in and warming the space between them.

"Okay, let's hear it," Emma said.

"He was way different than I expected."

"How so?"

"Well for one, he seemed exhausted. But more disorienting than that, he kinda brought up his own doubts about what NexTech was doing."

"What? What did he say?"

"Well, he said technology isn't good or bad, but how we use it that dictates that."

"True. But did he indicate what he thought about how it is being used here?"

"No, it's hard to really explain—it was more about his tone. And the questions he asked me."

"So how did it end?" Emma asked.

"We're going to meet next week. He said he wants to continue our conversation," Seph said smiling.

"Oh look at you! That's exactly what you wanted."

"I know, when things work out like this, it almost feels too easy."

Emma stood up and started towards the kitchen.

"Emma," Seph said, his voice low. She at glanced at him, her expression curious. "There's something I need to tell you. Something important."

She pulled her gaze back to him, giving him her full

attention. "What is it?"

Seph took a deep breath. "When I first joined NexTech, Lena in HR showed me some compatibility data. She told me we... you and I ... are highly compatible. Not just personally or professionally. We are compatible for marriage."

Emma blinked, her expression a mix of surprise and confusion. "They ... told you that? Why?"

"I don't know," Seph said honestly. "But I thought you should know. It felt important."

Emma leaned back in her chair, her arms crossed. "That's ... strange. I mean, it's flattering, I guess, but why would they even look into something like that? And why would they tell you? Why didn't they ask me first if I *wanted* this information? And who else has seen it?"

Seph shrugged, trying to gauge her reaction. "I mean, we scored over ninety percent compatibility for a romantic relationship. To be honest, it felt like they were trying to encourage, and even push me in the direction of pursuing that..."

Emma's lips pressed into a thin line. "So, you're saying the reason you've been spending time with me is because of a compatibility score?" Seph could tell she was angry. "Am I just an experiment to you?"

Seph's heart sank. He'd hoped this revelation might bring them closer and help take the relationship to the next level. He didn't intend for this information to upset her. But in that moment, Seph realized that during all these months at NexTech, he'd been categorizing the technology. The good tech, the tech that benefited him—he was happily using it. The bad tech, the tech that he felt restricted him, he was conflicted about. He realized he was no better than President Walker,

127

no better than all the other NexTech employees who were crossing the line on all these secret innovations.

Seph's mind was processing at such a rapid speed that he'd waited a few seconds too long to respond to Emma. She started to get up.

"Wait ... no ... this isn't an experiment," Seph pleaded. "Please stay..." But Emma was gone, already out the door.

Seph was in shock. The conversation had taken a turn he hadn't expected. He replayed the conversation in his mind and tried to figure out where he went wrong and why Emma was so upset. He realized the career algorithm that had affected her brother was basically a modified version of the relationship compatibility algorithm. And now it appeared as though he was trying to use the latter to justify their relationship evolving beyond friendship.

Seph grabbed his halophone from his room and typed a quick message: *"I'm so sorry. Can we talk more about this?"*

"I need space. I can't talk anymore today."

"Ok"

* * *

Seph had virtually no contact with Emma for several days. She called out sick from work with a headache. Seph knew that was just an excuse but since the nano chip could detect almost all illnesses, that was really one of her only options. Seph suspected that it might have even known she was lying.

Seph struggled to keep his mind focused on work, so he got up to walk the building and reset. As he was walking down an empty hallway, the sound of his footsteps muffled by the synthetic flooring. he heard faint voices coming from

128

an alcove near one of the maintenance doors.

"...*just vanished,*" a voice said sharply, low but distinct.

Seph slowed his pace, instinctively ducking into the shadowed edge of the hallway so he could listen.

"*Yeah,*" another voice replied, hushed and hurried. "*She told me she was going to bring up some concerns to Ramirez. Something about how the data was being used. Next day? Gone. Just like that.*"

Seph's pulse quickened. He recognized the voices—two analysts from the adjacent team, Nathan and Mira. They were usually buried in their screens, rarely stepping away from their desks.

"And no one's been able to reach her since?" Nathan asked.

"Not a word. Her halophone's been disconnected."

Seph edged closer, careful to keep out of sight. Nathan's voice dropped even lower.

"Did you ask Marlene or Lena?"

"I asked Lena, she told me Ava was sent to a treatment center because she was exhibiting signs of paranoia. But it just didn't sit right with me. Why wouldn't her phone still work?"

A loud clang echoed from somewhere deeper in the hallway, and both voices abruptly stopped. Seph quickly turned and continued walking, his head down and his heart pounding in his chest.

At lunch, Seph found Grace sitting alone at their usual table in the cafeteria, her halopad propped up as she picked at a salad. He slid into the seat across from her, his tray barely touched.

"Hey," he said, trying to sound casual.

Grace looked up, her sharp eyes narrowing slightly. "You okay? You look ... tense."

Seph hesitated, glancing around the bustling cafeteria before leaning slightly forward. "Have you ever … heard of anyone disappearing from NexTech? Like, just gone overnight?"

"Why are you asking that?" Grace's fork froze midway to her mouth.

"I overheard something. About a girl named Ava. She apparently raised concerns with her team lead, and the next day she was gone. No messages. No goodbyes. Just … disappeared."

Grace set her fork down, her expression hard to read. "Ava was on Ramirez's team, right?" Seph nodded. Grace's voice dropped to a near whisper: "I don't know all the details, but … it's not the first time. Our team got a report once about employees who were having psychotic episodes, specifically paranoia. And then a few hours later it was deleted and we were told to disregard it."

"Why doesn't anyone say anything? Report it?" Seph's stomach churned.

"Would you?"

The two sat in heavy silence, uncertainty filling the space between them. Seph's appetite was gone, replaced by a gnawing unease deep in his chest.

"But it could be real. Maybe people are experiencing a weird burnout from NexTech?" Grace said finally, her eyes serious. "If you're going to keep digging … be very careful."

Seph understood the warning, and more than ever he wished he had a way to contact June and Duke.

15

Seph

D ays later Seph was staring at his halopad when he saw someone out of the corner of his eye. There Emma was, arriving late and avoiding his eyes. Her hair was slightly disheveled, and dark circles under her eyes suggesting sleepless nights. She walked right by Seph and slipped into her desk, her usual upbeat demeanor replaced by a quiet, almost hollow presence.

Seph watched her from across the room, his concern growing with each passing hour. By mid-morning, he couldn't take it anymore. He approached her desk and gently placed a hand on the corner, just enough to get her attention without alarming her.

"Emma," he said softly. "Are you okay? Have you gone to the biotech department yet? You don't look well."

Emma shook her head, not meeting his gaze. "Not here," she whispered. "We can't talk here." Her tone was flat, her words clipped as tears filled the edges of her eyes.

Seph hesitated but nodded. "Okay. My place after work?"

Emma gave a small nod, and that was it. She turned back to

her screen, leaving Seph standing there, unease gnawing at him.

The rest of the day passed in a haze. Seph struggled to focus on his tasks, his mind constantly drifting back to Emma. Every scenario he imagined seemed worse than the last. By the time he left work, he was mentally exhausted, the questions swirling in his mind unanswered.

Emma arrived at his apartment shortly after him. She looked even worse than she had that morning, her face pale and her eyes rimmed red. As soon as he closed the door behind her, she broke down, tears streaming down her face. Seph guided her to the couch, his heart breaking as he watched her cry.

"Emma," he said gently, sitting next to her. "I'm so sorry for what I said the other day."

It took a few minutes for Emma to gather herself enough to speak. "It's everything," she began, her voice shaky. "Tucker … my grandmother … the system … you. I don't know what to believe anymore."

Seph furrowed his brow. "What happened with your grandmother?"

Emma took a deep, trembling breath. "She… she's been diagnosed with a rare disease. Something they said was manageable but expensive to treat. And she's ninety-two. The doctors told us there's no way to get approval for the treatment. The cost outweighs the benefit of her living a few more years."

Seph stared at her, horrified. "They … denied her treatment because of her age?"

Emma nodded, fresh tears spilling down her cheeks. "They said it's not suffering. She won't feel pain. But … it's not her

132

choice. She's still … she's still my grandma. She's the one who raised me when my parents were too busy. She's the reason I'm even here."

Seph placed a comforting hand on her shoulder. "I'm so sorry, Emma. That's… that's not right. None of this is right."

Emma shook her head violently. "And my mom? She agrees with it. She says it's practical, logical. That Grandma wouldn't want to burden us with the cost. That this is how people used to die. But how can she say that? It's not about logic, Seph. It's her life."

"What about your dad?" Seph asked quietly.

"He's detached," Emma replied bitterly. "He's all for following the rules. To him, the system is flawless. Efficient."

Emma's tears slowed as anger took their place. She turned to Seph, her eyes blazing. "What happens if I'm deemed useless by NexTech? Will they fire me? Decide my food's too expensive? Will I be discarded because I'm not efficient enough?"

Seph's stomach twisted. "Emma, no one's going to discard you. You're brilliant, you're…"

"But what if?" she interrupted, her voice rising. "What if one day, the system decides I'm no longer worth it? That I'm too old or too sick or too…" She buried her face in her hands, her words muffled. "I can't believe in this anymore. Everything I've trusted, everything I've worked for … it's all a lie."

Seph sat quietly, letting her words sink in. Emma had grown up in a world that celebrated the advancements of NexTech, a world where technology was seen as the ultimate solution. For her, the cracks in that system were new, jarring, and deeply personal.

He reached out and gently took her hand. "Emma," he said softly. "I know this feels overwhelming. And it's okay to question it. You should question it. None of this is easy, but you're not alone in this." She buried her face in her hands. "I have something I need to tell you too." Seph said, knowing he couldn't hold back information from her if he wanted her to trust him.

"Oh no, what else?"

"I overheard a conversation that Ava was poking around and brought concerns to Ramirez and no one has seen from her since. Her halophone is disconnected."

"What? Where did she go?" Emma was shocked.

"I don't know. I asked Grace if she knew."

"And?"

"She doesn't know for sure. Basically, there have been several employees who have all been reported for paranoia. They are sent to a treatment center, but no one ever hears from them again."

Emma looked up at him, her eyes wide. "How do you do it?" she asked. "How do you work for them, knowing all of this?"

Seph hesitated, choosing his words carefully. "Now that I am beginning to understand how evil it might be, I want to do something, to make sure our voices aren't completely drowned out."

Emma nodded slowly, her expression softening. "I just... I need time to process all of this. I don't even know where to start."

Seph wasn't fully sure what "all of this" meant. Did that include him? "Start by trusting what you feel," he said. "It's okay to be angry. To be upset. But don't let that stop you from believing things can change. That you can be part of that change."

Emma let out a shaky breath. "I don't know if I'm ready for that yet."

"That's okay," Seph said. "One step at a time."

They sat in silence for a while, the weight of their conversation hanging in the air.

Eventually, Emma's breathing steadied, and she leaned back against the couch. "Thank you, Seph," she said quietly. "For listening." She paused and took a deep breath. "I know you didn't mean to make me feel like an experiment. But I also don't like the idea of feeling like my choice in who I date or who I marry is being taken away."

"I understand that now," Seph replied. "But ... I want you to know that I had feelings for you before Lena told me about the compatibility score. I pretty much liked you since the first day we met and the feelings kept growing. For me, the score just confirmed what I was already feeling. It didn't feel like force to me. But I also know I picked the worst time to share this information."

Emma laughed. Seph was relieved to see her frown break.

"I was feeling something for you too. But I have to be honest, I can't even begin to think about anything romantic right now. I need to focus on what to do about everything else first." Emma said calmly.

* * *

The next morning, Seph was still groggy from their late-night conversation when his halophone buzzed on the nightstand. He reached for it reluctantly, squinting at the screen. A message from James Kent popped up, and Seph's heart skipped a beat:

"Seph, can you come to my office this morning? There's something I'd like to discuss."

Seph sat up, his exhaustion forgotten. He typed back quickly: *"Of course. What time works for you?"*

"9am. See you then."

Seph stared at the message, his mind racing. What could James want to talk about? Was it related to the emotional algorithm? Or was it something bigger?

Entering James's office, Seph sensed a change in the inventor's demeanor. Though still burdened, James appeared more energetic.

"Did you bring a halopad or any other device with you today?" James asked.

Seph pulled out his halophone and James reached for it. He add it to a few devices on his desk and carried them all over to what looked like a safe at the bottom of one of his bookshelves. James opened the safe, put the devices inside and walked back over to his chair.

"Seph I was intrigued by our last conversation. And I used the technology at my disposal to learn more about you."

Seph swallowed as he realized that the surveillance technology NexTech had developed might not just being used to stop criminals, but also to monitor NexTech employees.

"I heard your conversation yesterday with both Grace and Emma," James said.

Seph's mouth dropped open. He was too shocked to speak.

"Now, don't worry." James smiled with confidence. "I deleted those conversations, no one else will be able to find them. And if you need to have another one, make sure you don't have any devices around that are connected to NexTech or a cellular network."

Seph nodded, still in disbelief.

"But the conversations you had are what I needed to hear to know that I could trust you. You and your friends share very similar concerns to my own. So let's be honest, why are you working for NexTech?"

"Well, to be honest, I never really wanted to work here," Seph began. "I love technology, but I grew up in a family that was extremely concerned with the invasiveness of the nano chip. In fact, the only reason I decided to apply was to find out if the suspicions they had were true."

"So tell me, what did you find out? What do you think now?" James asked, leaning forward.

"It's taken me a long time to figure that out," Seph admitted. "When you strip everything away ... my core concern is that people willingly had a nano chip placed into their arm as a benefit to them but without knowing it, that benefit is going to be less and less beneficial over time. My fear is that the nano chip is going to be used as a weapon against us all. It will control, manipulate, and dictate every aspect of our lives." He paused. "It's like boiling a frog. It is happening so slowly, without checks and balances, without true transparency, that once people wake up and recognize what is going on ... it will be too late." He let out a deep breath ... waiting to see how James would respond and unsure if he was going to walk out of there with an advocate or an enemy.

"Seph, when we first met, I was in a dark place, consumed by the grief that what I'd created might do more harm than good. But in our last session, I sensed you shared a caution about what we're doing here that I haven't seen in others. You actually gave me hope that maybe, if others knew what you're seeing, we could take things in a different direction."

"If you could go back, knowing what you know now, would you choose not to invent the nano chip?" Seph asked.

James, sat back in his seat and looked out his window, lost in thought. Seph held his breath as he waited for his response.

"No, I would have invented it still. It has done incredible things. But I chose to keep inventing far past my need to. I should have stepped into the role of CEO long ago and spent my time ensuring the technology was not abused. That was my responsibility and I abdicated it to others," he said, matter-of-factly.

"If you disagree with how the nano chip is being used now, why do you still work here?" Seph asked.

James responded quickly: "I think it's the same reason you'd hoped for a second meeting." He smiled. "I have a better chance at turning things around from the inside than as an enemy. Most people are so zealous about what they're working on that they dive right in without considering the cost or the unintended consequences. I sensed in you a quality that I wish I'd had fifteen years ago. Maybe if I'd had that same caution then, we wouldn't be sitting in this office having this conversation right now. It's made me wonder if there might even be others working at NexTech right now that are also thinking of a way to … put boundaries on this technology."

"I know I'm not the only one. But I have no idea how to change things," Seph said.

"Come back on Friday. Let's work on this together," James suggested, his voice tinged with urgency.

Seph, sensing the significance of the moment, nodded in agreement. They were on the cusp of something ground-breaking, a potential turning point in their fight against the invasive system.

At lunch, Seph and Emma sat together. He spoke vaguely, knowing he could be under surveillance. "I had a second meeting with James today. He sees eye-to-eye with us about everything."

Emma paused mid-bite and looked at Seph. "Are you serious?"

"Dead serious." Seph paused eating as well. "In fact, I am going back on Friday to start working on a plan."

"I want in," Emma said.

"Well, I don't know if there is an open invitation yet, but as soon as there is something concrete, you'll be the first to know."

* * *

That Friday, James's office transformed into a brainstorming hub. Amidst the whir of computers and the flurry of notes, James shared his initial concept for altering the nano chip's functionality. It was a blueprint for deception, a way to feed the system false data while preserving the essential benefits of the chip.

Seph, intrigued yet cautious, listened intently. He was a part of something that could change the course of their struggle, but the weight of responsibility was heavy on his shoulders.

As they delved deeper into the technicalities, Seph posed a number of critical questions: "What if this technology falls into the wrong hands? Without universal adoption of the chip, aren't we risking a return to past dangers? What if someone with malintent used our technology to return to a life of murder and did so undetected?"

James paused, contemplating the gravity of Seph's concerns. "It's a risk, undoubtedly. But we are at a crossroads. We can either fight with conventional weapons or use their own against them. This is about giving people a choice, a chance to decide for themselves. I don't believe we would release this on everyone just yet. We would have to find a way to give people a choice."

The air in the room thickened with the realization of their undertaking.

"If we're wrong, the consequences could be dire," James continued, his gaze steady. "But the greater tragedy would be to rob people of their right to choose. We can't guarantee everyone will make the right decision, but denying them that choice … that's the real crime."

Seph absorbed James's words, understanding that their plan was a gamble, one that could either empower people or spiral out of control. But inaction was not an option. "So how cautious do I need to be about NexTech overhearing my personal conversations?" he asked.

"Well, it's like the crime algorithm. If you get flagged, you need to be very careful. But unless you do something suspicious, or raise a concern to the wrong person, no one is going to have time to sit in and listen to your conversations."

"But you found it," Seph pointed out.

"Well, you weren't flagged by the system. I flagged you. And then I deleted those conversations so no one else could hear. I can check daily and confirm no one is watching you or your friends."

"Thanks, that helps take some pressure off."

"But you still need to be careful, there could be real consequences." James said.

"Like what happened to Ava?" Seph asked. Still unsure what really happened to her.

James put down his pen. "Yes."

"And what really happened?" Seph said softly.

"Her manager reported her for exhibiting symptoms of paranoia. When that happened, she got immediately transferred to Apex Wellness Center."

"And what happens there? How many people has this happened to?"

"I honestly don't know for certain. Myles was part of a group that sponsored the creation of Apex under the passion for curing mental health. Their systems are completely separate from ours, so I have no visibility."

"Why can't we contact them?"

"Seph, I didn't think much of Apex until I saw some of the latest plans Myles and Walker are working on. I ended up looking into all the past employees who were transferred there. Almost all were part of the Innovation team led by Myles." James took a deep breath and continued: "I don't know exactly what is happening there, but I believe it is more of a facility to hold anyone with dissenting thoughts, and mental stability is just the disguise."

As their time waned, their resolve solidified. They were not just fighting against a system; they were fighting for the fundamental human right to choose.

16

James

J ames sat at the far end of the boardroom table, his fingers interlaced as he listened to Myles Fitz detail NexTech's newest initiatives. The morning sun streamed through the towering windows. Though the setting exuded power and innovation, James felt only unease. He'd built this empire to advance humanity, not to constrain it. Yet every decision made in this room seemed to lead to more control, more manipulation.

Myles's voice was crisp and confident. "The Career Aptitude Program has exceeded all projections," he said, his eyes flicking to a holographic chart that appeared in the air above the table. "Ninety-seven percent of participants have been placed into optimal training tracks, with parental satisfaction rates exceeding eighty-five percent."

"And the dissenters?" asked Brooke Yates, one of the board's more vocal members. His tone was sharp, as if dissent itself was an affront to the system.

"Minimal," Myles replied smoothly. "We've ensured their voices are contained to non-influential platforms. Public sentiment overwhelmingly supports the program. Parents appreciate the efficiency, and children are adapting quickly."

James's jaw tightened. *Adapting.* A sterile word for what he knew was coerced compliance. He leaned forward, clearing his throat. "And the feedback from the participants themselves?"

Myles's smile didn't waver. "A few outliers, but nothing statistically significant. The data speaks for itself, James."

Before James could press further, President Evan Walker entered the room, his commanding presence silencing the low murmur of side conversations. He moved with the confidence of a man who had the world at his fingertips, his tailored suit immaculate, his expression calculating.

"Good morning," Walker began, his deep voice filling the room. "I've just come from a cabinet meeting where we reviewed NexTech's latest contributions. The results are nothing short of extraordinary."

Myles's face lit up with pride. "Thank you, Mr. President. We're just getting started."

Walker nodded, then gestured for the holographic display to shift. Two new initiatives appeared, each accompanied by sleek, persuasive visuals.

"Let's talk about our next steps," Walker said. "First, we'll be introducing a Marriage Compatibility Program. Using NexTech's compatibility algorithms, all marriage applications will now require government approval to ensure long-term success. This will drastically reduce divorce rates, stabilize families, and create happier households."

The room broke into a burst of approval, but James felt his stomach clench. He stared at the hologram: a glowing ring encircling a happy couple, with data points mapping their "compatibility score."

"This isn't just about relationships," Walker continued. "It's about building a society rooted in stability and efficiency. Families are the foundation of our future, and this program ensures that foundation is unshakable."

James couldn't stay silent. "And what happens to those who don't meet the criteria?" he asked, his voice steady but cold.

Walker's eyes flicked to James, his smile thin. "They'll have the opportunity to improve their scores through counseling and developmental programs. If they still fail to qualify, they'll need to reconsider their options. It's for their own good."

James clenched his fists under the table. The words were dressed in benevolence, but the implications were clear. People's most personal decisions would now be subject to algorithmic approval.

"And what is even more exciting, is our compatibility score will be able to recommend matches for those who are single, without wasting time dating," Myles added.

"What happens to couples who choose not to marry and just want to live together?" Claire asked.

"Part of the new marriage law is that living together without marriage is not allowed," President Walker said. "But we will enforce this slowly and give everyone time to adjust. Claire it will be important for you to be on the forefront of making this a positive initiative, that everyone sees it as a benefit."

"And the second initiative?" Myles asked eagerly, his tone betraying none of the unease James felt.

Walker gestured again, and the display shifted. "Universal

Income Standardization," he announced. "This program will align individual incomes with their aptitude and job performance, as determined by a new NexTech program. Wealth redistribution will eliminate poverty and homelessness, creating a balanced and equitable society."

The room erupted in applause, but James remained silent, his mind reeling. The idea sounded noble on the surface, but he knew better. This wasn't about equality; it was about control. People's livelihoods would be dictated by data, their autonomy stripped away under the guise of fairness. Another plan that looks good on the outside but underneath can be manipulated in favor of a selected few.

"We'll start rolling out pilot programs in select regions next quarter," Walker continued. "With full implementation planned within the year. This is the future we've been working toward. Not long ago, the problem of homelessness was unsolvable. Now with the technology you have created, James, we can reset financial expectations across the board. We can ensure everyone has enough to keep a roof over their head and continue to reward those who really go above and beyond or have more skilled or risky positions."

Myles turned to James, his smile expectant. "Isn't it extraordinary, James? Your vision is finally coming to fruition."

James forced a smile, his heart pounding. "Extraordinary," he echoed, his voice hollow. And his eye caught Claire's. She was watching him intently.

The meeting adjourned, but James lingered in the boardroom, staring at the empty table. The weight of the morning's revelations pressed down on him, suffocating in its intensity.

A soft knock at the door pulled him from his thoughts. Claire stepped inside, her expression curious. "James, are you alright?"

He straightened, masking his turmoil. "Just processing everything. It's a lot to take in."

She nodded sympathetically. "I understand. But you should be proud. None of this would be possible without you."

Proud. The word rang hollow. James offered a polite nod, and Claire left, her heels clicking against the polished floor. Alone again, James felt the walls closing in.

That evening, James sat in his study, the soft glow of his halopad illuminating his face. He reviewed the files on the new initiatives, his unease growing with every line. The programs weren't just misguided; they were dangerous. It was the beginning of stripping people of their humanity, reducing them to variables in a system.

He quickly composed a message to Seph, someone who had become his unsuspecting ally. They needed to finalize a plan: *"We need to talk—9am."*

As he set the halopad down, James felt a rare sense of clarity. There was no more room for hesitation. NexTech had crossed a line, and he could no longer stand by. It was time to confront the abyss, to fight for the vision he had once believed in. The road ahead would be one of sacrifice, and he only hoped that it wasn't too late.

17

Seph

EEP. BEEP. BEEP.

The piercing sound pulled Seph from sleep, his heart thudding in his chest as he reached instinctively for his halophone on the nightstand. The screen was dark. Confused, he sat up, the dim light of early morning filtering through his blinds. The beeping continued, rhythmic and insistent, but it wasn't coming from his halophone.

Swinging his legs over the side of the bed, Seph rubbed his face, trying to clear the fog of sleep. He followed the sound to his desk, where his belongings lay scattered from the night before. His eyes landed on the old calculator—the relic Duke had given him months ago. The screen on the calculator flickered faintly, displaying a simple message: *"24 HOURS. LAT 38.8, LONG -105.2"*.

Seph's breath caught. His pulse quickened as he stared at the device, the weight of its implication sinking in. A meeting. From Duke or June—or perhaps both. It had felt like a lifetime since he'd talked to them. The timing couldn't be a coincidence.

He picked up the calculator, its edges smooth from years of handling. Turning it over in his hands, he let the memories flood back. Duke had given it to him just before leaving the city, a parting gift and a promise. *"If we need to get you a message, this is how we'll do it,"* Duke had said with a rare seriousness. Back then, it had seemed almost silly. Now, it was anything but.

Seph sat back on his bed, the cool morning air brushing against his skin as he stared at the coordinates on the device. His mind raced with questions: *Why now? What had changed?*

Before he could dwell further, Seph's halophone buzzed gently on the nightstand. The notification lit up the room with its soft glow. He reached for it, half-expecting another cryptic message. Instead, it was from James and had come in late last night while Seph was asleep.

"We need to talk—9am."

The urgency of the message sent a chill down Seph's spine. He wondered what was going on. Why was everything so urgent today? He swiped to unlock the screen, his fingers moving quickly as he typed a message to Emma: *"Need to see you tonight. My place."*

"Of course. Everything ok?" came the swift reply.

"I don't know yet, I'll explain later."

Seph placed the halophone down and leaned forward, resting his elbows on his knees. The noise of the city waking up reached his ears, a sound that usually brought comfort but now felt like background music to the storm brewing in his mind. His gaze drifted back to the calculator. The simplicity of the message belied its weight.

Seph got up and paced his small apartment. His thoughts swirled—the meeting with James, the mysterious coordinates, the broader implications of everything he'd uncovered at NexTech. The walls seemed closer than usual, the space too small to contain the gravity of it all. He showered and dressed, the mundane routine grounding him. As he left his apartment, the weight of the next twenty-four hours felt both reassuring and ominous.

Seph made his way to James's office. Every beep of the automated systems, every glint of the polished surfaces seemed to emanate with tension. Conversations were quieter than usual, almost hushed, as if the building itself had absorbed the weight of impending change. Even the normally efficient, impersonal greetings from passing colleagues felt tinged with unease. It was as if everyone sensed that something monumental was on the horizon, though few likely understood the scope.

When Seph reached James's door, it slid open silently, revealing the founder sitting behind his desk, his eyes distant, lost in thought. The light from James halopad cast sharp shadows on his face, emphasizing the lines of exhaustion and worry etched into his features.

"Close the door," James said without preamble, his voice steady but firm. He quickly got up and took both of their devices and put them in the safe at the bottom of his bookcase.

Seph closed the door and it sealed with a crisp clank. The room felt insulated, as if nothing beyond these walls mattered anymore. The gravity of whatever James was about to say hung heavy in the air.

James gestured for Seph to sit, but Seph remained standing, his own unease too restless to allow him to settle. James didn't

149

seem to mind.

"Things are moving faster than I anticipated," James began, his voice low but urgent. He leaned forward, resting his elbows on the desk. "The board ... they're pushing forward with new initiatives. Marriage compatibility scoring that will prevent couples with low scores to get married and universal income tied to aptitude and job performance, that will undoubtedly be used for manipulation."

Seph felt a sudden wave of nausea. He knew more programs were always on the horizon and eventually ones that crossed his ethical line would come about. But he had no idea it was moving so quickly. Hearing this from James, with such certainty, was a punch to the gut.

"They're not just tinkering at the edges anymore," James continued, his voice hardening. "They're ready to roll these out publicly within weeks. The Career Aptitude Program was only the beginning. They're consolidating control faster than we can counter."

Seph felt a surge of anger rising. "So what do we do?" he asked, his voice edged with frustration. "We haven't exactly had enough time to put our solution together, let alone test it."

James' gaze locked onto Seph's, his eyes sharp and calculating. "I have a plan I have kept in my back pocket that I was hoping I would never need. But I don't think we have a choice. And we might need some help."

Seph took a deep breath, steadying himself. "Well, I need your help to meet up with my Aunt June," he said, his voice more controlled now. "She sent me a cryptic message. A location. It looks like it is two hours outside the city. And I am supposed to meet her tomorrow morning. I don't have a vehicle that I can take, and I don't want to get tracked as I travel there."

James leaned back in his chair, his expression thoughtful. For a moment, he said nothing, his fingers tapping lightly on the desk. "I have a car—an old one, not connected to the NexTech system," he said finally. "We can use it to get there. Bring Emma. I think this will be the best opportunity to execute my plan."

The tension in the room seemed to thrum louder, an unspoken agreement settling between them. This wasn't just another step. It was the tipping point.

"Tell me more about this message," James said. "Why now?"

Seph pulled the old calculator from his bag and slid it across the desk. James picked it up, studying it with a curious expression. "Duke gave this when my aunt left the city," Seph explained. "He said if it ever beeped, it would mean something important. This morning, it did."

James turned the device over in his hands, his eyes narrowing as he read the flickering display. "Coordinates," he murmured. "The plan isn't public yet. The fact that someone sent this to you today..."

"What?" Seph asked.

"I just think there is a high probability that the person who sent you this message is in contact with someone from a very small circle of people."

Seph was now questioning if they were walking into a trap. The room started to spin and he started to feel like things were getting out of control.

James noticed Seph starting to breathe faster. "Hey, let me get you something to calm your nerves. I don't want your nano chip setting off any alarms." He went over to a small table that held several bottles of alcohol. Seph didn't drink and wasn't sure this was the time to start.

"I don't want a drink, I want to stay clear headed," Seph said, motioning towards the collection of bottles.

James laughed. "I am not planning on getting you drunk. I have a small stash of medication that we found out long ago masks the nano chips detection of a heightened state. It will actually calm you down, but it won't sedate you. Years ago, people battled high blood pressure at insane rates. So many drugs were created to control it. However, in the early days of testing the nano chip, this one posed a problem for us. It calmed all your biometrics down and masked how the person was really doing. These drugs have all been discontinued over the years … no one needs blood pressure medication anymore … and taking it when you're calm can actually reduce your heart rate too much. But that won't be a problem today."

Seph exhaled slowly, the weight of it all pressing visibly on him. "So, we'll leave tonight," he said as he drank the drink James had prepared. Almost instantly he felt himself stabilize.

"Just pack a few essentials, some food, water and maybe an extra set of clothes. In the event we're stopped, or the person on the other end of that message is not an ally, we need to be prepared to change course."

Almost unsure if he wanted to know, Seph said, "Are we coming back?"

"I hope so." James thought for a moment. "Seph, I hope the person on the other end of that message is your aunt. And if so, that means she is in contact with someone else who sees things the way we do and has been acting in the shadows. I don't know what this all means but what I am counting on is there are more people like you—like Emma, like June—that will be with us."

18

Seph

Seph wandered back to his desk, feeling surprisingly calm and sharp. He was grateful for whatever it was that James had given him. He needed the focus and clarity today of all days.

Seph sat in the dim glow of his workstation, his fingers hovering over the keyboard, every nerve triggering at full speed. The task before him wasn't just risky—it was outright dangerous. If anyone caught him breaching another employee's account, especially Emma's, the repercussions would be severe.

He'd spent the past hour meticulously disabling and rerouting security protocols. NexTech's surveillance was omnipresent, with every action logged and analyzed. He couldn't afford to leave a trace. Finally, he accessed Emma's workstation, her familiar login credentials lighting up his screen like a ghost. It felt intrusive, but there was no other way.

Seph took a deep breath, steadying his trembling hands. He typed quickly, keeping his message simple and to the point: *"Emma, Something is happening and I want you to come with me. Pack a backpack with some essentials and meet at my house. We are going to see my aunt. S"*

Satisfied, he set the message to appear as a routine system update, ensuring it would bypass NexTech's automated monitoring. It would pop up on her workstation blending seamlessly with the countless notifications that came through every day.

He sat back, exhaling sharply as the weight of the moment settled over him. The screen dimmed, and the soft glow of the city outside his window seemed to pulse with a foreboding rhythm. He knew he couldn't stay in one place much longer, he got up and went through the motions of getting lunch.

Emma walked by a few minutes after Seph sat down. "I got the ... update," she said, her eyes searching his face. "I'll be ready."

Seph nodded, grateful for her discretion. "Thank you," he said softly. He was relieved to know she was still on board and still trusted him.

Emma gave a small nod. "I'll see you tonight."

As she turned to leave, Seph felt a strange mixture of relief and dread. The wheels were in motion now, and there was no turning back.

* * *

After lunch, Seph returned to his workstation, his mind still swirling with thoughts of his conversation with James. As he settled into his chair, the soft chime of a new notification drew his attention. He glanced at the holographic display and saw a message marked urgent:

"HR Notice: Seph Thompson, please report to HR for an unscheduled meeting. Your presence is required immediately."

His stomach dropped. Meetings with HR had never been unscheduled before. Taking a deep breath, Seph locked his workstation and made his way down the quiet hallways toward the HR offices. Each step felt heavier than the last, his mind racing through possibilities. Had someone reported him? Had NexTech's surveillance flagged something suspicious?

When Seph reached the HR suite, Lena, was waiting for him in her glass-walled office. She greeted him with her usual composed demeanor, gesturing for him to sit.

"Seph," she began, her voice low but probing, "thank you for coming on such short notice. How are you doing?"

Seph took a seat, his posture guarded. "I'm fine. Is there an issue with my performance?"

Lena smiled faintly, tilting her head. "No, nothing like that. We've noticed some biometrics that indicated you might have been under an unusual amount of stress recently. It's nothing alarming, and I can see now that you're back to normal, but we like to be proactive about these things."

Seph's heart maintained a steady beat, though without the medication James had given him, he knew it would be sky high. Of course they were monitoring his stress levels. He quickly conjured a plausible explanation. "I've been dealing with some personal stuff," he said carefully, meeting her eyes. "It's nothing work-related, but it's been weighing on me."

Lena leaned forward slightly, her expression sympathetic but sharp. "Would you like to elaborate? We want to ensure that our team members feel supported."

Seph hesitated, then decided to stick as close to the truth as he could without revealing too much. "It's about my aunt. We've always been close, but recently we've been at odds about some things. It's … complicated, but I've let it affect me more than I should. I think I have a plan to work it out, though. I'm planning to talk to her soon."

Lena studied him, her eyes searching for cracks in his composure. Seph held her gaze, willing himself to appear sincere. She glanced at her halopad. Seph knew she was looking at his data.

Finally, she nodded. "Thank you for sharing that, Seph. You didn't have to, but I appreciate your transparency. It's important to me that you feel supported here."

Seph gave a small nod, unsure how much longer he could keep up the charade. "I appreciate that."

Lena leaned back in her chair, her tone shifting slightly. "Just to confirm, there's nothing amiss with your work or your relationships here? Everything is going smoothly with your team? And with Emma?"

Seph's chest tightened at the mention of Emma, but he kept his expression neutral. "Everything's fine, the team is great, I like what we are working on. Emma and I are good friends, we enjoy working together and are still getting to know each other, outside of work that is."

Lena smiled, though there was an edge of curiosity in her expression. "Good. That's what I like to hear. If anything changes, you know my door is always open."

"Of course," Seph replied, rising from his seat as Lena stood to see him out. "Thank you for checking in."

As Seph left the HR office, he felt the weight of the interaction settle over him. Lena's questions had been pointed, her probing subtle but effective. He knew he'd dodged a bullet this time, but the encounter left him more certain than ever that NexTech was watching his every move. He needed to be even more cautious—for himself and for Emma.

19

Seph

The rest of the day went surprisingly fast. Seph made sure to tidy up a few final findings, turn in a report to Martin and swing by Grace's department. Seph walked up to her workstation where she was looking at a nano chip under a microscope. "Hey Grace!"

"Seph! I haven't seen you in ages. I feel like every time I see you in the cafeteria your eyes are locked on that coworker of yours," Grace said with a knowing look in her eyes.

"Ha, yeah, I guess I got a little caught up in things. Well, I haven't seen you around so I'm just checking in, wanting to know how you've been enjoying it here." His eye glanced at the image of the nano chip in front of Grace. He wished he had more time to learn from her work and potentially use it to find a solution with James, but they were out of time.

"You know, I was actually a bit disappointed when I was placed here at first, but I have really come to love it. I like that

I can be hands-on part of the time. I didn't realize how much I would have enjoyed going into a medical field, but this role lets me work in tandem with the medical staff at the processing center when a nano chip is reported for malfunction," she said with pride.

"Wow, I had no idea you were involved on that level. So, are the malfunctions more often?"

"You know, it isn't that it's more often. It's actually more the fact that we're seeing such high adoption rates, that the volume of malfunctions is higher, but the percentage remains very low." She paused. "And what is very interesting—it's not actually proven yet—is that the issue isn't with the quality of the nano chip, it seems it's an issue with the host."

Seph was trying to read between Grace's excitement. Was she onboard with all that she had learned at NexTech? She wasn't showing any hesitation for their new employer.

"Wow, I hadn't considered that. Do you know what it is about a person that would not integrate well with the nano chip?" Seph asked, making a clear distinction between host and person.

Grace thought for a moment. "You know, we're still at the very early stages. We are currently brainstorming around the possibility that it is like an organ transplant from the past. The majority of the time, the compatibility was there and the person accepted the donated organ just fine, but there was a small chance that the body would reject the new organ. Eventually they developed medication to suppress that reaction and that was pretty effective."

"I'm glad I swung by, I feel so entrenched in emotional data that I haven't spent enough time getting to know all the other things going on here," Seph said, having lost hope that Grace was another ally.

"Well, you can always swing by my office, I am an open book." Grace smiled.

"See ya later, Grace. It's nice knowing we both landed in good spots."

"Back atcha, buddy." Grace swung back around and picked up where she'd left off.

Seph laid low for the last hour of the workday. On the way back to his apartment, he shot Callum a message: *"So how is the job search going?"*

"Ugh, don't get me started. I am starting to regret my life choices."

"That bad?"

"Man... I think companies pay way more attention to exam scores than I ever admitted before. I am actually thinking of going back to The Institute to speak with the career center. They offered any of us grads who haven't landed a job an assessment to refocus our energy in a different trade."

"Really? This soon?"

"You don't know what it is like out here. It's crazy expensive not to have any income coming in, and my parents are less than happy with my current situation."

"Dude, that sucks. Keep applying, I think something is just around the corner."

"I hope so."

The transpo came to a soft stop on Seph's street and he hopped out, took a deep breath, and headed into his apartment. He needed to think of just a few essentials to pack, without really knowing how long he would be gone, or if he would ever come back.

The sound of Emma's knock was sharp. Seph swung the door open, relieved to see her standing there with her bag slung over one shoulder. She stepped inside, her eyes scanning the small apartment as if looking for answers to unspoken questions.

"Alright, spill," she said, gesturing to his backpack leaned up against the couch. "Has something actually happened? Or did you lure me here under false pretenses just to take me on some romantic trip?"

Seph rubbed the back of his neck, stalling. "I can't tell which one would be better. But really, James will be here soon and I think I should wait to explain when he gets here."

Emma crossed her arms, leaning against the arm of the couch. "Okay, so no romantic getaway—noted. I'd like to have more than a vague sense of what's going on. I didn't really know what to pack."

Before Seph could respond, another knock sounded, followed by James stepping inside. He carried a single bag, his expression calm but unreadable.

"Good. You're both ready," James said, his voice even. He placed his bag next to Seph's and gave Emma a small nod. "Nice to meet you, Emma. Seph has told me a lot about you."

Emma stepped forward, her anticipation bubbling over. "Likewise." She shook James's hand and turned her focus to Seph, waiting for an explanation.

James glancing at Seph and back to Emma. "The less you know now, the safer you'll be. Once we're out of the city, I'll explain more. But for now, trust me when I say this: what we're doing is necessary."

Seph placed a hand on Emma's arm, his voice soft. "Emma, you can trust us."

Emma hesitated, her shoulders tense, before finally exhaling and nodding. "You gotta give me more than that. Where are

162

we going? Are we really meeting your aunt? And when are we coming back?"

"Seph got a message from his aunt to meet at an unspecified location, but we have the coordinates," James said.

Emma nodded but glanced at Seph. He knew she wanted more.

"We don't have all the pieces of the puzzle," he said, "but things are escalating at NexTech and we have a window now to contact June and Duke, and James has an idea to share when we get there."

James checked the clock on his halophone. "We're going there but using a route that will keep us out of high traffic areas in the event that people try to piece together my timeline. It will make sense later, but I don't want it to look like I had any help in my part of the plan. We will get there by 6am." He paused. "By the way, we can't bring any devices with us. I made a spoofing app that we can plug into each of our halophones and leave them here in Seph's apartment. When anyone looks, it will appear as if we are moving around the city like normal … at least until someone really studies the data … and notices our nano chips left the NexTech grid."

Emma and Seph handed their phones to James. He plugged in his spoofing device, pressed a few buttons and stepped back once he was done, their digital footprint covered.

"So do we know when we are coming back?" Emma hesitated.

"There are too many unknowns," Seph said. "I don't want to promise any timing in the event things don't go as planned. But don't you want to try to do something that could actually make a difference?"

"Okay, I guess it's my turn to find out what's at the bottom of the pool," Emma said with a smirk to Seph.

The three of them exchanged glances, a silent agreement passing between them. Without another word, they grabbed their bags and stepped out into the night, the city's hum fading behind them as they headed toward the unknown.

James's car was an antique by NexTech standards. Its metallic frame gleamed faintly under the streetlights, its design a relic from a time before connected vehicles dominated the streets.

Emma ran a hand along the smooth surface, her curiosity momentarily overriding her nerves. "This thing actually runs?" she asked, glancing at James.

He opened the driver's door and smirked. "Better than you'd think. It's off the grid, no trackers, no AI interference. Perfect for what we need."

Seph climbed into the back seat, settling his bag on the floor. "You've had this for how long?"

"Years," James replied, starting the engine. The sound was a low rumble, almost alien in a city where silent, electric vehicles reigned. "It was originally my great grandfather's. He worked as a mechanical engineer for Ford."

Emma slid into the passenger seat, her fingers fidgeting with the strap of her bag. "Why keep something like this?"

James pulled onto the street, his hands steady on the wheel. "Sometimes it's good to have a backup plan. You'd be surprised how many things can go wrong in a fully connected world."

The car sped through the city streets, its presence drawing a few curious glances. As they left the towering skyscrapers behind, the atmosphere inside the car shifted. The glow of the city was replaced by the rhythmic sound of tires on asphalt, the darkness of the open road enveloping them.

Emma broke the silence: "So, are we being followed?"

James shook his head. "Not yet. But we should assume they'll notice we're gone soon enough."

Seph leaned forward, resting his arms on the back of Emma's seat. "What do you think we'll find at the coordinates?"

James's grip on the wheel tightened. "Answers, I hope. But I can't guarantee anything."

The conversation lulled again, each of them retreating into their thoughts. Emma stared out the window, her reflection barely visible in the glass. Seph held onto the calculator, had fallen asleep in the back. James remained focused on the road.

A few hours later, Emma spoke again, her voice quieter this time: "Do you ever wonder if it's too late? If we've already lost?"

James glanced at her briefly before returning his gaze to the road. "It's never too late to fight back. As long as we have a choice, we have a chance."

The car continued its journey, the miles stretching out before them like a thread pulling them closer to an uncertain fate. The coordinates led them to a secluded clearing in the mountains, where a dim light shone from a small cabin nestled among the trees. The air was crisp, carrying the scent of pine and earth.

As the car came to a stop, Seph spotted two figures waiting outside the cabin. His heart leapt as he recognized June and Duke. He was the first to step out, his voice breaking the stillness: "June!"

She smiled, her relief evident as she rushed to embrace him. "Seph, it's so good to see you."

Duke hung back, uncrossing his arms for a hug. "You made

it," he said, his tone gruff but not unkind.

James and Emma emerged from the car, their presence shifting the dynamic. June's smile faded slightly as she eyed James. "So, you're the one who started all this."

James stepped forward, extending a hand. "James Kent. And you must be June." She hesitated before shaking his hand.

Duke motioned toward the cabin. "Come inside. It's safer to talk. This is a makeshift outpost we have been retrofitting for a few months. Halfway between my house, what we call The Refuge, and NexTech."

The interior of the cabin was modest but functional, with a makeshift command center set up in one corner. An old satellite computer hummed faintly, its screen displaying lines of code and encrypted messages.

As they settled around a small table, Seph began to recount everything he'd uncovered—NexTech's new initiatives, the data manipulation, and the cryptic message that had led them there.

When he finished, June leaned back in her chair, her expression unreadable. "We know," she said simply.

James frowned. "How? And who's your contact?"

Duke exchanged a glance with June. "We don't know exactly who it is. The messages come through that rig over there," he said, nodding toward the computer. "Whoever it is, they know things—things no one else should."

June added, "We've kept it quiet, only acting when absolutely necessary. But whoever this person is, they're deep inside NexTech—or the government." June looked at James "We actually wondered if it was you."

James's expression shifted "So you are saying I don't have a convincing sales pitch with all the interviews I have been doing?"

Duke responded. "Your sales pitch has actually been too good. No, one of the messages came through saying you could be trusted."

James had a strong suspicion who might be on the other end of those communications, confirming he was doing the right thing. June and Duke could be trusted.

"I've prepared a message," James began, "a comprehensive exposé of everything NexTech and the government have been doing. It includes proof of unauthorized surveillance, data manipulation, and plans for societal control."

Emma's eyes widened. "You're going to send that out to everyone?"

James nodded. "Not just that. Once the message is sent, a secondary signal will delete NexTech's entire database, every backup, and disconnect every nano chip. If people want to opt back in, they'll have to do it voluntarily, but this time with full knowledge of what they're agreeing to."

Seph looked at James, his voice shaky. "So everything will be erased?"

James's gaze didn't waver. "Then the system will have to be rebuilt to comply with the demands of the people. Finally, NexTech could have boundaries that allowed for innovation while protecting the rights humanity deserves. Before it's too late."

Emma frowned, crossing her arms. "That's asking a lot. What if they panic? What if society can't handle it? Why will they trust this information."

James met her gaze, his voice calm but resolute. "People deserve the truth. They deserve the choice. Freedom isn't easy, Emma. It's messy, uncertain. But it's better than living under a false sense of security. And I think I might be the only person people will trust to tell them this. NexTech made me the face of this thing. They will believe it coming from me."

Seph added "That is why you didn't want anyone to see us leave with you. Because you aren't ever going to go back."

James responded "No, I can't. I'll be arrested if I do."

"Will turning the system off cause any major catastrophe? Will cars crash or will people die?" Seph asked.

"No, we aren't taking down power. Disconnecting the chips and erasing the data won't cause any crazy disaster. Transpos will still be running and make it to their next stop, computers will stop working, it will cause some chaos as people won't know how to function without the technology they are accustomed to." James said.

"Hopefully enough chaos for them to wake up and realize what is actually happening." Duke added.

June, who had been silent until now, stepped forward. "He's right. If we don't do this, NexTech and the government will tighten their grip until there's nothing left. This is our chance to prevent a future we can't come back from."

Duke nodded in agreement. "We've been waiting for the right moment. If this doesn't wake people up, nothing will."

James turned back to the computer, his fingers hovering over the keyboard. He plugged his drive into the machine. "Once I hit send, there's no going back. This message will go out to every chip, every screen, every device connected to NexTech's network. The reset will be immediate."

The room fell silent, the weight of the decision pressing down on them. Seph took a step closer, his voice quiet but firm. "We're with you."

James gave a small nod, his expression softening. "Thank

you." He glanced at Emma. "You ready?"

Emma hesitated for a moment, then squared her shoulders. "Let's do this."

James pressed a key, activating the final sequence. A loading bar appeared on the screen, slowly filling as the command was sent from Duke's computer to the open halopad that was sitting on his office desk in his house hours away. The command went through successfully and the message uploaded to the NexTech network. The room seemed to hold its breath, every second stretching into an eternity.

A few seconds later, the screen flashed, and James's pre-recorded message began broadcasting. Across the world, every nano chip activated simultaneously, delivering the message directly to its users. Halophones lit up, holographic screens flickered to life, and James's voice resonated through homes, offices, and streets.

"Citizens," the message began, *"my name is James Kent. I am the creator of the nano chip and the founder of NexTech. Today, I need to tell you the truth."*

The video laid everything bare: the unauthorized surveillance, the manipulation of data, the plans for societal control through initiatives that sounded good with a sinister undertone underneath. It exposed the invasive ways NexTech and the government had integrated themselves into every facet of life without full transparency.

James's tone was calm but urgent. "None of this was done with your consent. Today, that changes. As soon as this message ends, every nano chip will be disconnected, and NexTech's database will be erased. If you choose to opt back in, you can do so. But the choice is now finally yours."

The message ended, and with it, the network went dark.

Devices powered down simultaneously, plunging the world into an eerie silence.

For the first time in years, the world was truly disconnected.

II

Part Two

20

Seph

The room was quiet as they sat in the aftermath of their digital attack. Seph could feel the tension hanging in the air as he finally let out a breath. He ran his hand over his forearm, focusing on the area where the nano chip was embedded. Did it feel different? Could he tell it was disconnected?

After James sent the signal, he turned the computer off which in turn closed the only light in the cabin. They sat in the darkness for what felt like hours.

"Do you think … it worked?" Emma's voice cut through the silence. She stood near the door, arms crossed, her expression matching the tension in the room.

James was the first to respond: "The signal went through successfully. Everyone is disconnected. The question is, were we able to really convince people they shouldn't reconnect? I am sure NexTech is already working on rebooting the system."

173

Seph exhaled, stood up and slowly walked outside. He strained his eyes to see if he could see the city from where they were. The sky looked darker than before, or maybe that was just his imagination seeking a physical representation for the havoc they had just caused.

He turned and met Emma's eyes as she remained in the doorway. "I don't know. But if it did, they'll be trying to figure out who did it. We shouldn't stay here."

James paced near the makeshift desk, his fingers drumming on the worn wooden surface. "We need to abandon this outpost. They might trace the signal to this old satellite computer. We should probably destroy it as we leave."

June nodded. "Duke, let's pack up everything we can and leave in ten. If they do eventually trace it back here, we don't want them to be able to tell who we are."

"They'll know it was me," James said, matter-of-factly.

"They will, but they won't know who was helping you. And we don't want them to connect anyone of us to you," June responded.

Seph looked at James. "What would they do?"

"I don't want to find out, I can never return to the city. They will have every camera and tracking device trained to detect my image. If they find me, they will arrest me, or worse. I don't want anyone here to have the same fate. June is right, we need to scrub this place of our presence. Not to protect me, but to protect each of you."

Without another word, they all started picking things up and loading it into their vehicles. As the group prepared to move, Seph and Emma found themselves outside, the rising sun painting soft orange hues across the distant city skyline. The stillness between them was palpable, a silence filled with

174

words unspoken.

Emma's eyes flicked toward the city, her face drawn with conflicted emotion. She clenched her hands at her sides as if bracing for a blow. *"I... I can't go,"* she whispered, her voice trembling.

Seph turned sharply, disbelief flashing in his dark eyes. "What do you mean? You have to. It's not safe here."

Tears threatened to spill as Emma shook her head, her breath hitching. "My parents... If I disappear now, they'll assume the worst. They don't understand. I need to make sure they understand that they have a choice."

Seph opened his mouth to protest, but before he could speak, Duke emerged from the shadows, his boots crunching against gravel. His expression was calm yet resolute.

"I'll take her to the edge of the city," Duke offered, resting a steadying hand on Seph's shoulder. His grip was firm, anchoring Seph in place. "She can make it home from there. No one will know she was gone."

Seph's shoulders sagged, the weight of inevitability pressing down on him. He turned back to Emma, his gaze fierce but softened by sorrow.

They stepped toward each other, their hands brushing before locking together. In that fleeting touch lay every unspoken promise, every shared memory.

"I don't want you to go back," Seph whispered in her ear, his voice rough with emotion.

"I know." Emma's voice cracked, and she fought the urge to fall apart. "But I can't leave them."

Their embrace grew stronger, desperate and unyielding, as if holding on could change what was coming. Then, slowly, reluctantly, they let go.

"James!" Seph shouted back into the cabin. "Emma is going to go back to the city to make sure her family doesn't re-connect. How can we stay in touch with her?"

James looked at Duke. "Do you have another satellite computer?"

"We do back at The Refuge," said Duke," but we try to use them in outposts similar to this so they can never be traced back to our location. You can never be too safe."

"Emma, once we get settled, I'll work with Seph to get an encrypted app going where we can send you a secure email," James said. "We will be an old friend from school you haven't talked to in a while."

"Thank you, James," Seph said. "Knowing we can communicate will make this easier." James gave Seph a smile, offering Seph comfort.

"Here's the key to my apartment just in case you need a safe space," Seph said, pulling the key from his pocket and handing it to Emma.

"Let's go, I want to get you back as soon as possible," Duke said.

Emma hugged June and James briefly. "Don't miss me too much," she said, hugging Seph one last time.

Without another word, Emma and Duke jumped into his cargo van and disappeared into the approaching dawn.

Seph stood rooted to the spot. Once again, another person he cared about was gone. An all too familiar feeling. He forced himself to hold back tears. There was no room for regret, no time for second-guessing. But as the rising sun illuminated the stark reality before him, Seph couldn't shake the feeling that he was leaving behind more than just Emma. He was leaving behind a part of himself—a part that only she truly understood.

Seph, June, and James finished packing up the last of the items in the outpost and jumped James's old pickup truck. They drove in silence, the rumble of the old engine blending with the distant call of wind through pine trees. The narrow road wound through a dense forest, towering evergreens casting shifting shadows across the cracked pavement. Mountains loomed in the distance, their snow-dusted peaks piercing the horizon.

"This place looks ... untouched," James muttered, his eyes scanning the remote terrain.

June, in the passenger seat, allowed herself a small smile. "It's why Duke chose it. No one comes out this far."

The truck rounded a final curve, revealing a secluded valley nestled between rugged hills. A scattering of rustic cabins stood beneath a canopy of towering pines, their weathered exteriors blending seamlessly with the natural landscape.

June guided them to a clearing near a large, wooden lodge. "This is The Refuge," she announced, stepping out of the vehicle. Her boots crunched against the gravel as Seph surveyed the area. It looked different than the last time he'd been there.

Seph followed June towards one of the cabins, noticing the sharp, clean air. It smelled of pine, earth, and distant woodsmoke—so different from the musty, manufactured atmosphere of the city.

"Come on," June beckoned, her voice softer now. "Let me show you around." She led them past the lodge toward a series of interconnected paths winding deeper into the forest. "This way," she said, pointing toward a stream glinting in the morning light. "We've got fresh water year-round from the mountain springs."

They walked further, passing small gardens carefully tended despite the rugged environment. "We grow what we can here," June explained. "Root vegetables, herbs... nothing fancy, but enough to get by."

Near the edge of the clearing stood a row of storage sheds, sturdy and fortified. "Supplies," June said simply. "Food, tools ... anything we can scavenge or trade for."

James nodded appreciatively, taking in every detail. "It's impressive. Well-hidden, self-sustaining," James commented.

June's face softened for a moment, touched by his acknowledgment. "It's built to last," she said quietly. "To be completely self-sustaining."

June led them toward a large wooden building with wide windows spilling light onto the ground outside. "This is the kitchen, it's where we eat all our meals." The faint hum of conversation and clinking dishes spilled into the cool morning air.

Seph hesitated at the doorway, catching a glimpse of the bustling scene inside.

"Everyone, this is Seph who most of you know. He's gotten a few inches taller, I'm sure. And this is James—you can trust him. Let's let them settle, but at lunch, I'll let them fill you in on everything that happened this morning."

June ushered them inside to join the others for breakfast. Long wooden tables stretched across the room, filled with people—twenty, maybe thirty—of varying ages. Adults talked in low voices while children laughed and darted between the benches. The smell of fresh bread and something savory wafted through the air.

Seph froze a few steps inside. The last time he'd visited,

there'd been fewer than ten people living there. Now, The Refuge was filled with life.

"Come on," Riley's familiar voice called out. He stood near one of the tables, grinning. "You're not going to stand there gawking all morning, are you?"

Seph managed a smile and followed Riley through the room. They joined two other teenagers at the end of a table.

"Do you remember Max and Lily?" Riley asked.

Seph studied their faces. Max had dirty blond hair, green eyes and a darker complexion. Lily looked almost identical with a softer jaw line and long hair pulled back.

"Did your parents work with Duke at the shop back in the city?" Seph asked, trying to remember if that was where he could place them from.

"Yep," Max said. "We moved out here nine months ago, once our dad wrapped things up there."

"It's an adjustment," Lily added, "but you get used to it pretty quickly."

The food was simple but filling—fresh bread, scrambled eggs, and some kind of root-vegetable hash. Seph found himself eating more than he realized, the tension of the past few days melting away, if only briefly.

Seph put down his fork as June approached. "Riley, Seph is going to bunk with you and Duke. Will you show him where your cabin is and help him get settled?"

Riley nodded, pushing away from the table. "Come on, Seph. I'll show you the deluxe accommodations."

As they walked along the path to the cabin, Seph was amazed how much has been added on in just a few years. The cabin was small but cozy, with three narrow bunks pushed against the walls. Sunlight filtered through the single window, casting golden streaks across the rough wooden floor.

"You can take that one over there," Riley said, pointing at the bed's clean crisp sheets. "The bathroom is just on the other side of this wall."

Seph placed his backpack on the bed and looked around. It was rough, the exact opposite of the high-tech environment he had grown accustomed to at NexTech.

Riley jumped in the shower while Seph grabbed his bag from James's car. As he unpacked his few belongings, Seph thought of Emma. He hoped she'd made it back to her house safely. He wondered how everyone in the city was reacting to the reset.

21

Emma

The city was chaos. Its usually synchronized flow had been replaced by frantic whirring and the distant wail of alarms. Haloscreens flickered with President Walker's face on every corner building, his expression composed but stern. Anxious murmurs passed through the crowded streets as Emma pushed forward, her hood pulled tightly over her head. Everywhere she turned, people clustered around outdoor displays or craned their necks upward at the massive projections blinking from skyscrapers. Processing centers glowed with harsh, white light, their entrances clogged with citizens desperate to find out how their nano chip had disconnected and how to reconnect it.

A sense of brittle fear hung in the cold night air. Emma kept walking, her sneakers striking against wet pavement, dodging panicked pedestrians who were either rushing to the centers or frozen in place by indecision. Above her, President

Walker's voice carried across the plaza, amplified by unseen speakers:

"Due to the unprecedented incident," he said, his voice smooth, *"criminals have taken advantage of the network outage. Our advanced monitoring systems were temporarily disabled. Without the nano chip, society is vulnerable. We urge everyone to remain calm and stay inside until we can get everything back online securely."*

Emma glanced at a nearby family clustered in the glow of a storefront display. The mother clutched her child while the father stared at the screen, his lips moving silently as if repeating Walker's words to himself.

"James Kent's disconnection was a result of a mental breakdown," Walker continued. *"His nano chip detected early signs of instability, but before intervention, he acted. To ensure public safety, I urge all citizens to make plans to reconnect as soon as processing centers and the NexTech system are fully back online. We anticipate this being within the next twenty-four hours. The nano chip is essential for maintaining order and peace."*

Lies. Every word. Emma's stomach twisted, and her hands balled into fists inside her coat pockets. Walker spoke with the polished charm of someone who had rehearsed every line, every inflection. He didn't stumble, didn't hesitate. It was terrifying how convincing he sounded. She could tell the crowd around her believed every word he was saying.

"Until we can get everybody connected to the NexTech system through reconnecting their nano chip, essential services, including transpo, hospitals, and commerce systems, will not be functioning. We will broadcast again once the processing centers are open. I urge you all to be safe and do not let our world turn to chaos. Everything will be back online soon."

182

A soft chime ended the broadcast, and the haloscreen shifted to looping footage of calm, smiling citizens scanning their wrists at processing centers—a stark contrast to the panicked reality Emma was witnessing. A new message overlayed the footage: *"Processing Centers Opening Soon".*

She kept walking. Her goal was Seph's apartment. It felt impossibly far away as she pushed through the sea of frightened faces.

By the time she reached Seph's building, Emma's legs ached and her throat felt raw from breathing in cold air. A drone buzzed past her head, its red sensor light flickering as it scanned the crowd. It paused briefly over her, hesitating, before moving on. Emma pressed her hand to her chest, trying to steady her heartbeat.

Seph's apartment felt impossibly still. Emma moved quickly to the counter where James had left their halophones. She picked up Seph's and disconnected the location spoofing device. Messages flashed across the screen: system notifications and error logs. She turned his off and put it in her bag. She then took her own phone, unplugged the spoofing device and tried to turn it off and back on. Once it lit up, it displayed a connection error. There was no way to make a phone call or send a message to her parents. She knew by now they would be worried for her. She had to get home.

Before she left Seph's apartment, Emma looked around for something metal that she could break James's halophone with. She didn't want to leave it there in the event it would get traced back to Seph, and she didn't want to be caught with it. She put it on the floor and slammed the foot of a dining chair on it. The phone shattered with each blow. She carefully picked up the pieces and put them in a paper bag. She would need to drop these in a public trash can on her way home. This was the best time to get rid of this evidence.

Emma exhaled slowly, her hands shaking as she thought of going back outside. Seph had been right, James had been right—they were at the edge of something irreversible.

Her halophone buzzed in her pocket. A single notification flashed: *"Transpo services temporarily offline. Standby for updates."*

Emma sighed with relief, realizing that her phone was starting to come back online. But without the transpo, she would have to walk home. It was only a few miles away, but today, that felt like eternity.

When Emma arrived home, her parents were in the living room, the haloscreen painting their faces with the cold light of another presidential address. Her mother was sitting rigidly on the couch, clutching a blanket, while her father stood near the window, staring out at the flickering cityscape below.

"You're home!" her mother exclaimed, relief in her voice.

Emma stepped into the room, gave her mom a long hug, her coat still damp from the mist outside. "Yeah. I—" she paused, her voice failing her. "Have you been watching?"

Her father turned away from the window, his face tight with stress. "We've been watching all morning."

Her mother's eyes darted back to the screen as Walker's face faded into footage of citizens lining up at processing centers, scanning their wrists under the glowing arches. "I'm so glad you are okay. We heard it wasn't safe out there." Her mother's voice was shaking but firm. "We need to get reconnected as soon as possible."

Emma froze. "What?"

"It's for our safety," her father added, stepping closer.

"Without everyone getting reconnected to the nano chip, the safety we've all experienced free of crime and disease, that would go away."

"But—what about what James Kent said?" Emma's voice wavered. "The control, the surveillance. This isn't just about safety, Dad, it's about power."

Her father's jaw clenched. "Safety comes at a cost, Emma. And it's one worth paying."

"No." Emma shook her head. "It's not. You don't see it, do you? President Walker's not protecting us—he's controlling us. Every move we make, every choice—we won't even own our own thoughts."

Her mother's voice cracked as she whispered, "Emma, today has been a lot to handle. We've never had an attack like this before. We did hear James's message, but not everything he said was true. Your dad works for the government, he would know if those claims were true."

She stepped back, shaking her head slowly. "I don't think I can reconnect."

Her father's voice was sharp now. "Emma, don't be foolish. This is about survival."

Emma's pulse pounded against her throat. The people she loved most—her parents, who had raised her with such care—were slipping away into the same fear that gripped the city. They weren't choosing to be blind. They were terrified.

Emma turned and walked away, ignoring her mother's pleading voice as she climbed the stairs to her room. She locked the door behind her and pressed her forehead against it, tears blurring her vision.

Outside her window, the city glowed cold and blue, every screen a reflection of a system tightening its grip. Somewhere

185

out there, Seph was settling into a life off-grid with no idea how things were for her here. *Had she made a mistake coming back?* She shook that possibility out of her head. She needed to rest and have a conversation with them when they weren't all exhausted and in shock. It had taken her weeks to realize Seph's concerns were real. She had to find a way to convince them.

Emma woke to the smell of bacon and fresh bread wafting up from the kitchen. Her eyelids felt heavy, but the scent nudged her out of bed. Sunlight spilled through her curtains, soft and golden, painting warm streaks across her desk and floor. For one disorienting moment, she felt normal—like she'd simply overslept on a lazy Sunday morning. But then it all came flooding back: James disconnecting the nano chips and erasing the database; the streets full of frightened faces; President Walker's voice echoing over haloscreens. Her parents quickly disregarding James's concerns.

Pressing her palms into her eyes, Emma forced herself to stand. She grabbed her halophone and saw the service was back online. She scrolled through her missed messages and then checked her email. Nothing from Seph, nothing important.

The kitchen was loud with clinking pans and the sizzle of bacon. Her mom hovered over the stove, flipping pancakes onto a growing stack. Her father sat at the kitchen table, scrolling through updates on his halopad. Tucker, her fourteen-year-old brother, was perched on a stool, stuffing a forkful of eggs into his mouth while absentmindedly sketching on a scrap of paper.

"Morning, sunshine," her mom said with forced brightness as she noticed Emma. "I made your favorite—chocolate-chip pancakes."

Emma managed a small smile as she slid into the seat across from Tucker. Her dad glanced up from his halopad and gave her a nod. Tucker, on the other hand, looked up and grinned through a mouthful of eggs.

"Morning, Em. You missed the first batch, but these are pretty good, too," Tucker said, muffled through chewing.

Emma reached for the stack of pancakes her mom set in front of her, pouring syrup absentmindedly over the pile. She wasn't sure if she was hungry, but her stomach growled in protest as she picked up her fork.

"So…" her dad said after a moment, setting his halopad face down on the table. "How are you feeling this morning?"

Emma swallowed a bite of pancake and took a breath. "Better. I think I just needed some sleep."

"Good," her mom said, relief flickering across her face. "You had us worried last night."

"Yeah," Emma said softly, setting her fork down. "Last night was … intense. Everything James and President Walker said— it's a lot to process."

Her dad nodded, his brow furrowed. "It is. And I won't pretend we're not worried about the situation. But Emma, we've been through scares before. Things always stabilize."

Emma hesitated, choosing her words carefully. "What if… what if this time it's different? What if James Kent wasn't lying? What if there really *is* something dangerous about the way the nano chip is being used?"

Tucker perked up from his sketching. "It wouldn't shock me!" he said eagerly, his pencil paused mid-line. "We don't need the chip! Why should some tech decide what we do, where we work?"

"Tucker," their father said, his voice firm but calm. "You're fourteen. You don't understand how much easier life is with the nano chip. How much safer. The systems we rely on—they all run because of it."

"Doesn't mean it's right," Tucker muttered, returning to his drawing.

Emma looked at her parents, her voice steady. "But what if Tucker's right? What if we're relying on something that isn't as safe as it seems? What if President Walker's assurances are just … distractions? What if this isn't about safety at all?"

Her mother sighed, placing the spatula on the counter and turning to face Emma. "Honey, the nano chip has done so much good. Think about the diseases it's stopped. The crimes it's prevented. Our world was chaos before NexTech created the chip. Do you remember hearing stories about the epidemics, the violence in cities? People used to fear walking home at night. Parents feared sending kids to school. Schools had emergency drills to respond to an active shooter."

Emma nodded. "I know. I'm not denying the good it's done. But that doesn't mean we should trust it blindly. There's a line somewhere, and I think—no, I *know*—we're crossing it."

Her father's expression softened as he leaned forward, resting his forearms on the table. "Emma, listen. Your mother and I don't agree with *everything* the government does. We have our concerns occasionally too. But pulling away entirely? Refusing to reconnect? That's not a solution—it's isolation."

"It's not about isolation, Dad," Emma pressed. "It's about keeping our ability to *choose*. Every update, every new initiative—it's another piece of our freedom handed over to a system we can't control."

Her mother looked away, her hands wringing the dish towel

she'd been holding. Tucker's pencil scratched lightly against paper, the only sound filling the silence.

Her father let out a slow breath. "Emma, these are important questions. And I'm proud of you for asking them. But you can't expect everyone to see things your way overnight. This technology isn't perfect, but nothing is. That's why it's so important for people like *you* to be part of it. People who ask hard questions. People who don't just accept things because they're told to."

Emma frowned. "What do you mean?"

Her father leaned back in his chair. "I mean … maybe you should talk to someone at NexTech, someone higher up. Bring these concerns forward. You work there, Emma. You have a voice. Maybe you can help change things from within."

Emma's stomach twisted at the suggestion. If only he knew how far down the rabbit hole she'd already gone.

Her mother chimed in gently, "You've always been so sharp, so thoughtful. You see things other people miss. Maybe you can help make the system better, instead of running from it."

Emma's eyes flickered between her parents. They weren't dismissing her outright. They weren't blind believers. But they also weren't ready to see the full picture—not yet.

Tucker chimed in, setting down his pencil. "I still think we should all just ditch the chips and move to the mountains or something. Live off the grid, grow potatoes. It'd be awesome."

Emma couldn't help but smile faintly.

Her father chuckled softly, though his eyes remained serious. "Emma, you're smart. You'll figure out what feels right. Just … be careful. This is bigger than any one of us."

Emma nodded slowly, her appetite gone despite the plate of pancakes still in front of her. The conversation had given her clarity, but also a grim realization: convincing her family wasn't going to happen overnight. They weren't going to just pack up and leave because she asked them to.

Her mother reached out and squeezed her hand. "We love you, Emma. And we trust you."

Emma forced a smile. "I love you too."

As the conversation faded, Emma felt the weight of the divide between her reality and theirs settle heavily on her shoulders. Her parents weren't enemies. They weren't ignorant. But they were tethered to a system they had grown to depend on, and breaking free wouldn't be easy.

Tucker grabbed his sketchbook and hopped off the stool, pausing as he passed Emma. "If you ever *do* decide to ditch the system, take me with you."

She gave him a small, sad smile. "Deal."

As the family settled back into their routine—her father scrolling through updates, her mother cleaning dishes, Tucker sprawled on the couch with his sketches—Emma felt a pang of loneliness.

This wasn't going to be easy.

But she wasn't going to stop trying.

22

Seph

Seph woke to the sound of hammering echoing through the cool morning air. Sunlight filtered weakly through the dense canopy of pine trees outside his cabin window. The air was sharp and cold, carrying the scent of woodsmoke and damp earth.

Rubbing the sleep from his eyes, Seph stepped outside and squinted against the light breaking over the treetops. The Refuge was alive with activity. Figures moved purposefully between half-built cabins, while others hoisted solar panels onto angled frames. Smoke curled lazily from the central lodge's chimney, promising breakfast.

"Morning, kid." Duke's voice carried over the noise as he approached with a pair of leather gloves and a heavy canvas tool belt slung over one shoulder. His face was creased with exhaustion, but his eyes were sharp. "Got good news for you—Emma made it back to the city, safe and sound."

Seph let out a breath he didn't realize he'd been holding. Relief flooded his chest, and for a brief moment, the ache in his shoulders lessened. "Thanks, Duke. I was worried."

"She's tough, just like you," Duke said, clapping Seph on the shoulder, "but we've got a long day ahead of us. Here, put these on."

Seph slipped on the gloves and followed Duke to a stack of lumber. Together, they began carrying heavy planks to the edge of an unfinished cabin foundation. The work was grueling, repetitive, but oddly grounding. The hammering of nails and the rhythmic whir of saws filled the silence between them.

"The physical labor here takes some getting used to," Duke said after a while, leaning on his hammer. "But your body will adjust quickly. Clear skies, honest work, people looking out for each other, this is how we were always meant to live."

Seph nodded, his brow damp with sweat despite the chill in the air. "Do you think... do you think she'll come back? Emma, I mean. With her family?"

Duke sighed, wiping his hands on his pants. "I hope so."

"I hope James's message was enough to cause a resistance that will force the government to change the tech and have more transparency for people to consent before new initiatives are unleashed," Seph said.

"But people in the city—they're tethered to that life, to those systems," Duke responded.

"Cutting those cords—it's not easy."

Seph didn't reply, but his gaze drifted toward the tree line. He hoped Emma would find a way to convince her parents quickly, and he wondered how many others they'd be able to awaken to the truth behind NexTech's perfect facade.

Lunch in the communal dining hall was a comforting affair. Long wooden tables stretched across the room, piled high with bread, root vegetable stew, and boiled eggs. The chatter of conversation filled the space—children laughing, adults exchanging quiet words between bites.

Seph settled at a table with Riley, Max, and Lily.

Riley was halfway through a sandwich, crumbs clinging to the corner of his mouth. "Well, you made it through the morning without dropping a solar panel on someone's head. Proud of you, buddy," he said with a grin.

Max and Lily laughed.

"How's it been settling in?" Max asked, dunking a chunk of bread into his stew.

"Better than I thought," Seph admitted. "It's quieter here. Simpler. I didn't like that about this place a few years ago, but now there is a peace to it."

Seph chewed his bread in silence as he listened to them discuss what they were each working on, glancing around the room he saw the mix of faces—old and young. There was something raw and honest about the way these people lived. It was so different from the polished, hollow veneer of the city.

Riley leaned over to Seph, lowering his voice. "Hey, James wanted to talk to you after lunch. He's been in the tech cabin all morning—says he's onto something with the satellite."

Seph's stomach tightened. "Did he say what?"

"Nah," Riley said with a shrug. "But I am not sure I would have known what he was talking about even if he did."

The tech cabin was not what Seph had in mind. It was filled with bundles of wires, blinking lights, and stacks of dusty computer equipment salvaged from decades past. This was far from the latest equipment he was used to working on at NexTech.

James sat hunched over a flickering monitor, his face illuminated by pale blue light. His fingers flew over the keyboard, his brow furrowed in intense concentration.

June stood nearby, arms crossed, her sharp eyes scanning a large map pinned to the wall.

"Seph!" she greeted, her face softening. "Come in."

Seph stepped carefully over cables and tools strewn across the floor. James barely glanced up from the screen.

"We're close," he muttered, "so close."

"What are you working on?" Seph asked.

James paused, scribbling a note before answering: "I've been running an app—something to mask our location. But I can't test it properly without connecting to an external satellite network. And I can't do that from here."

June stepped forward, gesturing to the map. Red Xs marked several locations scattered around the forested region surrounding The Refuge.

"These are our outposts," June explained. "Minimal infrastructure, but each one has a satellite uplink. We've used them in the past to send encrypted messages without drawing attention here."

Seph walked over to the wall where the map hung. He saw a dozen markers indicating outposts. Then he noticed closer to the city several question-mark symbols on the map. "What are these marks here?" he asked.

"Those are places we scouted that could be potential rendezvous points for anyone in the city trying to escape," June said. "We haven't had time to build out the infrastructure, but our plan was to create locations that someone could reasonably walk to in a day or two from the city, and then trigger a call for us to come pick them up."

"Wouldn't the nano chip send the signal meaning NexTech could figure out where people were leaving from?" Seph asked.

"We hadn't figured out all those details. We were just scouting for exit locations and these were all possible. I'm not sure if we will even need this anymore," June said hopefully.

Seph stared at the map, studying where the outposts were and the potential escape points near the city. He was impressed with how much work Duke had been able to accomplish over the years.

James pointed at one of the closer Xs. "This one's about two hours away. If we can access the uplink there, I can test the masking program, check city broadcasts, and maybe get a message to Emma."

"Can I go with you?" Seph interjected.

"Yes," James said without hesitation. "I need someone I can trust to come with. And it's always best to have an extra set of eyes make sure I am not missing something critical."

"The roads aren't safe, Seph. Patrol drones are increasing their range. You two need to be careful. I don't want you to get caught with James," June said.

Seph took a deep breath and nodded. "We'll be careful. When do we leave?"

"Tomorrow morning," James replied. "Early, before the sun is up."

* * *

The sun was dipping below the horizon as Seph and James

packed supplies into an old off-road truck. Canvas bags filled with tools, spare batteries, and rations were stacked carefully in the back.

Riley hovered nearby, double-checking their inventory. "You've got food, water, tools, and the radio. Stay on the marked paths, alright? Don't take shortcuts."

Duke handed Seph a worn map, the edges frayed and faded. "Stick to this. If anything feels off, turn back."

"How far out will this radio work?" James asked.

Seph looked at the device in James's hand, it was another old piece of technology nobody used anymore; a communication tool that could go undetected from today's modern-day surveillance.

"It will only cover you about halfway there, but it may still come in handy. And you can let us know when you are on your way back," Duke said.

June appeared briefly, her face tight with worry. "Don't stay longer than you have to. Test what you need, send your message, and get back here."

Seph adjusted the straps of his backpack, wishing it wasn't so complicated just to find out how things were going in the city.

They finished loading the truck and headed inside to get a few hours of sleep before they left.

* * *

The road twisted through dense trees, gravel crunching under the truck's wheels. Seph sat in the passenger seat, his hands gripping his knees as the forest seemed to close in around them. "Do you think we convinced people?" he asked, breaking the silence.

James glanced at him briefly before turning back to the road. "To be honest, I have no clue. And I know Walker would have been quick to combat my message with his own."

They fell silent again as they maneuvered around a fallen tree, the truck's engine growling as they pushed on.

23

Emma

The subtle vibration of the car's electric engine felt deafening as Emma sat in the back seat, staring out the tinted window at the sprawling government services building. The mirrored facade glinted in the pale morning light, and a steady stream of citizens moved in and out of the towering structure, their faces set in tight, resigned expressions.

Her parents sat in the front—her mother twisting her wedding ring, her father gripping the steering wheel. They had avoided the long lines at the city's processing centers by scheduling an appointment directly at the government building, reserved only for government workers and their families.

Emma swallowed hard. This was happening.

Her mother turned around. "Are you ready, sweetheart? It'll be quick. Just a little pinch, and then everything will be back to normal."

Normal. Emma's stomach turned. She forced a nod. She hated that she was doing this, but she needed to give her parents a little more time. She hoped playing along for a little while would give her the chance to convince them to leave with her. She couldn't imagine leaving her family while she escaped.

Her father's voice was steady but firm: "You're doing the right thing, Em. It's better this way—for all of us."

She wanted to scream, to tell them that *nothing* about this was better. But instead, she just nodded. She needed time. Time to find proof. Time to convince them.

As they walked through the grand glass doors of the building, the faint scent of antiseptic hung in the air. The marble floors gleamed under bright overhead lights, and digital kiosks guided citizens toward various processing zones. A *"chip reconnect"* sign hung above an archway, glowing soft blue.

A polite woman in a crisp white uniform led them to a smaller, private room. It felt sterile and clinical, the kind of place designed to make people compliant.

Emma sat in the reclining chair, her heart pounding as a nurse entered. He was middle-aged, wearing NexTech scrubs with the company's logo stitched neatly over his chest. He wheeled over a cart with small, silver instruments arranged in precise rows.

"Alright, Miss Miller," he said with a too-bright smile. "We'll get you reconnected in no time. Now, since your chip was fully disconnected, we'll be replacing it entirely. So the first poke will remove the old device, and the second will put in the new one."

Emma froze. "Replacing it? Not just reconnecting it?"

The nurse's smile didn't falter. "Yes, the reset was a perfect opportunity to upgrade older chips. Something that would have happened in the next few months, but now we can kill two birds with one stone. Nothing to worry about. You'll barely feel it."

She glanced at the gleaming silver device he picked up—a needle-like instrument attached to a sleek glass cylinder. It looked sharper, more intricate than what she remembered from her first implantation.

The nurse pressed a cold alcohol swab against the skin on her forearm. "You'll feel a slight pinch and a brief burning sensation."

The needle slid in, and Emma bit down on her lip as a sharp, electric pain flared up her arm. It was over in seconds, but her skin tingled, and an ache pulsed beneath her veins.

The nurse pressed a small bandage over the site and gave her another practiced smile. "All done. Give it a few minutes, and your system will reconnect. Your halophone will get a message shortly with your digital certificate or reconnection."

Emma's forearm throbbed as she stood. Something felt *different*. She couldn't explain it, but the chip didn't feel … neutral. It felt *active*, like a tiny heartbeat under her skin. This was definitely different than the first time.

Her mother hugged her tightly as they left the building, her father clapping her shoulder with a relieved smile. She looked at the bandages on their arms. "Did it feel different to you?" she asked them.

"It's been so long, I honestly don't remember," her mom said, rubbing her back. "I'm just glad it's over and we're connected again."

The sterile scent of NexTech's corporate offices felt sharper than usual as Emma walked through the glass doors. The receptionist barely glanced up when she scanned her wrist under the security arch. Her new chip pulsed faintly, the arch lighting up green.

The office was quieter than she'd expected. Rows of cubicles stretched out in neat lines, but only about half were occupied. The glow of haloscreens and the faint tapping of keyboards echoed softly.

Martin was already seated at his desk when Emma arrived. His shirt was rumpled, and there were deep shadows under his eyes.

"Morning, Martin," Emma said hesitantly.

Martin glanced up and gave her a tired smile. "Emma. Good to see you back. I was starting to think I'd have to run this whole floor by myself."

"Where is everyone?"

Martin sighed, running a hand through his disheveled brown hair. "Only about fifty percent of staff have come back. Some are still waiting for their reconnect appointments, but almost twenty percent haven't even reported—their status is unknown." He hesitated.

Emma swallowed. "Are they being searched for?"

Martin gave her a long look. "Officially? No. But unofficially? I think so. I don't think it is clear yet if they are hurt, lost, or choosing not to get reconnected."

Before Emma could respond, Marlene appeared at the edge of her cubicle, her presence sharp and unyielding.

"Emma," Marlene said, her voice clipped, "welcome back."

"Thank you," Emma replied cautiously.

Marlene's sharp eyes flicked across Emma's desk. "Where's

Seph? He hasn't responded to our outreach. We're trying to track down all employees who haven't returned."

Emma's heart skipped a beat, but she forced herself to stay calm. "He's still waiting for his reconnect appointment. You know how long the processing center lines are."

Marlene studied her for a moment, her lips pressed into a thin line. "Oh good. I'll mark down that we are expecting him to be back in a few days. Let him know that if the processing lines don't clear up, he can come here, and we can get his chip connected through our on-site medical suite. He should have all that information in his inbox."

"I'll let him know," Emma said evenly.

Marlene gave a curt nod before disappearing down the hallway.

Emma slumped into her chair, her pulse racing, unsure how long that excuse would still work.

The afternoon dragged on, with Emma finding herself staring out the floor-to-ceiling windows of the NexTech tower. Below, the city was still filled with chaotic movement: drones hovering above congested streets; haloscreens projecting Walker's face on every corner. Her thoughts drifted to Seph—his quiet determination, the way he always seemed to see straight through her defenses.

Did she... like him? Like, like him?

Her feelings were layered and every time she felt a deep connection with him, she'd pushed the thoughts aside. But she knew that when Seph was around, the world felt less suffocating. She'd never felt so seen, so understood.

Seph wasn't just her friend. He was her safe space. And she missed him.

* * *

When Emma got home, she found Tucker sprawled on the couch, his halophone balanced on his chest as he scrolled absently through some app. "Hey, Tuck," she said, flopping into the armchair across from him.

"Hey," he muttered, eyes still on the screen.

She waited a moment before asking, "So ... have you decided about your training program? Mechanical repair isn't exactly what you wanted, right?"

Tucker sighed and set his halophone down. "I don't know, Em. I mean, it's fine. I like working with my hands, but ... it's not *me*. And now everything's been pushed back because of the reset."

Emma nodded thoughtfully. "Do you think you could ask to retake the career assessment exam?"

"Maybe," Tucker said quietly. "But I feel like it won't matter. The system will just push me back here again. Like ... maybe this is what I'm supposed to do, whether I like it or not."

Emma frowned. "Life isn't supposed to feel like that, Tucker. You should have a choice."

Tucker looked up at her, his face serious. "Do you ever feel like we're not really free? Like James said, we're all just cogs in some giant machine?"

Emma's breath let out. "Yeah, Tuck. I do."

That night, Emma lay awake in her bed, her new nano chip pulsing faintly under her skin. She couldn't shake the feeling that something about it was *wrong*.

The city outside her window buzzed with light and motion, but all Emma could feel was the weight of the impossible task of convincing her parents. But one thought stayed with her as she drifted into uneasy sleep:

Seph, please be safe.

24

Seph

The outpost was barely more than a shack pressed against the hillside, its roof angled awkwardly to blend in with the trees. Vines tangled with the solar panels, and the door creaked as James pushed it open.

Inside, the air was stale, and the sun shone through cracks in the walls. An ancient-looking terminal sat in the corner, wires snaking across the floor.

James powered it up, the screen flickering to life. Seph adjusted the solar panels outside until the terminal's glow steadied.

"Here goes nothing," James muttered, typing rapidly. The screen filled with scrolling text as he scanned broadcasts and pulled up city forums. The terminal's glow cast sharp blue shadows across James's face as he hunched over the screen, his fingers dancing across the keyboard.

Seph leaned against the doorway, the cold wind from

outside brushing against his back as he watched lines of code and snippets of text flash across the screen. "Anything yet?" Seph asked, his voice full of anticipation.

James didn't answer immediately, his eyes flicking across the data as it loaded. Then, with a sharp exhale, he spoke: "The city's message boards are chaos. Most of them are just reposts of President Walker's speeches or people complaining about the lines at processing centers." He paused, scrolling further. "From what I can piece together, it seems that shortly after my message went through, President Walker gave an address that encouraged people to remain calm and stay inside while they worked to reset systems and begin reconnecting the nano chips. He discredited everything I said, of course, saying I was mentally unstable."

"Did people believe him?" Seph was angry.

"Hard to know. It seems like it was chaos for a few days, and still may be—a little. NexTech says they have reconnected forty percent of all the nano chips, but I don't know if that's true." James kept scrolling.

"Right, they could just be saying that to make it seem like nobody is actually concerned." Seph hoped that number was just propaganda.

"Exactly, or, it could be that my message didn't work. And people either don't care or just don't want to believe it." James sighed. "It does look like there are some skeptics out there…"

Seph stepped closer, his eyes narrowing as he scanned the fragmented posts on the screen:

@FreedomChoice92: *I'm not reconnecting. I think James is right.*

@SeekingAnswers: *Something's wrong. They didn't reconnect my chip, they replaced it with an upgrade! What is this new* *chip?*

@DisconnectedSoul: *They want us to believe James Kent is crazy, but what if he's not? What if he's right? I can't shake the feeling that we're being lied to.*

But for every one of these voices, there were dozens—hundreds—drowning them out:

@CitySafeUser: *James Kent is a terrorist. He put lives at risk. The chip is what keeps us safe. I'm reconnecting first thing tomorrow.*

@Walker4Life: *If you're not reconnecting, you're part of the problem. Society doesn't work without structure.*

Seph rubbed a hand over his face. "They're scared, James. And fear … it's louder than reason."

James nodded grimly. "President Walker's narrative is winning. And the lines at the processing centers indicate that people want their safety blanket back. The fear of losing access to basic services—it's too much for most people to resist."

"Wait, what did that say?" Seph pointed at a link.

James clicked it and opened a news article. They were reporting that criminal activity was up for the first time in years, showing both petty theft and violent attacks—even murders—spiked when the reset happened. They were working to make arrests but didn't have the sophisticated systems working, so many suspects were on the loose.

"Do you think that's true?" Seph asked. "Did we cause that?"

James paused. "My suspicion is that there probably were some attacks and theft during the chaos. But I think they're bolstering these numbers to incite more fear and panic." He paused again. "Nothing gets people to act quicker than fear does. But Seph, even if it's true, we didn't force anyone to hurt others."

Seph let out a slow breath. "What about NexTech? Are there any employee forums? Internal chatter?"

James typed quickly, accessing secure threads marked with corporate signatures. The screen flickered as restricted files loaded. "Looks like internal communication is controlled tightly, but there are whispers … a few employees wondering about the upgrade process, others talking about longer hours and increased security protocols." James paused, glancing briefly at Seph. "There's no mention of anyone else being involved in the reset. No red flags. That's good."

Seph nodded, relief washing through him.

James hesitated, then said, "We should reach out to Emma to see if she responds while we're still here. She might have more insight for us."

A cold sweat prickled at the back of Seph's neck. He needed to know she was okay. "Yes," Seph said. "let's send her a message."

James began typing, his words appearing on the screen:

To: Emma Miller
From: Stephanie Lang
Subject: Catching up

Emma, it's been too long since we talked. I have been staying inside while things in the city settle down. Are you staying safe too? I heard forty percent have already reconnected—do you think that is true? How is your family? Hoping to see you soon once things settle down.

—Stephanie

James hesitated over the keyboard, glancing at Seph. "Anything you want to add?"

Seph stepped forward, his body tense as he stared at

the blinking cursor. He thought about Emma: her fierce determination, her quiet courage—the way she'd looked at him before they'd said goodbye.

"Tell her … we can come back for her if she needs to get out."

James nodded, typing out the final line:

P.S. Let me know when you're ready to hang out. You can come over to my house.

The message sent with a faint chime, and the screen dimmed slightly as the data encrypted and disappeared into the satellite relay.

"Do you think she'll respond?" Seph asked quietly.

"She will," James said firmly. "We can stay for a few more hours before heading back."

For a moment, neither of them spoke. The cold wind whistled faintly through the cracks in the outpost walls, and the terminal's soft hum filled the silence.

Seph crossed his arms over his chest, his gaze locked on the dark screen. "James … do you ever think about what happens if we fail?"

James didn't look away from the screen. "Every day."

Seph swallowed hard. "And…?"

"And we keep going anyway," James said simply.

They scrolled through more articles and public forums, reading more of the same comments. Seph was anxious for Emma's response. "Can you refresh the email again?" he asked.

"Seph, I just did thre minutes ag—"

A notification chime came through, indicating a new email:

To: Stephanie Lang
From: Emma Miller

Subject: Re: Catching up

Stephanie, it's so good to hear from you. I'm safe! My parents and Tucker are good too. Yes, I do think forty percent is fairly accurate, and fifty percent of employees are already back at NexTech. I'm looking forward to getting together soon—I miss you. But I am busy with my family right now, and will need to wait for things to settle down. Work is busy as well, as all our initiatives are getting reprioritized after the reset.

Talk soon, Emma

"Wait, she is back at NexTech?!" Seph exclaimed.

"If she has to stay longer, she probably didn't have a choice." James leaned back in the chair. "She can't do anything to bring on suspicion."

Seph nodded, stepping back toward the door. "Let's leave. We've done what we can here."

James powered down the terminal, the screen flickered off. Together, they gathered their equipment, the weight of what they had to share with the others at The Refuge hanging over them.

The Refuge's main lodge was warmer than usual, a roaring fire crackling in the stone hearth as shadows flickered along the wooden walls. The long meeting table was crowded— James, June, Duke, Riley, and a handful of other leaders were scattered around it, their faces etched with concern.

Seph sat near the end, his elbows propped on the table, head bowed as he stared at a map splayed across the surface. The mood in the room was heavy—they'd just finished updating the group on what they'd discovered.

James spoke first, his voice sharp with frustration: "Forty percent. Already. And that number is growing every hour. Processing centers are clogged, but people are still waiting.

Willingly."

Duke crossed his arms, leaning back in his creaky chair. "Forty percent in less than a week. Another week, and it'll be seventy. Two more, and we'll be lucky if anyone remains disconnected."

"They're scared," June said quietly, her arms wrapped around herself. "President Walker is painting this perfect picture of safety and order, and they're clinging to it because the alternative feels unbearable."

Seph finally looked up, his voice quiet but firm. "But it *is* unbearable. They're walking right back into a cage. And this time they are choosing it."

A long silence followed his words, broken only by the occasional crackle of the fire. No one wanted to admit it, but Seph knew they were all thinking the same thing—James' reset had failed. The signal had gone out. The nano chips had been turned off. And still, it hadn't been enough.

James ran a hand through his disheveled hair, leaning heavily on the table. "I thought the evidence I had would be enough. I thought if people had even a moment to feel what it was like to be … *free* … they'd fight to keep it."

"They don't know how to fight, James," Duke said, his voice low but steady. "We've all been conditioned to rely on the nano chip. To trust our government leaders."

"So what should we do now?" Riley asked, his voice cutting through the stillness. He sat across from Seph, his usually bright demeanor dimmed by the weight of the conversation. "Do we just … give up?"

"No," June said firmly, her eyes blazing with conviction. "We can't give up. We have to keep trying."

"And we have someone on the inside," Duke said, his words

heavy with meaning. "Someone who can walk through those doors and not raise suspicion."

Silence fell again. Seph's stomach knotted as he anticipated what was coming.

"Do you think Emma can find out what they are planning to do next?" Riley said hesitantly. "She's already there. She's on the inside. She could—"

"No." Seph's voice was sharp and immediate, cutting through Riley's suggestion like a blade. "Absolutely not. Emma's already risking enough just being in the city to try and get her family out. I won't let her be a pawn in this."

James sighed, rubbing his temples. "Seph, listen—"

"No, *you* listen." Seph's chair scraped loudly against the wooden floor as he stood. "She's already doing enough. She's walking a tightrope every day, trying to convince her parents, trying to keep her head down at NexTech. And if they catch her—if they even *suspect* she's helping us—we have no idea what is at stake. She could get arrested. Or worse."

"Seph—" June started, her voice gentle.

"No!" Seph's voice cracked slightly as he slammed his hand on the table. The others flinched, and Seph took a deep breath, trying to steady himself. "We can't ask her to do this while we sit in safety. It's not right."

The room was silent again, everyone staring at Seph. His chest rose and fell with quick breaths as he clenched the edge of the table. "She's not expendable," he said softly, his voice breaking slightly. "None of us are."

Duke leaned forward, his voice calm and steady: "Seph, we're not saying Emma should do anything reckless. But she's already *there.* She has access. She can move through NexTech without raising suspicion. You know as well as I do how rare that is."

Seph shook his head, staring at the map without really seeing it. The thought of Emma risking herself—of her being caught, of something happening to her—made his stomach churn.

"I'll go back," he said suddenly. The words hung in the air, sharp and unyielding.

James frowned. "Seph—"

"I'll go back," Seph said again, his voice firmer this time. "I can get inside NexTech, I haven't been gone long enough to raise suspicion. Out of everyone here I am the only one who can get back in. This way I can make sure when I leave again, Emma doesn't stay behind."

June looked at him with wide eyes. "Seph, you'd be walking straight into a nest of vipers. If they catch you—"

"They won't," Seph said firmly. "I know how to keep my head down. I know what they'll be looking for. And I know how to get out."

The others exchanged uneasy glances. Duke's brow furrowed deeply as he studied Seph's face. "You understand what you're saying, right?" Duke asked carefully. "This isn't just about sneaking around an office building. NexTech isn't just a company—it's *the* company. They see everything, hear everything. And if they catch you—"

"I know the risks," Seph interrupted. "I'm not asking Emma to carry this weight. I can do this."

James leaned forward, his elbows braced on the table. "Seph, you have to understand—if you go back, there's no guarantee you'll make it out again. You'll be walking through those doors as a ghost—a ghost they might already be hunting."

Seph met James' eyes, his voice steady. "If I don't go, we'll lose everything. You said it yourself—we need information to plan what is next. If much more time goes by, we won't have this option."

The room was still, the crackle of the fire the only sound.

Duke exhaled deeply, rubbing a hand over his stubbled jaw. "Alright," he said finally. "Alright, Seph. If this is what you're choosing, then I'll support you. We'll get you to the edge of the city, and if something feels off—even slightly—you pull back. Understood?"

Seph nodded. "Understood."

June's face was pale, her lips pressed into a tight line. "We'll leave a few radios outside the city at a few of these locations where we previously scouted. Seph ... if it gets too dangerous, you have to promise us you'll leave, get to one of these points and make contact."

Seph hesitated before nodding. "I promise."

James leaned back in his chair, pinching the bridge of his nose. "It would be helpful if we knew who at NexTech was sending those messages to you all previously. Someone on the executive level, or with access to the executive level, was sending those. And it would be helpful for us to know who that is."

"And by coming back," Seph added, "it will throw off any scent that I was working with James."

"And Emma?" June asked softly. "If she chooses not to leave, how long will you stay?"

Seph's chest felt heavy. *Emma.* The thought of seeing her again made his heart race.

"I'll make sure she leaves this time," Seph said quietly. "Anyone that I know wants a way out, I'll make sure they leave with us too."

The meeting adjourned, and Seph stepped out into the cold night air. The sky was clear, the stars scattered in sharp, brilliant patterns across the expanse. His breath misted in front of him as he walked aimlessly toward the edge of the clearing, his boots crunching against frost-tipped grass.

He thought of Emma—her sharp wit, her quiet strength, the way she always seemed to see through him. He thought of her in that sterile office building, surrounded by people who couldn't see the walls closing in around them.

He didn't want to go back. Not really. But he couldn't stay here while others risked their lives. He couldn't let Emma carry this burden alone.

Somewhere deep in the forest, an owl hooted softly. Seph closed his eyes and exhaled. Tomorrow, he'd prepare. But tonight, he let himself feel the fear. The uncertainty. The ache of missing Emma.

Please don't let this be a mistake, he thought.

25

Emma

To: **Emma Miller**
From: **Stephanie Lang**
Subject: **Re: Re: Catching up**

Emma,

I'm going back to work in two days. Can we meet for dinner tomorrow night at my place?

Miss you.

—Stephanie

Emma stared at the message on her halophone, her thumb hovering over the screen. Her heart hammering against her ribs as she read the short email again.

Seph. He was coming back. Tomorrow.

A mixture of relief and dread tangled in her chest. She wanted to see him, to know he was okay, but the thought of him walking into the city—into NexTech—made her stomach churn. Why was he coming back? Did they have a plan now that they realized erasing everything didn't work?

The morning sunlight poured through the floor-to-ceiling windows of NexTech Tower. Around her, employees moved with a strange mix of exhaustion and forced enthusiasm. The reset had left its mark on everyone, whether they wanted to admit it or not.

Emma pushed her hair behind her ears and opened her email inbox. Messages flooded in—memos from upper management, updates on system protocols, reminders about reconnect appointments for those who hadn't yet complied.

Stifled conversations floated over the cubicle walls. Emma glanced up as a group of employees huddled by the coffee station, their heads bent together as they whispered furiously:

"—saw the broadcast again this morning. Walker said it's over sixty percent now. More people reconnected overnight."

"Yeah, but did you see the new processing center footage? Some people have been waiting in line for two days. They're camping out there."

"It's insane. Why would anyone wait that long? I would just wait until things cooled off, if I couldn't get it quicker through my employer."

Emma turned away, trying to focus on her work, but their voices stuck with her. *Sixty percent.* It was happening faster than she expected.

Mid-morning brought a lull in productivity, and Emma found herself cornered near the break room by Martin. He clutched his coffee mug with both hands and his shirt wrinkled.

"Emma!" he said with forced cheer. "You're looking ... well. How are things holding up over there in your corner?"

She managed a smile. "Fine, Martin. Still catching up on all the updates."

He lowered his voice, glancing around as if someone might overhear: "It's madness out there, isn't it? People are losing their minds. My sister works at one of the processing centers, and she says they're running twenty-four hours now, full capacity, all the time."

Emma nodded, unsure how to respond.

Martin sipped his coffee, his expression growing serious. "Do you think Kent was telling the truth? Or was he just delusional?"

Emma froze for a moment before shaking her head slowly. "I... I don't know, Martin. It's hard to believe."

He sighed. "I feel bad for him. Spent his life a hero and ended as an enemy after a mental break."

Before Emma could respond, a chime rang out across the office—a soft, melodic tone that signaled an incoming announcement. The haloscreens positioned around the office flickered to life, and the NexTech logo filled the displays. A soothing chime played again before the screen transitioned to a live broadcast. A woman in a polished gray suit appeared on screen, her hair styled into perfect waves, her expression calm but commanding.

"Good morning, NexTech employees. As we all know, the recent system reset has caused unprecedented disruption to our society. We've seen resilience, determination, and strength from every corner of our community. But we also know there are still questions—doubts that linger in the minds of many."

Emma noticed a growing unease settling over her body as the woman continued:

"NexTech is committed to innovation AND transparency. Today,

we are introducing a new initiative: The Reconnection Forum. This forum is for all NexTech employees to come and hear from leadership, and to voice any questions or remaining concerns. We believe in empowering our team members to shape the future of our systems and our society."

The screen flashed to the meeting details:

"The first forum will be held today at 2:00pm in Theater B. Together, we can ensure a better, safer future."

The screen faded to black, and the office murmurs began immediately.

By 2:00pm, Theater B was almost completely filled and Emma noticed they were already opening up overflow in the cafeteria. She slipped into a seat near the back.

At the front of the room, Lena from HR stood beside Myles, the head of NexTech's Innovation team. Lena was poised, her smile bright and approachable. Myles was lean, sharp-featured, and dressed in a suit so perfectly tailored it seemed sculpted onto him.

Lena stepped forward, clapping her hands softly for attention. "Thank you all for coming today. This space is for open dialogue. Please know this is a safe space. No question is too big or too small."

Myles stepped up next, his piercing gaze sweeping the room. "We're here because we care about NexTech, about our world, and about the systems we've built. But no system is perfect. And if recent events have shown us anything, what we do here at NexTech is even more important than ever.

"Due to the recent departure of James, the board has selected me to replace him as the leader of NexTech. I have been in touch with President Walker, and we have been working tirelessly to come up with a plan that ensures the nano chip and its data will not be used to harm anyone. Now, let's start off with some questions."

Emma shifted uncomfortably in her chair as the first person stepped up.

"What happened with the reset? How was someone able to shut down the nano chips? Aren't they supposed to be secure?"

Myles nodded thoughtfully. "Security is our top priority, but no system is immune to exploitation. What matters is that we learn from it and ensure it doesn't happen again. Because of what happened, we have expanded our Cyber Security team, we are rapidly getting new personnel up to speed. We were able to identify how this happened, James had written this code in the very early years, and it went undetected."

"Was everything really erased?" the next employee asked.

"Unfortunately, James permanently deleted all the data that had been collected by the nano chips. But he was not able to delete all the programs and algorithms that we built. So, we've been able to get all our systems back up and running. That is why we can continue right where we left off, once everyone reconnects," Myles responded, with a positive bounce in his voice.

Another employee raised their hand. "What if Kent was right? What if the chip is being used for more than just safety and health? What if we're giving away more than we realize?"

Myles looked over to Lena, and her expression softened as she spoke: "I know these fears are real, and they're valid. NexTech is committed to transparency. Typically, we would never give share this type of personal information in a forum like this, but this is an unprecedented circumstance and the board authorized me to share with you today. Over the last few months, James's nano chip was detecting some heightened emotions and paranoia. Looking back, we believe he was experiencing extreme burn-out from overworking all these years. The board tried to ease his burden and take things off his plate, we thought that would help. But in the end, we should have done more. It's terribly tragic that he was led to destroy something he created."

Myles nodded. "This is why one of the priorities here is to focus on curing mental health. We have done so much for other diseases, and now it's time to cure these terrible illnesses of the mind."

Emma felt like the walls were pressing in as Myles's eyes scanned the crowd. For a moment, she thought he would look directly at her.

Around her, a few hands went up. More questions kept coming. Emma kept her hand down, clasped tightly in her lap.

As the crowd began to disperse, Emma slipped out through the side doors and into the hallway. Her mind was spinning. Lena and Myles seemed genuine—they were very, very good at pretending. But to her, the forum felt like a performance, a way to placate employees, to soothe their unease with carefully curated answers.

As she walked back to her desk, she looked out the windows and saw the lines of people still waiting outside to reconnect. She wished she could scream loud enough for them to snap out of it and go back home.

26

Seph

The faint rumble of Duke's old cargo van filled the silence as it rattled along the narrow, cracked road leading toward the outskirts of the city. The trees lining the roadside were thinning now, their dense branches giving way to flickering haloscreen billboards and drone patrol lights cutting through the predawn gloom. The city skyline loomed ahead—sharp, metallic, and unyielding.

Seph sat in the passenger seat, his backpack clutched firmly against his chest. His eyes stayed fixed on the horizon, where the clouds above were glowing in hues of pale orange.

"This is as far as I can take you," Duke said, his gravelly voice breaking the silence as he eased the van to a stop near an abandoned service station.

Seph turned to face him, swallowing hard. "Thanks, Duke. For everything."

Duke grunted, his hands still gripping the wheel. "You know

the risks, kid. You don't have to do this."

"Yes, I do." Seph's voice was steady, even if his heart was not. "It's the only way."

Duke nodded slowly, then reached into the glove box and pulled out a small, encrypted drive. "James prepped this. If you can get into one of their terminals, plug this in. It might give him a backdoor."

Seph took the drive, its metallic surface cool against his palm. "I'll do my best."

Duke's eyes softened, and for a brief moment, Seph thought he might say something else. But instead, Duke simply extended a hand. Seph shook it firmly before slipping out of the van and into the cold morning air.

It took several hours for him to walk back to his apartment. He couldn't use the transpo since his nano chip was still disconnected. Seph climbed the narrow stairs to his old apartment, his key clutched in one hand. His heartbeat was loud in his ears, each step echoing in the stillness of the empty hallway.

The familiar door came into view, its chipped paint and worn handle somehow grounding him.

The door was unlocked.

He turned the handle and stepped inside. The apartment was dimly lit and everything felt frozen in time—exactly as he'd left it.

Then he saw her.

Emma stood near the window, her arms wrapped around herself as she stared out at the city below. When the door clicked shut behind Seph, she turned sharply. Their eyes met, and for a split second, neither of them moved.

Then Emma rushed forward, throwing her arms around

him. The force of her hug nearly knocked him back a step, but he held her tightly, burying his face in her hair.

"You're here," she whispered, her voice trembling.

"I'm here, but aren't you supposed to be at work?" Seph said, his arms wrapping around her.

"I made up an excuse, I had to see you." When Emma finally pulled back, her cheeks were streaked with tears, her eyes searching his face like she was trying to memorize every detail.

Before he could think, before he could second-guess, Seph leaned in and kissed her. It was hesitant at first, but Emma leaned into him, her hands clutching the collar of his jacket as if she could anchor him there forever.

When they pulled apart, Emma laughed softly through her tears. "I was worried I might never see you again."

Seph brushed a strand of hair away from her face. "I'm not going anywhere. Not yet."

They sat on the worn couch, their knees touching, as they each took turns updating each other on everything that had happened since they were last together.

"I have to go to NexTech tomorrow," Seph said finally. "I have to blend in, act like nothing's changed. I want to start digging to see what I can find out. I am not sure how long we will get."

Emma nodded, though her hands twisted together in her lap. "Just be careful, okay? You have to stay invisible. If they suspect anything, they will not hesitate…"

"I know." Seph pulled his halophone from Emma's bag, its familiar weight resting heavily in his hand. "I'll be careful." When he turned it on, the screen lit up with missed notifications, buzzing softly as messages flooded in.

Seph scrolled through the backlog of notifications until he

spotted the string of messages from Callum:

"Dude, where are you? NexTech hired me! Cybersecurity team— crazy, right?"

"They've been onboarding dozens of us. You wouldn't believe the chaos."

"They asked about you, by the way. Said you haven't reconnected yet. I told them you were probably stuck in line. You good?"

"Seph, seriously. Are you ok? Where are you?"

Seph's stomach clenched as he read the messages. Callum was walking right into NexTech's tightening grip, and he didn't even know it.

Seph stared at the last message for a long moment before setting the halophone down.

"Callum's on the cybersecurity team now," he said softly.

"Honestly, having a friend on that team may turn out positive for us," Emma said. "It might be good to have a few trustworthy allies to help."

"I just don't want to get him in trouble."

"Seph, you have to give people a chance. Remember?"

He opened up the thread with Callum and responded:

"See I told you you'd land a job soon."

"But sorry to leave you hanging, I got caught helping a friend and my phone just reconnected today. I'll be at work tomorrow—we need to catch up in person."

* * *

Seph approached the looming glass facade of NexTech Tower, his backpack slung over one shoulder. Employees streamed in through the grand entrance, their faces tired but focused. He walked through the security checkpoint, knowing full well what would happen. As soon as he scanned his wrist, the arch above him flashed red.

"Sir, your nano chip isn't active," a guard said, stepping toward him.

"Yeah, I know. I've been stuck in line at the processing centers for days. I couldn't wait anymore—I needed to report in." Seph kept his expression neutral.

The guard frowned but nodded. "Come with me."

Seph was led to Lena from HR, who greeted him with her usual polished smile—though her sharp eyes lingered on his face a beat too long.

"Seph," she said smoothly. "It's good to see you back. But you know you can't work without an active nano chip."

"I understand," Seph replied calmly. "I was stuck in line at the processing centers. The delays were ridiculous. Emma told me that Marlene said I could come here to get reconnected and skip the line."

Lena studied him before nodding. "Alright. Let's get you taken care of." She turned to the security guard and said, "Thanks, I'll take him from here."

They took the elevator to the third floor where the medical lab was. The sterile white of the medical bay made Seph's skin crawl. He sat in the chair as a nurse prepared the needle-like instrument.

"This will be quick," she said with a reassuring smile. "We're using upgraded chips now—better stability."

He watched the two-step process as his old chip was removed and then watched as the new chip slid in with a sharp pinch, followed by a slow, burning sensation under his skin. Seph gritted his teeth and forced himself to stay still. That burning sensation definitely didn't happen the first time, he would have remembered. Emma was right.

"All set. Welcome back," the nurse said.

Martin greeted Seph with tired relief: "Man, it's good to see you. You missed a mess."

Seph settled into his old desk, keeping his expression neutral. "Yeah, I heard. What's been going on?"

Martin leaned closer, lowering his voice. "We're working with the Innovation team now." He paused to wait for Seph to react. "And with Myles Fitz directly. He is overseeing the implementation of our emotional data algorithm to cure mental health."

Seph nodded. "They're using our algorithm?"

"Yeah. But it's not just that. Ours is part one. There's another team—one that's figured out how to send signals *back* through the chip: chemical triggers, brain responses. If our emotional algorithm detects instability, the chip can send a calming signal straight to your brain. Instant relief."

Seph felt his stomach drop. "And it works?"

Martin shrugged. "Well, I haven't seen it in action yet. Everything is still a bit of a mess around here. We should get more insight soon."

All Seph could think was, *They are going to control us with our emotions.*

Later that night, back in his apartment, Seph told Emma everything: "They're not just monitoring emotions—they're controlling them," he said. "If someone gets angry, if they feel rebellious, NexTech can just … *turn it off.*"

Emma's face was pale. "This isn't about mental health. It's about obedience."

Seph nodded. "They're creating a population that won't fight back. That won't *want* to fight back."

They sat in silence, the weight of their realization pressing down on them.

"We have to get out, we shouldn't have come back," Emma whispered.

Seph squeezed Emma's hand in his. "We will. We will need help, and there are a few things I have to do first. But we will."

27

Seph

The sun was just rising as Seph awoke. The muted haloscreens flickered outside, broadcasting President Walker's most recent address: seventy-five percent of the nano chips were now reconnected. His new nano chip thrummed faintly beneath his skin, and he couldn't shake the unsettling feeling knowing it was capable of even more.

Seph picked up his phone and sent out two messages:

"Callum, let's meet up for coffee today."

"Grace, can you have lunch today?"

Seph's mind was cemented in the fact that time was limited—he had to plan a way out of the city, and he needed help from trusted friends in order to do it safely.

* * *

As Seph arrived at the coffee shop just a few doors down from

NexTech, he was nervous to see Callum.

"Hey, you look familiar!" Callum said.

Seph turned around and paused when he saw his friend. Callum was dressed in a NexTech security uniform: a grey suit with the company logo etched in the chest and *"C. Coleman"* stitched underneath. Seph almost didn't recognize his clean-shaven face and slicked-back hair. The sharp style, paired with the crisp uniform, gave Callum an air of authority Seph wasn't used to seeing on his old friend. His usually carefree demeanor was now replaced with a focused, almost mechanical presence, as if the uniform itself had pressed a new identity onto him. Yet behind the polished appearance, Seph caught a flicker of something familiar in Callum's sharp, blue eyes—a spark of the easygoing guy he was used to.

"Who are you, and what have you done with Callum?" Seph said jokingly.

"Ha ha… It's still me, I just had to look the part."

The friends embraced and took a seat outside.

"So what happened when the reset happened? Why did it take you so long to respond?" Callum asked.

"Man, it's a long story. I don't even think we would have time to get into half of it before we have to head back to work. But I promise I'll tell you everything later," Seph said.

"Oh, so now you're willing to hang out with your old pal since he works at NexTech?" Callum said half-jokingly.

"Really, things got crazy when I started here—actually before. My aunt moved out with Duke."

"Wait, she went off grid?" Callum's eyes widened.

"Yep, so I had to hunker down and do my best to get a good job so I could afford to stay in the city myself." Seph looked around to make sure no one was listening.

"Dang, I had no idea. Why didn't you say anything before?" Callum asked.

"I don't know. I was overwhelmed and kept thinking we would catch up, and then so much happened, I didn't even know where to begin," Seph answered honestly.

"And I thought my unemployed journey was just too low-brow for you," Callum said.

"You know I've never been like that." Seph paused, thinking back on the years of friendship they'd had, through good and hard times, they had always remained supportive of one another.

"But I do want to have a deeper conversation about everything. I know you are just starting out here, but there are some things from James's message that I wanted to talk about." Seph braced himself for Callum's reaction.

"I was honestly expecting that you had completely drunk the NexTech Kool-Aid and would have discredited all of that..." Callum said.

"Let's not get into it here. Can you come over tonight? I'm rounding up a few friends to hang," Seph asked casually.

"Name the time and place and I'll be there." Callum nodded and took another sip of his coffee.

"Perfect, see you at 6." Seph stood up and Callum followed as they headed back into NexTech for the day ahead.

* * *

At lunch, Seph found Grace sitting at a table near the windows. She looked more tired than the last time he saw her. Her normally perfect, curly brown hair was unkempt. "Hey, Grace, how are you doing?" he said, taking the seat across from her.

231

"To be honest, been better. I was thankful for your message this morning."

"Oh no, sorry to hear that. What's wrong?"

Grace let out a sigh, looked around and then her eyes met Seph's. "Let's just say, it's been A LOT since the reset."

"I can imagine. Did they have you helping with the reconnection?"

"No, although we get reports each day on the progress."

Seph could tell she was hesitating with what to share as she poked at her salad. "You know, I have had my doubts too." He watched as her eyes lit up. He knew he'd hit the nail on the head.

"What did you do about it?" Grace asked.

"I kept looking until things made sense."

"And it eventually did?"

Seph stared at her for a while. Then he shook his head. Her eyes widened and they stared at each other, communicating in silence.

"Why don't you come over tonight after work?" Seph said. "Callum and Emma are coming over to hang out. I think it will help take your mind off the *pressures of work*." He hoped she understood what he was trying to say.

"I'd like that," she said, nodding in understanding. "Just text me your address. I don't think I've been to your place before."

* * *

The apartment was dimly lit by the faint glow of the kitchen light when Seph opened the door for Grace. She stepped inside, her sharp eyes scanning the room.

"Seph, Emma," she said by way of greeting.

232

"Hey, Grace," Emma replied from across the room. "It's good to see you."

A knock at the door came moments later. Seph opened it to see Callum, his hair still looking as crisp as it had that morning.

"Hey," Callum said quietly as he stepped inside.

"Hey, Callum, this is Emma." Seph gestured towards Emma.

"I've heard good things about you." Callum smiled.

They settled into the living room. Emma sat on the side of the worn couch, Grace took the armchair, and Callum perched uneasily on the edge of a dining chair pulled from the kitchen.

Seph hesitated before sitting down. "Before we get started, I need to put all devices in the other room. I don't want to take any chance of someone else listening in."

"Okay … you're being weird now," Callum said.

They each pulled out their halophones and handed them to Seph. After putting them in his room, out of ear shot, he settled into the couch next to Emma. "I asked you both here because I trust you. And because NexTech is doing something dangerous, something that goes beyond monitoring or safety."

Emma continued, her voice steady but low: "The emotional algorithm isn't just monitoring emotions—it's designed to *manipulate* them. When the system detects anxiety, anger, or fear, it sends signals through the chip to shut those emotions down."

Callum stared at them, his face pale. "That's … not possible. Is it?"

Grace leaned forward, her brow furrowed. "It is. I've seen the schematics for the new chips. The old ones couldn't send signals—they could only receive data. But these new chips?

They're different. They're *active*. They can transmit."

Emma's voice cracked slightly. "It's not about helping people, Callum. It's about making them compliant. Obedient. And no one will even realize it's happening."

Callum ran a hand over his face. "James wanted to wake people up. That was the point of the reset. But instead, he gave NexTech the perfect excuse to tighten their grip. Everything they're building now is under the guise of 'fixing the system.'"

"Exactly," Emma said.

Seph felt confident that Callum had connected the dots quickly. "As soon as I started at NexTech, the stuff I was seeing didn't add up. The nano chip was being used in severely invasive ways without public consent."

"I remember," Grace said. "You were asking questions way back then, ones I dismissed."

"I was, but I didn't know a fraction of what I know now." Seph shared with the group how he'd grown suspicious of NexTech's intentions and then about his involvement with James and the reset.

"Holy cow!" Callum exclaimed.

"I don't even know what to say…" Grace added.

"I know it's a lot," Emma said. "I've been trying to convince my parents, but they haven't really been able to handle it. It's a lot."

"Honestly, why did you come back?" Grace asked, looking at Seph.

"I just kept hoping that we could make a difference. That we could stop this," he said thoughtfully.

"People are way too far gone," Callum said, "especially those that have had the nano chip for a long time. They buy everything President Walker says."

"Well, when we came back, we realized it was even worse than we thought," Emma said.

"Emma and I realized that we couldn't stay here and fight this … not with the emotional manipulation coming. I knew I needed to see if you two would come with us," Seph said.

"You know I'm in," Callum said quickly. "No way I'm going to end up like some emotionless drone."

"Same," Grace added.

Seph leaned forward, resting his elbows on his knees. "We may never have an opportunity like we do now to find out information about NexTech's next moves. We won't be able to stop the system from within, but maybe this information will help us find a way to change things when we get to The Refuge.

Callum nodded, his sharp blue eyes flickering with unease but also resolve. "I'll monitor the security logs and backend systems. With my clearance, I can access restricted files and see if there are any red flags."

Grace tucked a loose curl behind her ear, her brow furrowed in thought. "I'll dig into the chip data—schematics, update logs, and anything else new about the latest nano chip everyone has. If I can figure out how the new chips are communicating with the system, maybe we'll find a way to shut it down or at least disrupt it."

Emma sat next to Seph, her voice steady despite the tension in her posture. "Martin's already hinted at the updates they're planning—if I can see who's calling the shots, we'll have a better understanding of their endgame."

Seph's jaw tightened as he spoke. "I'll focus on getting access to one of the secure terminals. James's encrypted drive isn't going to be useful if we can't plug it in. And we still need to figure out who at NexTech made contact with The Refuge."

The group went silent as the enormity of their plan settled over them. There was no guarantee of success, and failure wasn't an option they could afford. Each role carried its own risks: discovery, exposure, punishment.

Emma spoke softly into the silence, her eyes locked on Seph: "And I'll keep trying to convince my parents to leave when the time comes."

Callum let out a low whistle. "This feels … massive. Like something way bigger than us."

"It is," Grace said firmly, her gaze steady, "but we're already in it. We either do this, or we let them take everything."

The group exchanged glances, their expressions a mix of fear and fierce determination. Seph felt the weight of their trust settle on his shoulders. He couldn't let them down—not Emma, not Grace, not Callum.

"Let's meet again on Friday," Seph said, his voice steady, "same time, same place. We can't talk about this anywhere outside of my apartment and we need to keep each other updated."

They nodded in unison, the fragile alliance forged in trust and necessity solidifying under the dim light of Seph's apartment.

Grace and Callum left separately, disappearing into the rainy night.

Emma lingered for a moment longer, standing near the door. "Seph, do you think we can really do this?" she asked softly.

He stepped closer, his voice low but steady. "We have to try, Emma. We can't let them turn us—everyone—into puppets."

Emma nodded, her eyes glistening with unshed tears.

They were running out of time. But for now, they had a plan.

And they had each other.

28

Emma

The kitchen was warm with the scent of roasted vegetables still hanging in the air. Emma's mother moved methodically around the kitchen cleaning up, her back to her daughter, while Emma's father sat at the kitchen table, scrolling through his halopad.

Emma was nervous—she'd just come back from Seph's house and it was late, but she needed to talk to them. She leaned against the counter, her arms crossed over her chest. She'd rehearsed this conversation a hundred times in her head, but now, standing in her childhood kitchen, the words felt tangled and heavy in her throat. "Mom. Dad. Can we talk?" She paused. "Without devices."

Her mother turned slightly, spatula in hand, her brow creased. "Of course, sweetheart. Dinner's almost ready, but we can talk now."

Her father looked up from his halopad, his expression calm

but curious. "What's on your mind, Em?"

Emma pushed away from the counter and walked to the table, grabbing their devices and taking them to the other room. She walked back in and pulled out the chair across from her dad. Her mother turned off the stove and joined them, sitting down beside her husband.

"I need to tell you something about work," Emma began, her voice was an octave higher than normal, "About NexTech. About what we're building."

Her father fidgeted with his hands in front of him. Her mother leaned forward slightly, her lips pressed into a thin line.

"As you know, I've been working on the emotional data algorithm," Emma continued, "the one they're saying is supposed to help people—detect anxiety, depression, keep everyone emotionally stable. So, no one has a mental breakdown like James Kent supposedly did. But that's not all it does."

She paused, taking a deep breath. Her parents watched her intently, their expressions unreadable. "The nano chips are not just detecting emotions. The new ones are designed to also send signals directly to people's brains. They're manipulating chemical responses. If someone feels angry, or anxious, or sad, the chip can just … switch that emotion off by sending a signal to counteract it."

Her mother's hand flew to her mouth, and her father's brow furrowed deeply.

Emma pressed on. "It's not about helping people. It's about *control*. They're creating a population of people who will never question anything, who will never feel anger, never rebel, never even think about resisting. And no one will even realize it's happening, 'cause as soon as that emotion arises, they'll turn it off."

The silence in the kitchen was heavy. Her mother's hand trembled slightly as she lowered it back to the table.

"If this goes forward," Emma said, "we're going to lose what makes us *human*—our ability to feel, to choose, to fight back when something is wrong."

Her father's voice was low and steady. "Emma … if what you're saying is true, that's deeply concerning."

Her mother nodded slowly, her eyes wide. "But … how do you know this? Are you sure? Could it be … exaggerated somehow?"

Emma shook her head. "I've seen the data. I've heard it from Myles myself. He talks about the project and the good it will do, but it will just as easily control people through their emotions."

Her father leaned back in his chair, his eyes flickering across the room as if calculating something in his mind. Finally, he nodded slowly. "I have a few connections, people who might know more than we do. I'll reach out first thing in the morning. Quietly."

Emma's heart fluttered with a spark of hope. "Be careful, I don't want you to get in trouble for poking around."

Her mother's voice trembled slightly. "Emma, the same goes to you."

Emma hesitated. "I know, I'm going to keep working. Keep watching. But unless there's a way to stop this, I'm going to find a way to remove my nano chip and leave. And I hope you will come with me too."

Her mother reached across the table and took Emma's hand, squeezing it tightly. "Just … please be careful. Please."

Her father's gaze met hers, sharp and serious. "If something feels wrong—if you feel like you're in danger—you come to us. Immediately."

Emma nodded, "I will."

* * *

"Emma," her dad said, shaking her awake.

"Dad—what time is it?" she asked.

"It's 7am. Let's go for a drive," he said quietly. "Leave your halophone inside."

Emma froze—she knew her father must have found something out. He didn't explain further, but his eyes said enough. She quickly got up and threw on some clothes.

When she stepped outside, her father had already started the car. Emma climbed in and they pulled out of the driveway in silence. The city lights receded into the rearview mirror as they took a quiet road out toward the edges of town. The streetlights grew farther apart, and the sky above them turned orange with the sunrise.

For a long time, neither of them spoke. The only sound was the steady movement of the car.

Finally, her father spoke. "Emma ... you need to be careful. More careful than you've been."

She turned to look at him, a knot was forming in her stomach. "What do you mean?"

"I reached out to someone. An old contact. He didn't have many details, but something's happening, Emma. They're cracking down on anyone who's poking around NexTech's systems, questioning things, or talking in support of what James did."

Emma swallowed hard. "What do you mean by 'cracking

down'?"

Her father hesitated, gripping the steering wheel tighter. "There have been arrests. Quiet ones. People are disappearing, Emma. If they catch anyone showing even a hint of intent, anything they can interpret as motive against NexTech or the government, they're calling it *domestic terrorism.*"

The words hit Emma like a punch to the gut.

"They're not taking chances this time," he continued. "Whatever happened with James—it scared them. They're making sure it doesn't happen again."

Emma stared out the windshield, her mind racing. She'd known it was dangerous. She'd known there was risk. But hearing it from her father, spoken so plainly, made it feel suffocating. "I can't live like this, Dad," she said softly. "I can't live in a place where they control everything and get rid of people who get in the way. If I can't stop it … I'll have to leave."

Her father glanced at her briefly before turning his eyes back to the road. "I know."

The weight of those two words hung between them, heavier than the night air.

"You're an adult now, Emma," he said after a moment. "I can't stop you from leaving. But I don't want to see you arrested. I don't want to see you disappear."

"I don't want that either." Emma's voice cracked. "Will you and Mom leave with me?"

"I work for the government. I took an oath to serve. If everyone in my position left, there would be no one here to try and bring back a balance to the system."

"But Dad, James already tried to change things. It didn't work. You guys can't stay."

"I know it is hard to see things from my perspective but

I'm not ready to abandon the advancements we've made. Before NexTech, your mom tried every medical treatment for depression. None of it worked. You haven't seen half of her struggles, Em. They're finally getting close to the cure. I don't think she would make it outside the city. It was so much worse before we moved here."

They drove in silence again, the faint sound of the tires on the pavement filling the space where words failed.

When they returned to the house, Emma's mother was waiting in the kitchen, her halophone still resting untouched on the counter. She looked up as they walked in, her eyes searching their faces. "Everything okay?" she asked hesitantly.

Emma nodded. "Yeah, Mom. We're okay."

Her father kissed her mother's forehead and retreated upstairs without another word. Emma lingered, her mother watching her closely.

"Emma," her mother said softly. "Are you… are you sure about what you're doing?"

"I'm sure." Emma nodded.

"Then just … promise me you'll be safe." Her mother stepped forward and pulled her into a full body hug.

Emma closed her eyes to hold back tears and whispered, *"I promise."*

Back in her room, Emma sat on the edge of her bed, her father's words replaying in her head over and over: *"If they catch anyone showing even a hint of intent … they're calling it domestic terrorism."*

She thought about Seph, about Grace, about Callum. About the quiet network they were building within NexTech's walls.

They were walking on a knife's edge, but she couldn't stop now.

If they didn't fight this—if they didn't try to stop it—there wouldn't be anything left to fight for.

We'll find a way, she thought. *We have to.*

29

Seph

Seph's halophone buzzed as he stepped into the NexTech lobby. Employees flowed through the entrance in synchronized waves, their movements quiet and efficient. He pulled the device from his pocket and glanced at the screen:

"Group Chat: Emma, Callum, Grace

Emma: Be careful."

His heart raced. Emma wasn't one to send warnings without reason. He quickly typed back:

"Seph: Understood."

Pocketing his phone, he moved with the crowd toward the elevators. Scanning the walls he noticed the cameras and nano chip sensors, a reminder of the eyes always watching.

The conference room on the fiftieth floor was expansive, its walls made entirely of glass overlooking the sprawling city below. Long rows of sleek black chairs faced a holographic presentation screen suspended in the air.

Seph and Emma sat toward the middle of the room, near the back, trying to blend in.

Myles strode to the front of the room, his confident smile as polished as his tailored suit.

"Thank you all for being here today," Myles began, his voice smooth and commanding. "This is an exciting day for us. For months now, we've been perfecting our mental-health stabilization program, and I'm proud to share that we've reached a major milestone."

The holographic screen flickered to life, displaying graphs, charts, and video clips of individuals sitting in pristine white rooms with haloscreens strapped to their wrists.

"Our initial trials involved volunteers subjected to emotionally intense stimuli—films, conversations, and guided visualizations designed to provoke anger, sadness, anxiety, and joy. What we discovered was extraordinary. The emotional algorithm was able to detect spikes in their emotional responses thanks to the emotional-analysis division. Recently, as most of you have heard, we transitioned to combine this program with one to help stabilize extreme or unwanted emotions."

The screen transitioned to a clip of a young man watching a tragic movie scene. Tears streamed down his face, his chest heaving with emotion. But then, all of a sudden his breathing slowed. His expression smoothed out, neutral and placid.

Emma shifted uncomfortably beside Seph.

Myles continued: "But it doesn't stop there. We are beginning to run controlled trials on individuals suffering from severe anxiety and depression. Individuals who have lived years battling these conditions."

The screen flickered again, showing before and after clips of patients. The "before" showed them pale, hollow-eyed, wringing their hands. The "after" showed them smiling, standing confidently, their expressions almost eerily calm.

Franky raised his hand. "Who are the individuals selected for these trials?"

"We partnered with a foundation called Apex Wellness Center and have several individuals there who are now reporting a hundred percent emotional stability. They're free from their burdens, able to live normal, happy lives," Myles said with a smile.

Seph felt a cold chill creep down his spine. He raised his hand, unable to contain his skepticism. Myles nodded for him to speak.

"Do these individuals report feeling ... numb?" Seph asked, without thinking. "I mean, how do they feel, *not feeling?*"

Myles's smile faltered slightly but recovered quickly. "That's an excellent question. What we've found is that emotional stability outweighs emotional chaos. These individuals are now productive, happy members of society. Isn't that the goal? To reduce suffering?"

"But isn't it also important to *feel*? Aren't emotions, real emotions, what make us human?" Emma chimed in.

Seph nudged Emma with his foot, trying to signal her to simmer down.

Myles's smile turned icy. "Oh, I see your concern. I must not have been clear in my presentation. We are not creating a program that will turn off *all* emotions. Even those who have signed on for this trial are still reporting normal emotional responses. It is only the extreme reactions we're eliminating." He now addressed the whole room: "And to be clear, we still have to extend out our trials to more individuals and finetune our algorithm. We need you to help figure out what threshold of emotional response is acceptable, and what requires the nano chip to intervene."

The room fell quiet. Seph felt like Myles was asking this group of engineers to play God. He glanced around the room trying to read everyone's opinion, trying to dissect if they were buying this.

"We're entrusting this group to continue pushing hard and collaborating as we finesse this system." Myles continued.

Marlene, who was sitting in the front row, stood up and addressed the room: "Can you all imagine being part of the team that eliminates mental-health disorders? All that pain and suffering can finally end."

Seph watched as heads nodded and the room rumbled into a cheer, an obvious departure from his own reservations.

* * *

Back at his desk later that afternoon, Seph's computer pinged with a new notification.

"Incoming Message: Be careful with your questions."

His eyes widened as he stared at the text. The message had no sender information. The text box was sterile and untraceable.

Seph's fingers hovered over his keyboard. He quickly opened a diagnostic window, attempting to trace the origin. Lines of code streamed across his screen, his eyes darting back and forth. But every path led back to a dead end. Whoever sent the message was high up, executive-level access at least.

His halophone buzzed with another notification.

"Emma: Want to go for a walk in five minutes?"

Seph closed the window and shut down his terminal, his pulse thrumming as he stood and slipped away from his desk. But before Seph could reach Emma's desk, Lena intercepted him in the hallway. Emma stood beside her, her face carefully blank.

"Seph," Lena said smoothly. "Could I have a moment with both of you in my office?"

The two of them exchanged a quick glance before following Lena down the hallway. Her office was pristine, filled with soft, ambient lighting and a faint floral scent.

Lena gestured to two chairs in front of her desk and sat across from them, her hands folded neatly on the glass surface. "I wanted to talk to you both about something unique," Lena began, her tone polite but firm. "You two have been working together for some time now, haven't you?"

"Yes," Emma said cautiously.

Lena tilted her head slightly, her eyes sharp. "You know, the compatibility algorithms from your nano chips are among the highest we've ever seen. Ninety-six percent romantic compatibility is extremely high. And yet..."

Seph felt his stomach drop.

"And yet," Lena continued, "you're not officially in a relationship. Not dating. Not romantically involved at all. Why is that?"

Seph looked at Emma.

Emma hesitated. "I, I haven't wanted a romantic relationship. It's complicated."

Lena's smile was thin. "Complicated? Or resistant?"

Seph forced himself to laugh lightly. "Sometimes things just don't work out the way the algorithm predicts."

Lena studied them both for a long moment, then nodded. "I'd like to invite you both to participate in a session with our Relationship Insights team. It's an experimental program, but it's been very ... enlightening. To be honest, you are the only couple who has scored over ninety percent and has not chosen to engage in a romantic relationship. It would be helpful for them to meet with you."

Emma opened her mouth but Seph cut her off: "We'd be happy to."

Lena's smile returned. "Good. I'll have them schedule a session for tomorrow. It's important we understand why two people with such remarkable compatibility haven't ... connected. For data purposes, of course."

"Of course," Seph said smoothly.

Lena dismissed them, and they walked out of her office in silence.

Once outside, Emma turned to Seph. "This is too much, Seph. It's invasive. It's disgusting."

Seph nodded, his jaw clenched. "I know. But if we refuse, they'll suspect something. We can't risk that right now."

Emma's shoulders sagged. "We'll go. But afterward, we're coming back to your apartment, and we're figuring out our next move. We need to update Callum and Grace."

Seph reached out and squeezed her hand briefly before letting go. "Agreed."

30

Emma

mma's halophone buzzed on the edge of the break room counter as she finished her coffee.

The notification read:

"Reminder: Relationship Insights Program—Today, 10:00am— Conference Room 14A. Attendance is mandatory."

Emma stared at her reflection in the dark surface of her coffee. Realizing they were not going to stop until they controlled every part of her—her emotions, her career, her health choices—was cataloged and controlled. And now they wanted this? What she felt about Seph? She hated that she had to play along and give them something of hers that was so personal.

The conference room was smaller than Emma had expected, with two plush chairs facing each other in the center of the space and a long table set up against the far wall. Three NexTech employees—two women and one man—sat behind the table, a haloscreen glowing faintly in front of them.

The lead examiner, a woman with sleek hair pulled into

a bun and a tender smile, gestured for Emma and Seph to take their seats. "Welcome, Emma. Seph. Thank you for your willingness to participate in this session. We're here today to better understand the emotional and relational dynamics between pairs with extraordinarily high compatibility scores. Your participation will help us refine our relationship algorithms for optimal emotional outcomes."

Emma's palms felt clammy as she lowered herself into one of the chairs. Seph sat across from her, his expression calm, but she could see the tension in his jaw.

The lead examiner folded her hands together. "Let's begin with some basics. How would you describe your relationship with each other?"

"We're ... close. We trust each other." Emma hesitated, glancing at Seph.

Seph nodded. "We work well together. We rely on each other."

The examiner typed something into her halopad. "Have you ever considered pursuing a romantic relationship with one another?"

Emma's cheeks flushed, but she kept her voice steady. "I think ... it's crossed both of our minds. But things are complicated. Our jobs, our lives—it's not that simple. The timing hasn't been right."

"Have you ever kissed?" the examiner asked without hesitation.

"Yes." Emma's breath felt stuck, but she forced herself to answer.

The examiner smiled faintly, as if that was the answer she was hoping for. "And how did it make you feel?"

Emma's stomach churned. This wasn't normal. This wasn't

right. But before she could speak, a strange calmness began to wash over her, like a warm blanket had been draped across her mind. The tightness in her chest eased, the embarrassment faded, and her pulse slowed.

Her voice felt distant as she said, "It felt ... nice. It was comforting."

The examiner glanced briefly at the other two staff members, who made notes on their screens.

Seph's eyes flickered toward Emma, and she could tell he felt it too—that subtle shift, an artificial calm.

They were using the emotional response algorithm on them. *Right now.*

The questions continued:

"Do you hold hands?"

"Do you talk about your feelings for each other openly?"

"Would you describe your bond as romantic, platonic, or somewhere in between?"

Emma answered them all, her voice steady but hollow. The calmness smoothed over every jagged edge of discomfort. She was aware of it—aware that this wasn't *her.* But the algorithm made it hard to care.

Seph's voice was similarly flat, his answers measured and even. They were performing exactly how NexTech wanted them to.

Finally, the lead examiner leaned back in her chair. "We're going to give you two a few minutes alone to talk about your potential for a more serious relationship. Sometimes these conversations are better without observers. Take your time. Be honest with each other."

The three examiners stood and left the room, the faint sound of the door clicking shut behind them.

But Emma knew they were still watching. Still listening.

"Emma…" Seph leaned forward, his elbows resting on his knees.

She knew he wanted to say what she was thinking, but didn't want to be overheard. "I know." Emma nodded faintly, her voice a whisper.

She stared at Seph for a long moment, trying to fight the unnatural calm that clouded her emotions. But she felt it slipping, breaking through the haze just enough for her voice to crack as she spoke.

"I like you, Seph. More than you know. But I don't like this part of me being … *an experiment.*"

Tears welled in her eyes, despite the algorithm's grip on her mind. She fought against it, letting the raw edges of her emotions cut through the fog.

For a moment, Seph was silent. But then something shifted.

A wave of warmth flooded through Emma's chest, sudden and overpowering. She gasped as an electric rush of attraction, affection, and longing surged through her. She could see it in Seph's eyes, too, full of desire.

Without thinking, Emma whispered, "Seph, hold me."

He crossed the space between them, pulling her into his arms. Their embrace was intense, desperate, charged with an emotion that felt far too sharp to be natural. And then his lips found hers, and Emma felt herself pulled under, every nerve in her body alive with something that felt like fire and lightning all at once.

But just as quickly as it came, the surge began to fade. The sharpness dulled, the fire cooled, and they both pulled away, breathing hard, their faces inches apart. And then she remembered the group that she imagined watching her from the other side of the wall.

Emma's mind was spinning. The emotions had felt real, but the timing, the intensity—they had to be manufactured.

The door clicked open, and the examiners returned, their smiles filled with satisfaction.

"Thank you both," the lead examiner said smoothly. "I think we've learned everything we needed from this session."

She typed something on her halopad. "We'll be marking your relationship as 'romantic' and passing it along to HR. Congratulations."

Emma and Seph walked in silence through the narrow corridors of NexTech, side by side but not touching. She was still in shock from what happened. The fluorescent lights seeming brighter than normal, and employees passed them without a second glance.

When they finally stepped out into the open air of the street, Emma turned to Seph, her voice low and sharp. "They manipulated us, Seph. They *forced* us to feel that. What we felt, it wasn't ours."

Seph's jaw clenched, his fists tight at his sides. "I know. And they were watching every second of it."

Emma shook her head, tears pooling in her eyes again. "How can they *do* this to people? How can they play with something so sacred and call it progress?"

Seph reached out and gently took her hand. "We can't let them get between us. We have to fight back, together."

31

Seph

Seph's apartment felt small with the four friends crammed into the living room. Grace sat cross-legged on the floor, her notebook balanced on her knee as she jotted down notes. Callum stood near the window. Emma sat beside Seph on the couch, their shoulders just barely touching. Seph was aware of the tension his body was holding.

It had been less than an hour since Grace and Callum arrived, but the weight of what they were discussing felt suffocating. Seph had already filled in the group about the experience with the Relational Insights team.

"Alright," Seph said, his voice low but firm, "let's go over the other things we've learned. Emma, you start."

Emma cleared her throat and shared everything her dad had discovered about the increasing arrests. "They're starting to target people with *intent.*"

Grace frowned. "Intent? That's terrifyingly vague."

Emma nodded. "My dad said they're calling it 'domestic terrorism.' If they suspect anyone is working against them, they're taking them away. Quietly."

Seph felt a cold knot in his chest. "And then there was the message I got, *'Be careful with your questions.'* Someone's watching me. I don't know who, but they were either in the meeting with Myles or heard about it afterwards."

Callum stopped pacing and turned to face the group. His face was pale, and dark circles clung under his eyes. "There's something else," he said quietly. "I found internal memos in the cybersecurity logs. They're planning a mass arrest. Not just people actively resisting, but anyone who *doesn't* have a chip."

Emma's eyes widened. "What do you mean?"

"They've decided it's too dangerous to let people live without a nano chip as it puts those with the chip in danger. They're calling it a 'public safety risk.' In fourteen days, they're going to start sweeping the city, door to door, checkpoint to checkpoint. Anyone who doesn't have a chip will be arrested, forcibly implanted with one, and then sent back home."

The room went still. No one spoke, no one moved.

Emma's voice was barely above a whisper. "Because once they have the chip, they can make them compliant. They can manipulate their emotions. They can *erase* the fear or distrust about what's happening."

Callum nodded. "Exactly. The memo said they're giving everyone 'ample time' to reconnect. Fourteen days. After that, there's no more pretending this is voluntary."

"Are they announcing this ahead of time?" Seph asked angrily. His mind raced. *Fourteen days.* That was all they had. The city was already a net tightening around them, and soon it would snap shut.

"No, if they announced it ahead of time, they fear people would just leave or hide," Callum said.

"We have to leave," Seph said firmly. "Before the sweeps start. Before they notice we're missing."

"It's not that simple. The moment we stop showing up to work, they'll flag us. We need to be careful, calculated." Grace sighed heavily and stood up. "I might be able to figure out a way to either disable our chips without detection or mask the signals they're sending to our brains. But I'll need time—days, at least. But I can't promise it'll work."

Emma nodded. "Do it, Grace. Whatever you can figure out. We need to find a way to get these nano chips out and leave."

The group stayed in Seph's apartment well into the night, hashing out what they needed to do before they could escape.

As they wrapped up, Grace and Callum left first. Seph noticed Emma sitting by the window, staring out into the neon-lit cityscape.

"We need to talk," he said softly, sitting down beside her, their shoulders brushing. "Emma," he said carefully, "Lena and her team are watching us. Every interaction, every conversation. They expect us to act like a couple now."

Emma sighed, running a hand through her hair. "I know. And honestly, the way they talked about it, it's like they don't even care if it's real—as long as their fake emotions help 'compatible couples' take the next steps."

"I know, but we have to play along. Hold hands at work, laugh and joke, purposely let them see us ... *together*."

Emma winced slightly. "It feels so fake. I feel like they are taking something from me before it's even mine."

"I know," Seph said quietly. "But if we don't, they'll start digging deeper. It's not worth the risk."

"What do you think they are going to do with this?"

"I think once everyone has the nano chip, they will roll out the compatibility program that James knew about before the reset. But I think this time they may match people without them even applying, and then they will just turn on the emotional response the way they did to us."

For a moment, neither of them spoke. The quiet hum of the appliances in the apartment filled the silence between them.

"Do you ever wish things were different?" Emma asked suddenly.

"Everyday…" Seph laughed, thinking that was obvious.

"I mean with us," Emma said, looking Seph in the eyes. "I used to think we had a chance at being something real. Then things got complicated and the timing didn't feel right. I wanted to push anything with us … to later. But now I feel like it's even more complicated."

"But what we feel for each other is real," Seph said defensively.

"Is it?" Emma said. "How do we know they didn't start feeding us these feelings before?" She turned her gaze back to the window.

"Let's get through these next few days, Emma. And when we're out of here, when we're somewhere safe, maybe we can figure out what's real and what isn't."

Seph reached out and took her hand, his fingers wrapping gently around hers. And he watched as she looked at his hand in hers, working out if his touch was real or manufactured.

32

Emma

Emma awoke with the sun before her alarm went off. For a moment things felt peaceful and calm, then she remembered the events of the day before and that calm quickly faded.

She walked over to Tucker's room and found him cross-legged on his floor, fiddling with a small metal puzzle he'd been carrying around for weeks. "Tuck," Emma said, sitting on the edge of his bed. "I need you to listen to me. Really listen."

He glanced up, his sharp green eyes locking onto hers. "I'm listening."

"Things are changing, and they're changing fast. I don't know if I can stop them. And if I can't, I might have to leave. And if that happens, I want you to be ready to come with me." Emma took a deep breath.

Tucker set down the puzzle carefully, his expression unreadable. "You mean leave the city? Like, for good?"

"Yes." Emma swallowed hard. "If you really mean it when you say you want to live off-grid, away from all of this, then you need to be ready. No hesitation. No second-guessing."

"I'm in," Tucker said without hesitation. "You know I'm in. I've been saying it for months, Em. I don't want the nano chip. I don't want to be part of this."

"Okay. But it's going to be dangerous, Tuck. I don't know exactly when we will have to leave, it could be tomorrow or next week. You just need to be ready, and you can't tell a soul."

Tucker gave her a lopsided smile. "I'm better than you might realize at keeping secrets, Em. I'm with you."

* * *

At NexTech the energy in the office felt heavier than usual as Emma walked through the glass doors. Employees moved like quiet robots. She spotted Seph near the elevators, leaning casually against the wall with his arms crossed, waiting for her.

Their eyes met, and Emma took a steadying breath before walking straight up to him. Without hesitation, she leaned in and pressed a soft kiss against his cheek.

"Morning," she said calmly, her voice carefully measured.

"Morning, love." Seph smiled faintly, his expression relaxed but his eyes sharp with awareness.

A soft cough interrupted them. Martin stood nearby, holding a halopad and wearing a grin that stretched a little too wide across his face.

"Well, well," Martin said, raising an eyebrow. "Looks like HR let me in on the secret. Congratulations, you two. One of the first couples in the new program! Exciting stuff."

"Thanks, Martin," Emma said, forcing a smile.

"Don't let me interrupt," he said, winking before walking away.

As he disappeared, Emma let out a slow breath.

Seph leaned closer, his voice low: "It's working."

Emma nodded, her hand brushing briefly against his arm. She was attracted to Seph, not just physical attraction but she felt connected to him on a deeper level. As she stood there, with her body close to his, she wondered how much of her feeling for him was hers and how much was part of the larger experiment happening in this building.

The day dragged on, Emma and Seph sitting together during breaks, laughing at each other's jokes with just a little too much enthusiasm, making sure to touch at every opportunity. Every touch sent goosebumps down her body. She tried to ignore the feeling, knowing it may not be hers, but she couldn't help allowing the anticipation of the next touch to cross her mind.

At lunch, they sat side by side in the cafeteria, sharing a plate of food. Grace passed by briefly, giving them both a wink before grabbing her lunch.

In the late afternoon, Emma and Seph were called into Lena's office. The space was pristine, organized with the faint scent of something floral lingering in the air. Lena sat behind her glass desk, her posture perfect and her smile razor-sharp. "Emma, Seph, thank you for coming," Lena said smoothly. "We just have a few administrative things to finalize."

She slid two halopads across the desk toward them. Emma picked hers up and scanned the screen. It was a standard NexTech relationship contract, filled with clauses about workplace behavior, reporting requirements, and mandatory emotional monitoring sessions.

"Just sign at the bottom," Lena said, her voice calm.

Seph and Emma exchanged a glance before they each signed their names with quick flicks of their fingers.

"Excellent," Lena said, retrieving the tablets. "Oh, and one more thing, I've spoken with Claire who leads PR here. She's overseeing the rollout of our new marriage compatibility initiatives, and she's very interested in speaking with you both. She believes your story could be inspiring."

Emma's stomach twisted. "What do you mean by 'story'?"

Lena's smile didn't waver. "Your relationship. Two employees, perfectly matched by the algorithm, thriving in both work and love. It's exactly the image we want to project as we prepare to announce the new marriage laws."

"Oh…" Emma forced a smile, unsure how to respond.

"What are the new marriage laws?" Seph asked.

"You know, I'm not as close to those details as others, so I don't want to misspeak." Lena leaned back in her chair. "But our goal is to improve lives, and if we can help people find partnerships that don't end in divorce or a messy breakup, that will be very important for our quality of life."

Emma watched as Seph nodded, indicating he was satisfied with that answer.

"Wonderful," Lena said, standing. "Claire's expecting you in Conference Room 7C in an hour. I also let Martin know of your participation with this and to expect there to be a productivity impact to your work."

Claire was everything Emma expected from a NexTech executive—polished, poised, and sharp as glass. She sat at the head of a long conference table, her presence commanding even in stillness.

"Emma, Seph," Claire said with a smile, "thank you for coming."

They both nodded, taking their seats across from her.

Claire wasted no time. "We're preparing to announce new marriage laws based on compatibility scores. The idea is simple—why leave love to chance when we can optimize it? You two are an excellent case study, and we'd like to showcase your story."

Emma's pulse quickened, but she kept her face neutral. "What would that involve?"

"Public profiles, perhaps a few promotional videos. Maybe even a segment on one of the news broadcasts. It's important that people see the emotional algorithm as a force for good. We went wrong in the past with this—we need to get on the frontend of public perception. Get everyone excited about its potential before we roll it out."

Seph nodded slowly. "We're always happy to help."

"I'll have the details sent to you." Claire leaned back in her chair, smiling, her eyes flicking between the two of them. "You know, James Kent used to speak very fondly of you, Seph."

Emma's heart skipped a beat as she glanced between Seph and Claire and then back to Seph. His face frozen, not giving up any surprise at the mention of James.

Claire continued, her smile sharpening. "He always said you were sharp. Loyal. Someone who paid attention to the details. It's unfortunate how things turned out with him."

The silence hung heavy in the room.

"Thank you both for your time. I'll be in touch." Claire stood, smoothing the creases from her blazer.

As she walked out of the room, Emma and Seph remained

seated, the air crackling with tension. Emma wondered if she knew about their involvement with deleting the database and resetting the systems.

Emma went home with Seph after work. They were finally alone, truly alone for the first time all day. She stood in his kitchen, her arms wrapped tightly around herself as if trying to hold her emotions in place. Seph leaned against the edge of the counter, his head lowered, his fingers tracing absent patterns across the chipped surface.

"She knows," Emma said. "Claire knows about you. About us. She wasn't just reminiscing about James—she was warning you."

"If she's trying to help, she's being careful about it. And if she's trying to trap us, she's being even *more* careful," Seph said.

Emma turned to face him, her eyes glistening faintly in the dim light. "Do you think she's the one who sent you that message?"

Seph's brow furrowed, and he shook his head slowly. "I don't know. Maybe."

Emma crossed the room in slow, measured steps until she stood just a foot away from him. "Seph … this feels like a trap closing around us. Every move we make, every word we say—it feels like they're watching, waiting for us to slip. I don't think we should have come back."

His shoulders sagged slightly, and for the first time, Emma saw the exhaustion etched into his face. It was the weight of everything they were carrying, everything they were fighting against.

"They are watching," Seph said quietly, "but not here. Not right now."

His words hung in the air.

Emma took another step closer until there was barely any space between them. "I hate this, Seph. I hate feeling like every glance, every word, every *touch* is something they're cataloging, analyzing."

Seph reached out slowly, his hands resting gently on her upper arms. His touch was warm, grounding, and she felt a shiver run through her.

"I know," he said. "But they don't get *this*. They don't get to own this moment. Not here. Not now."

Emma let out a shaky breath, her eyes locked on his. "Seph … I'm scared."

He pulled her into his arms, wrapping her tightly against his chest. Emma let her head rest against him, her arms coming up to clutch at the fabric of his shirt. They stayed like that for a long moment, their breathing slow, their heartbeats steadying in the stillness of the room.

"They won't win," Seph whispered into her hair. "They won't take this from us, we will get out before they do. They won't take *us*."

Emma pulled back just enough to look up at him. The faint light caught the edges of his face, his sharp features softened by the vulnerability in his eyes. Without thinking, without questioning, she leaned in and pressed her lips against his.

The kiss was slow, tender at first—a quiet understanding passing between them. She wanted to remember what it felt like kissing him, if it could be something that was just theirs. But then it deepened, filled with everything unsaid, every fear, every hope, every desperate plea for time to stop.

Seph's hands cupped her face, his thumbs brushing against her cheeks, and Emma felt herself melting into him. But even as the warmth spread through her chest, a cold knot of conflict filled her stomach. The kiss felt *real*, achingly real, but at the same time, it felt like something *they* wanted.

When they finally pulled apart, Emma rested her forehead against Seph's, her breath coming in soft and uneven. "I hate that I love this," she whispered. "I hate that this feels so good, because it's *exactly* what they want."

Seph brushed a loose strand of hair from her face. "They might want this, Emma. But they don't *own* this. What's between us, that's ours. No algorithm can replicate it. No program can manufacture it."

"I want to believe that," she said softly.

They stayed like that for a long time—wrapped in each other's arms, the city still moving quietly outside. But in that small, fragile moment, Emma let herself believe Seph's words. Even if only for a moment.

33

Seph

Seph felt like life was on hyper speed, like he couldn't fully catch a breath. Every day he was balancing the new tasks at work, planning their escape, his fake relationship, and Emma's feelings. He felt like his own needs were on the back burner. He couldn't even open up that box with all the other plates he was juggling.

As he stared at the list of outstanding work tasks in front of him, he didn't hear Martin approach behind him.

"Hey Seph, how's your morning going?" Martin asked.

"Shoot—you scared me!" Seph said, startled.

"Oh, sorry about that. Didn't realize you were so in the zone already!"

"Me neither. Maybe I need some coffee. Something I can help you with?"

"Well, I just wanted to touch base with you about our current project. I just met with other team leads to figure out how we divide and conquer."

"Oh great, excited to hear what we will be working on." Seph tried to sound enthusiastic.

"Since we were working on anger before, they asked us to see how our program can do at detecting panic," Martin said.

"That is a good use case, I actually had thought about a while back. But I haven't dug into it yet."

"I was actually thinking about your big breakthrough for detecting emotions," Martin explained. "The key there was that we needed to wait to analyze the emotion. But I think with panic attacks, we need to figure out how to detect the early signs and trigger before someone reaches a true panic level."

"That makes a lot of sense. Once you hit level ten, it's already too late," Seph added.

"Exactly, we need to send signals when someone is at a four or five and stop the panic from starting." Martin smiled.

"Do you think the solution is really sending signals to calm someone?"

"What do you mean?" Martin looked at Seph quizzically.

"I mean, I understand if someone is at level ten, having a panic attack, it would be amazing to be able to calm them down. But if someone is at a four or five, wouldn't it be better to alert them on their nano chip and give them time to calm down naturally? Maybe instruct them to go on a walk or meditate?" Seph was hoping he wasn't revealing his cards too much.

"Well, I don't know why that would be needed," Martin said, puzzled.

"You don't think it would help to train someone how to overcome anxiety on their own?" Seph was unable to hide his disbelief.

"Do you know someone who has struggled with severe mental illness, Seph?" Martin paused and then continued his thought. "They can spend hours of their day trying to manage it with meditation, diet, exercise and to be honest, it has little impact. With what we're doing with the nano chip, all that energy can be refocused in enjoying life, not managing a time-consuming condition."

Seph knew there was no point in arguing with Martin. His mind was already made up.

"I hadn't thought of it that way," Seph said quietly, trying to naturally back off from his argument.

"Don't worry about it, Seph. What we're doing, it's a lot to consider. I'll send you a couple of documents that talk more in depth about what I'm looking for. We'll want to go back through some of our data and old sessions to see where we can pinpoint fear and cross-reference the Innovation team plans."

"I'll get right on it," Seph responded as Martin headed back in the direction of his office.

Seph turned his attention back to his computer as a new notification popped up on his screen:

"Video Shoot Prep – Starts in 15 minutes
Location: Studio D"

Seph had forgot about his meeting with Claire to prep for the PR campaign about his relationship with Emma. He'd have to dig into the documents from Martin later. He logged out of his computer and headed for the elevator.

Seph stood outside Studio D, his hands tucked into his pockets as he waited, trying not to let his nerves get the best of him.

The door slid open and Claire was there. "Seph, come in."

Seph hesitated for half a heartbeat before stepping inside. The door closed automatically behind him, and the noise from the corridor disappeared. The studio was sleek and he couldn't help but be impressed by the camera equipment and multiple greenscreens and digital backgrounds they must use for their video shoots.

"We don't have much time," she said, gesturing to a small side door. "Leave your halophone here and follow me."

"Where are we going?" Seph asked but Claire didn't respond. His pulse quickened, but he followed her without hesitation.

She led him to a narrow storage closet that held equipment for the studio when not being used. The air was cooler there, the faint hum of old machinery vibrating beneath the floor.

Claire turned to face him, her expression raw for the first time since he'd met her. "We're safe here. For now."

"Safe, what is this place?" Seph's heart was hammering in his chest.

"A blind spot. One of the only ones left in the building," Claire said. She crossed her arms tightly over her chest. "You need to listen carefully because I won't have time to repeat myself."

Seph nodded, swallowing hard.

"Not everything is as it seems here, Seph. Some of us—very few—see what is *really* happening, what NexTech has become. And we're trying, in our own way, to stop it. Most who were disconnected have already reconnected to the NexTech system. They're planning mass arrests, Seph. Anyone who hasn't connected will be labeled a dissenter—a threat to public safety. NexTech will have the legal authority to detain them and forcibly implant new chips."

Seph already knew this, but he was shocked Claire was sharing this information with him.

"And the worst part? They've already updated the emotional-suppression algorithms in the new chips. Soon, people won't even *want* to resist. They'll feel ... calm, content. Even when they should be terrified. Any day now, they are going to turn on a program that will force everyone's nano chip to send calming signals. Each day the signal will get stronger, so that by the time the arrests start, no one will be concerned. Each time a new initiative rolls out, like these marriage laws, they will do the same thing."

"Why are you telling me this?" Seph asked.

"Because I know you were working with James. I managed to erase the evidence so no one else saw. But your questions and your proximity to James before the reset has you on a watch list."

Seph swallowed, his heart beginning to pound. "So you are the one who contacted The Refuge?"

"I did. I 've had to be extremely careful. No offense, but James was reckless with his timing. He escalated things between Myles and Walker that maybe we could have handled with a little more ... tact."

"Who is behind these plans for control?" Seph asked.

"It's always been Walker, Myles, and a close circle of friends. They want total power, total control. President Walker is the public face, but Myles is the brains behind it all. He is twisted."

"So, what's your plan?" Seph asked.

"We don't have time for that. You and your friends need to get out of the city while there is still time. Then I'll make contact when the time is right," she said calmly.

"James gave me an encrypted device to plug into a terminal

272

so he can get backdoor—"

"No!" Claire interrupted. "That is the kind of thing that will get you caught. When you get back, tell James not to make any more moves until he hears from me."

Claire reached into her pocket and pulled out a small glass jar. Inside was a white powder, that looked similar to the one James had given Seph the day before the reset.

"That's from James office, isn't it?" Seph asked.

"Yes, I was able to grab it. You and your friends might need this to get out of the city undetected. Don't try and take out your nano chips until you're on the city's edge. Take this to help you get there without raising any flags. You have to make it look like everything is fine—you're just going on a hike or running errands or something believable." Claire put the jar in Seph's hand.

"Claire … you have to come with us," Seph said suddenly. "We can get you out. There's still time."

But she shook her head. "No, Seph. I can do more good here. Someone needs to pull the right strings when the moment comes. I can keep some things hidden, slowing them down, giving people like you a fighting chance." Her voice softened. "But you need to promise me something."

"Anything," Seph said without hesitation.

"Don't do anything else stupid. You guys need to get to The Refuge and wait." Something tired and sad flickered across Claire's face.

"I promise," Seph said, knowing it would be hard to convince his aunt, Duke and James of the same.

"Good. You remind me of someone I used to know—a boy with fire in his chest and steel in his spine."

"Who?" Seph asked.

She stepped back, her hands falling to her sides. "We need to leave now, Seph. We're out of time."

Seph hesitated, his heart aching at the finality in her voice. "Claire…"

"Go," she said firmly. "And Seph? Leave tomorrow."

Seph turned and walked back through the narrow closet, his footsteps quick but heavy. When the studio door slid open, he stepped back into the corridor, the sterile NexTech air hitting him like a slap, the ordinary noise of a busy day filling his ears again. He glanced back at Claire, but she had already gone.

The walk back to his workstation felt endless. Seph's mind raced, a sinking feeling pooled in his gut with the weight of what Claire had told him. The scale of it all was suffocating.

He stopped at a quiet corner of the floor, leaning against a cold metal pillar and taking a deep breath. The small glass jar in his pocket felt tempting to take now, but he knew he needed to save it for when it really mattered.

He closed his eyes and focused on the image of The Refuge, the smell of the woods, the sound of the wind. He took slow, deep breaths, forcing his body to calm. Seph opened his eyes, his resolve hardening into something sharp and unbreakable.

They had to leave.

34

Seph

Seph's small living room was cluttered with maps and supplies for their escape. Callum, Emma, and Grace were leaning over the coffee table looking at the map. Seph tapped a finger against three routes marked in red, each one winding through different parts of the city.

"These spots right here will be the easiest ones for us to get to. Duke and June have already scouted them," Seph said. "They were working on putting a radio in so we could make contact if we need to leave."

"I sure hope it's there when we get there," Emma said, sitting cross-legged on the floor, her fingers tracing the edge of the worn city map. Her brows were furrowed, and her lips pressed tightly together.

"Callum, do you know which is the safest way out of the city?" Seph asked.

"Honestly, no. They've already started putting up checkpoints on a lot of the main routes out. But I'll memorize these routes and then cross-reference the logs tomorrow morning at NexTech."

"This is it," Seph said, his voice low and steady. "We don't get a second chance at this."

Everyone nodded, but no one spoke. Seph knew they weren't ready to leave yet, they all thought they had more time, but it was now or never. "Route one takes us through the industrial sector. It's the most direct, but also the most populated. Route two follows the river, but there really aren't places to hide. And route three skirts the perimeter of the city, using an old service railroad tract. It's the longest route, but it also has a lot of old service stations we could pop into if needed."

Emma looked up, her voice quiet but firm. "What happens if we get caught?"

"We have to stay calm and say we are just out on an adventure. Maybe we can say we are playing flashlight tag or something?" Grace suggested.

"And we will have all taken James's calming powder, so if we are questioned, our vitals will remain calm and they will believe us," Seph said.

"But we also shouldn't pack much," Callum added. "That will look suspicious if we're carrying suitcases.

"No, a backpack each at most," Seph said. "Everything else we have to leave behind."

"I think we should take the transpo to the farthest point we can, then stick to either the river or the old railroad track. Those seem the most plausible for us to be playing a game." Emma suggested.

"Callum, you have to be thorough when you look tomorrow,

276

we need your intel to finalize our plan." Seph added.

"So one more normal day at work, and then we will leave," Emma stated.

"Yes, we should leave right as it is getting dark," Seph said.

"I'll grab Tucker and come right over." Emma looked sad.

Seph realized his friends all had to say goodbye to family. Leaving wasn't as easy for them as it was for him.

Grace cleared her throat. "I've been analyzing the chip data. If we're far enough from NexTech's surveillance grid, I think I can remove the nano chips without triggering an alert. But I will also need to bring an extraction device. When it removes the nano chip, it also turns it off. If we don't have that, the nano chip keeps sending a signal that it was improperly removed and it would get picked up by any drones doing a patrol."

Seph frowned. "You think?"

Grace met his gaze. "I mean, I've watched dozens of videos and seen it done in person. But I've never done it myself."

"How far out do we need to be?" Callum asked.

"At least fifty miles. Maybe more," Grace replied.

Seph sighed, rubbing a hand over his face. "That's a long way to go undetected. But each of our rendezvous points are over fifty miles away. We should try to make it there, radio for help, and then remove them."

Callum shifted, his large frame casting a long shadow against the wall. "We'll make it work. We don't have a choice."

Emma glanced between Callum and Grace, her fingers twitching against the fabric of her pants. "You said earlier … you've felt something different. The emotional suppression. Tell me what you mean."

Callum exchanged a glance with Grace before speaking. "It's subtle at first. You don't really notice it until you stop and think about it. There were moments this week when I should have felt … terrified, angry. But I didn't. It was like those emotions were there, but they were a few levels deeper than normal. Just a little bit unreachable."

"Same for me." Grace nodded. "There were things I should have been panicking about, but I just felt … calm."

Emma's face went pale. "They're already running the suppression protocol. And if they're doing it on us, they're doing it on everyone."

"That's why we need to get out. The longer we stay, the more they will turn up the signal. Soon, we won't even *want* to leave." Grace's voice was firm and steady.

Seph reached into his jacket pocket and pulled out the small glass jar Claire had given him. The powder inside seemed to glow in the evening light. "We'll take this when we're about to leave tomorrow." He placed the jar carefully on the table. "Maybe it won't just calm our vitals but also block the emotional signals they are sending."

Grace picked up the jar, studying it closely. "This is … old. Pre-update formula. Where did James get this?"

"He didn't say," Seph replied. "But it worked for me before, almost immediately. It lasted about twelve hours."

Seph looked around the room, meeting each person's eyes in turn. "We leave tomorrow night. We'll meet here after our shifts. One backpack each—essentials only. No halophones, no trackers. Once we're out, we're ghosts."

"This is it, then. We either make it out tomorrow, or we don't make it out at all." Grace sighed, running a hand through her hair.

No one spoke after that. The air was too heavy, the stakes too high. One by one, they began to pack away the maps, the scattered supplies. Seph lingered for a moment, staring down at the routes they highlighted on the map.

He walked Emma to the door, his hand resting lightly on her shoulder. "Get some rest," he said quietly. "Tomorrow's going to be ... a lot."

Emma nodded, her voice barely above a whisper. "You too."

When the door finally closed behind her, Seph let out a shaky breath and tried to calm his breathing again. He packed a small bag and brushed his teeth and tried to settle into bed. As he lay there, he thought of all the things he needed to do the next day, but he fought the urge to get up, he knew he needed sleep.

The room was cold. Seph could feel the faint draft against his skin as he stood at the edge of a massive theater. Rows upon rows of plush red seats stretched endlessly in every direction, each one occupied by a figure silhouetted against the pale glow of the screen. Above them, gilded letters shimmered in the dim light spelled: KINGDOM

The title on the screen pulsed gently, casting a golden hue over the faceless audience. The air was thick, heavy with the faint scent of stale popcorn.

Seph wasn't sitting. He stood in the narrow aisle, his breath shallow, his chest tight with urgency. The screen was playing something—vast landscapes of green fields and perfect skies, smiling faces, and voices speaking in warm, reassuring tones. It looked peaceful, idyllic even, but Seph's gut twisted with unease.

He began moving, weaving through the packed rows of people, his voice trembling as he spoke: "What day is it? What time is it?"

No one responded. Some faces turned slightly toward him before snapping back to the screen, their expressions slack, almost lifeless. Others waved him away dismissively, as though he were an insect buzzing in their ear.

He leaned closer to an older man in the front row, gripping the edge of his seat. "Please—what day is it? Do you even know where you are?"

The man's lips twitched, forming a ghost of a smile. "It's always today," he muttered, his voice hollow, before turning his head back toward the golden glow of KINGDOM.

Seph stumbled backward, his breath coming in shallow, uneven pulls as he scanned the endless crowd. There were hundreds of them—maybe thousands—eyes glazed over, lips parted slightly as if drinking in every flicker of light from the screen.

A child no older than six turned in their seat and looked at Seph with wide, questioning eyes. The little girl tugged at her mother's sleeve, pointing at him. But the mother shook her head slowly, her gaze never leaving the screen.

"Don't you care?" Seph's voice cracked, his hands trembling as he addressed the faceless crowd. "Don't you want to know what's really happening out there? Don't you care what's outside this theater?!"

His voice rose, echoing through the cavernous space, but no one flinched. No one answered.

The film on the screen shifted—it was too bright now, the colors oversaturated, the smiles too sharp. The music swelled, drowning out Seph's voice with saccharine orchestration.

"Listen to me!" Seph screamed, his voice breaking. "You have to look away! Just for a second! Please!"

The crowd responded in unison this time. A low, soft hiss of "Shhhhhh...." washed over him, like wind rustling through dead leaves.

Seph froze. The sound felt alive, crawling over his skin and tightening around his throat. The golden light from the screen intensified until it filled the entire theater. It was blinding now, scorching his retinas.

"Stop!" he shouted, shielding his eyes.

The light roared like a wave crashing against him, swallowing his voice, his body—everything.

Seph woke with a sharp gasp, his chest heaving, sweat dripping down his temples. His halophone buzzed faintly on the nightstand, its pale blue light casting strange shadows across his bedroom. He sat up, clutching the edge of the mattress as he tried to steady his breathing.

Why does no one want to find the truth? The thought was a blade, sharp and clear in his mind.

Because the truth was uncomfortable—it was messy, uncertain, and required effort.

The theater was safe. Warm. Predictable.

Seph buried his face in his hands, his shoulders trembling—not from fear, but from something heavier. A sadness so deep it felt like it was hollowing him out from the inside.

He couldn't save them. No matter how hard he tried, how loud he shouted, most people would choose the golden glow of KINGDOM over the harsh light of reality.

35

Seph

Seph walked alongside Emma through NexTech's sprawling glass atrium. It was there last day at work. Their last day of pretending. Employees moved around them quickly, their steps mechanical.

Seph's shirt collar felt too tight around his neck. He glanced sideways at Emma. She walked with her head high, her expression composed, but he could see the tension in her shoulders, the slight tremor in her hands. They were both pretending. Every word, every gesture, every glance was choreographed. The weight of their plan pressed heavy on Seph's chest, but there was no turning back now.

"Are you ready?" Emma asked as they approached the security gates.

Seph forced a smile. "As ready as I'll ever be."

They scanned their wrists under the glowing arches, the faint chime of their nano chips being authenticated. The security gate slid open and they stepped inside, blending seamlessly into the crowd of employees funneling toward their respective floors.

But Seph felt every camera, every drone, every pair of eyes fixed on them.

The interview setup was pristine—a sterile, white room with cameras mounted on every corner, soft lighting casting a flattering glow on their faces. A NexTech banner hung behind the chairs where Seph and Emma now sat side by side.

Lena stood off to the side, her arms crossed, her sharp gaze fixed on them. A technician adjusted the microphones clipped to their collars while another fiddled with the camera angles.

"Relax," Lena said, her tone clipped but even. "You both represent NexTech's resilience, confidence. Remember that."

Emma's smile was frozen, tight around the edges. Seph tried to mirror it, but his stomach churned.

The interviewer entered, an overly polished man with a perfect haircut and an enamel NexTech pin on his lapel. He introduced himself as Kyle, his smile practiced.

"Seph, Emma—it's wonderful to have you both here today," Kyle said, settling into his chair. "The two of you will become quite the symbol of NexTech's commitment to unity and progress."

"Thank you, Kyle," Emma said smoothly. Her voice was steady, but Seph could see the slight rigidity in her shoulders.

Kyle launched into his script—questions about their experiences at NexTech, how they felt during the recent "incident," and what their hopes were for the company's future.

Emma spoke first, her words careful and measured, painting a picture of optimism and gratitude. Seph followed, his answers just as rehearsed, just as hollow.

"And of course," Kyle said with an overly charming smile, "everyone wants to know—how's the relationship going? You two seem like such a perfect pair."

Seph froze for a split second, but Emma squeezed his hand lightly under the table—a warning, a lifeline.

"It's going great," Seph said, forcing a laugh. "Working here together has been amazing. NexTech feels like home, and Emma makes it feel even more so."

Emma smiled, and the cameras captured it, but Seph could see the cracks behind her eyes. Every word felt like glass splintering on his tongue.

The interview wrapped up shortly after, Kyle's smile never faltering as he shook their hands and congratulated them on their "inspiring" relationship. As soon as the cameras stopped rolling, Seph felt like he could breathe again—but the weight in his chest remained.

Claire approached them as the crew began packing up equipment. "Good work. That will go a long way." Her sharp eyes flicked between them. "And good luck."

"Thank you," Seph said.

Seph followed Emma out of the studio, his pulse pounding in his ears.

A few moments after they made it back to their desks the overhead lights dimmed slightly, and the haloscreens around the office flickered. Conversations died out as President Walker's face filled every screen. His expression was calm, polished, and utterly cold.

"Good Afternoon, NexTech Family. I wanted to thank each and every one of you for your hard work. With the recent attack on NexTech, your hard efforts brought back public safety and societal stability quicker than we even knew possible. We were tested and

you all rose valiantly. We are strong, and stronger together. "

The words settled over the office like a blanket of frost.

"We have some exciting new initiatives we will be rolling out very soon, including chips for everyone over five years old. As a way to prepare and thank you for your efforts, I will be on campus tomorrow and look forward to showing my appreciation in person."

Seph could feel Emma's gaze on him from across the floor, her eyes wide. And then they both felt it, a calm came over them. Seph even felt like it would be nice to see President Walker tomorrow.

Seph clenched his fists under the desk, begging the calm suppression to go away. They had to get out before it was too late.

* * *

The cafeteria was unusually quiet for midday. Employees sat huddled together, their eyes glued to the haloscreens mounted on every wall. President Walker's face covered the screens in between looping corporate announcements.

Seph carried his tray to the far corner of the cafeteria, where Grace and Callum were already seated. Emma slipped in beside him, her tray untouched.

For a moment, they sat in silence. No one wanted to be the first to speak. Around them, the low murmur of employees filled the air, but it all felt distant—like background noise in a fading dream.

"We're still on track," Callum said quietly, his voice barely above a whisper. His sharp eyes darted around the cafeteria, scanning for nearby listeners.

"My work has been wrapping up nicely today." Grace

nodded, her face resolute.

"Hey, why don't you guys each try my drink?" Seph said holding out a bottle of soda.

"What is it?" Grace asked.

"Something that will help you think clearly," Seph said "It's really good. A bit of a celebration considering President Walker will be here tomorrow."

Grace nodded, understanding what Seph was saying. He'd put James's powder in the soda because he felt the apathetic signals already beginning. They each took a big swig.

"Is that enough you think?" Callum asked, handing the bottle back to Seph.

"For good measure let's each do one more." Seph took another sip and passed it around.

"Hey, do you guys want to play a game of flashlight tag tonight?" Seph asked.

"I'm in," said Callum.

"Same," said Grace and Emma in unison.

"Callum, you want to pick the spot?" Seph asked, looking him in the eyes.

"Yeah, I've got two ideas where we could have a good time. Maybe we can meet up at your place and pick between them?"

Seph knew that everyone was ready. Grace had what they needed and Callum had found two routes that should be safe for their escape. They continued eating in silence. When they finally stood and parted ways, Seph felt the finality of it settle deep into his bones. This was it.

As he sat at his NexTech workstation for the last time, Seph felt every tick of the clock, every second crawling past. Each movement, each glance, each exchange felt like walking across a frozen lake, the ice creaking and splintering beneath his feet.

When the day finally ended, Seph stood up, and walked to the elevator without looking back.

36

Emma

The sun was already beginning to set by the time Emma turned the key in the lock and pushed open the front door of her family home. The familiar creak of the hinges echoed in the quiet entryway, and the smell of her mother's lavender candles lingered in the air. For a brief moment, she stood still, letting the illusion of normalcy wash over her. It felt fragile, like glass balanced on a knife's edge, ready to shatter with the lightest push. "Tucker?" she called as she closed the door behind her.

A shuffle of footsteps came from upstairs, and moments later, Tucker appeared at the top of the staircase. His expression was sharp, alert—he looked older than his fourteen years in the dim light.

"We're leaving tomorrow," Emma said.

"I've already packed a bag. Not much, just clothes, snacks, and a first-aid kit."

Emma's chest ached as she reached out and squeezed his shoulder. "Good. We're going to finally be somewhere safe, Tuck."

He looked up at her, his wide, brown eyes filled with something heavy—trust, fear, and something else that made her want to break down right there.

"Are they coming with us?" he asked, his voice barely above a whisper.

Emma paused as she glanced toward the living room, where the faint flicker of a haloscreen illuminated the walls. Her parents were in there, she knew it. Watching another of Walker's speeches or one of NexTech's curated broadcasts.

"I don't think so," she said honestly. "But I have to try one more time."

Tucker nodded and gripped the backpack straps tightly.

Emma leaned down and pressed a kiss to the top of his head. "I promise," she said.

Tucker turned and disappeared back up the stairs, leaving Emma standing in the silence of the entryway. She took a deep breath, straightened her shoulders, and walked into the living room.

Her parents were sitting side by side on the couch. Her mother's hands were wrapped tightly around a cup of tea, her knuckles white. Her father sat stiffly, his elbows propped on his knees as he stared intently at the haloscreen. Walker's face filled the display, his calm and calculated voice washing over the room:

"The nano chip isn't just about safety—it's about order, about peace. We cannot let the selfish actions of a few endanger the stability we've worked so hard to build. Compliance isn't a choice; it's a duty."

Emma cleared her throat, and her father's head snapped up. Her mother blinked slowly, turning her head toward Emma with an expression so vacant it made Emma's skin crawl.

"You're home," her father said, rising to his feet. "Are you alright? Did anything happen on your way here?"

"I'm fine, Dad, I was at a friend's house," Emma said carefully. "But we need to talk. Right now."

Her father hesitated, glancing at the haloscreen. Walker's face still glowed in the corner of the room.

"Can we turn that off?" Emma asked, her voice firmer this time.

Her father sighed but grabbed the remote and powered down the screen. The silence that followed was deafening.

"What is it, Emma?" her mother asked, her voice distant, like she was speaking from far away.

Emma swallowed hard and clenched her hands at her sides. "I need you both to listen to me. Really listen. I know you think everything is going to be okay—that if we just follow the rules and stay quiet, everything will go back to normal. But it won't. You have to see that."

Her father's brows furrowed, and he crossed his arms over his chest. "Emma, we've been through difficult times before. NexTech has always stabilized things."

"It's not the same this time!" Emma's voice cracked, and she took a shaky breath. "They're forcing people back into the system. They're controlling emotions now, Dad. They're taking away the *choice* to feel, to doubt—anything that might make people question what's happening."

Her mother's gaze remained dull, unfocused.

"Emma," her father said, his voice low, almost pleading. "Everything is going to be all right. I was worried too, but the more I watch Walker, and the more I think about all the good. Those concerns have faded. It's so much safer now."

"Dad…" Emma shook her head, tears gathering in her eyes. "That calmness isn't yours."

Her father paused and looked away.

Emma turned to her mother, her voice softer now. "Mom … please. Please tell me you see what's happening. Tell me you feel it too."

Her mother's lips trembled slightly, and for a split second, Emma thought she saw something flicker behind her tired eyes—a spark of recognition, of understanding. But then it was gone.

"I'm just … so tired, Emma," her mother said, her voice trembling. "I'm tired of being afraid. I feel better."

Emma's stomach dropped. The suppression algorithm was working. It was already working on her mother, dulling her fear, erasing her doubts. It wasn't her mother's fault, but the realization still hit Emma like a punch to the chest.

"Mom, that's not real. It's not you," Emma said softly, tears spilling down her cheeks.

Her mother looked away, her gaze fixed on the dark screen of the haloscreen.

"I can't leave," her father said firmly. "She won't make it out of the city."

Emma wiped the tears from her face and stepped back, her voice trembling. "You're wrong. And I'm so … so sorry, but I can't stay here and watch everyone turn into robots."

Her father's face crumpled slightly, but he said nothing. Her mother simply stared ahead.

Emma turned and walked upstairs, her steps slow and heavy. She found Tucker sitting on his bed, clutching his backpack against his chest. His eyes were red, like he'd already been crying.

"Are they coming?" he asked delicately.

Emma shook her head. "No, Tuck. They're not."

"Okay." Tucker nodded slowly, his face pale and serious.

She crossed the room and sat down beside him, pulling him into a tight hug. He clung to her, his small frame trembling in her arms.

"I'm going to keep you safe," she whispered into his hair. "I promise."

They sat there for a long moment, the quiet of the house pressing in around them. Finally, Emma pulled back and looked him in the eyes. "Are you ready?"

Tucker nodded. "Yeah. I'm ready."

When Emma walked back downstairs, her parents were still sitting on the couch. Her father stared at the dark screen, his face hollow and distant. Her mother had fallen into a deeper trance. Emma paused at the bottom of the stairs, clutching Tucker's hand tightly.

"This is your last chance," she said, her voice barely above a whisper. "Please."

But neither of them responded.

Emma felt heavy as she turned toward the door, her fingers squeezing Tucker's hand as they stepped outside into the cool night air. The door closed behind them with a soft click, and Emma forced herself not to look back.

They walked down the driveway in silence, the city lights painting the horizon ahead of them. Tucker's backpack bounced lightly against his shoulders with each step.

"Are they going to be okay, Em?"

"I hope so." Emma took a shaky breath and squeezed his

hand tighter. "We have to focus on us today, then we can figure out how to help them once we are safe."

They disappeared into the night, leaving the warm glow of their family home behind them. The street was quiet, the distant hum of drones the only sound breaking the stillness.

Emma didn't let herself cry again until they were far enough away that the house was just a faint silhouette. And even then she kept walking, toward freedom—fragile and distant as it felt—it was still within reach.

37

Seph

The city was draped in shadow when Seph stepped through the apartment door and locked it behind him. He opened his backpack and went through the contents one more time. He had everything he needed: several changes of clothes, two water bottles, a couple of protein bars, and a small flashlight. "Is everyone ready, no turning back?" Seph asked.

No one spoke, but they all nodded. Tucker tightened his grip on the strap of his bag, his knuckles white.

Callum walked over to the coffee table and spread the map out one last time. "Alright, let's go over this before we head out."

The group huddled around the map, which had key locations marked out with faint red lines and circles.

"This is our route," Callum began, pointing to the southern edge of the city map. "The last stop at the transpo will put us out by Stonecrest High School. Once we hit the river access point, we'll take the maintenance catwalk along the edge. It's exposed, but it keeps us out of any checkpoints or heavy drone patrol zones."

He traced his finger along the map. "The walking path here," he tapped a small red circle, "is where we'll need to be the most careful. If there's drone activity, we wait it out. No risks. But this is the point when it will be the most obvious we are leaving the city."

"How far is the outpost from here?" Grace asked.

"It's here." Seph tapped a point, this is the closest one from that exit. "Old relay tower. Once we get there, we will have somewhere inside to stay and wait for Duke to arrive. Hopefully they already have the radio there and we won't be waiting long."

"What about backup routes?" Emma asked

"There aren't any," Callum said bluntly. "This is it."

Silence followed his words, each of them letting the reality sink in.

One route. One chance.

Seph interjected. "We can do this. We have to."

Seph glanced around the circle, at each face lit by the pale glow of the lamp—Grace's sharp determination, Callum's steady resolve, Tucker's fragile courage, and Emma's quiet strength. He reached out, placing his hand flat on the map. "We stick together. No matter what happens, we don't split up."

Everyone nodded, their hands slowly joining his over the paper map, their small pact unspoken but deeply felt.

* * *

The night wrapped around them like a blanket as they slipped out of the apartment building. Seph led the group toward the transpo, his steps careful but purposeful. Tucker walked just behind him, Emma's hand lightly on his shoulder. Grace and Callum brought up the rear.

It took twenty-three minutes to make it to the stop they targeted near the edge of the city.

"Alright, this is us," Seph said.

"Who's gonna win?" Callum said as he turned on his flashlight and leaned into their cover.

"Something tells me you are a little more competitive than the rest of us." Grace laughed.

They stepped onto a side street and moved like shadows, slipping through narrow alleys and ducking under scaffolding. At one point, they paused behind an overflowing trash container as a patrol drone glided overhead, its red sensor light sweeping methodically across the alley, logging nano chips it sensed in the area.

Seph held up a hand, and everyone froze. Tucker squeezed his eyes shut, his small frame trembling slightly against Emma's side.

The drone hovered for what felt like an eternity before moving on, its red light fading into the night. Seph let out a silent breath and gestured for the group to move.

"Do you think it saw us?" Tucker asked

"It probably picked up our nano chips, but at this point we haven't done anything it would have to report," Grace said.

"I can't wait till we are out of the city and can take these nano chips out," Emma said.

"There are things I am going to miss about mine," Callum added.

Seph clapped Callum on the back. "Let's keep moving."

They crept forward, sticking to the shadows, their breaths coming in short, sharp bursts. Every corner they turned felt like stepping onto thin ice, every shadow a potential threat.

"Right there, that's the river access point we are looking for," Callum said excitedly.

"Okay, so the maintenance catwalk should be close," Seph said.

"Yeah this way," Callum instructed the group. Seph was amazed at his friend's sense of direction.

"I guess your *Call of Duty* skills have actually come in handy," Seph joked.

"Who would have ever guessed that?" Grace added, laughing.

They reached the maintenance track that followed the outskirts of the city. It was darker where they were as the city center was dimming with every step.

"I think we can pick up speed. I am not seeing any drones in any direction." Callum looked around in the sky.

"Good, we needed some good fortune tonight," Seph replied.

"You guys good to jog?" Callum asked.

"You bet!" Tucker said enthusiastically.

"Anything to get out of here quicker," Emma added.

Seph looked at the group and saw they were all sweating. "Let's drink some water first, then we can pick up speed without anyone falling into dehydration."

"Dang, another reminder of how I'm missing my halophone. I can't check my hydration levels," said Callum.

"Get used to it, I don't think you'll have it back anytime soon," said Grace.

They all took gulps of water and reset for a few minutes,

taking in the silence.

"Ready?" Callum asked.

"Ready!" they said in unison.

Callum set the pace and they all followed in single file. Seph pulled up the rear making sure no one fell behind unseen in the dark. His breathing had started to get heavier and he wanted to stop, but he focused on slowing down and reminded himself to keep putting one foot in front of the other.

"How much farther?" Grace strained.

Callum slowed and they all formed a circle as they panted.

"We might need to slow down a bit," Seph said. "Have you been working out?"

"Yeah, I started running every day when I wasn't having luck applying for jobs," Callum said. "But I think we're close, I think the walking path we are looking for is about a quarter of a mile up."

"Let's check the map, just to be safe," Grace said.

Seph pulled it out of his backpack and Emma pointed the flashlight at it.

"See, we are right here." Callum pointed to a spot on the route. "We just passed that old vacant manufacturing plant you see here, and so we should literally be about five hundred yards from the path that we will take to cross the city limits."

"Wow, this is getting exciting," Tucker added.

"I think we should push through," Seph said. "I know the rest of us are wiped, but I want to keep moving. I don't want to get this close and then get caught."

"Okay, let's go, we got this," Callum said, encouraging the group.

They slowly jogged in the direction Callum had suggested. Seph pulled out his flashlight to see if there was a path.

"It should be right here," Callum said.

But there wasn't anything there, just thick and overgrown bushes that would be hard to trek through. They all turned on flashlights and started looking.

Seph walked a few feet away from the group and spotted the flicker of something silver.

"Over here. I think this might be it."

His flashlight found the metal that had caught his eye. He used his hand to dust off a sign that read: *"Burke Trail."*

"Good find!" Callum said.

"I guess your calculations were off." Grace gave Callum a friendly elbow.

"You guys ready to leave the city?" Seph asked.

"Ready as I'll ever be," replied Callum.

"Let's do this," Emma added.

They turned their flashlights off and stepped onto the old walking path that led them out of the city. It was nearing dawn when they finally stumbled upon the old relay tower. The structure loomed out of the fog, its rusted metal frame creaking faintly in the breeze. The base of the tower was surrounded by cracked concrete and overgrown weeds, the remnants of a world that had been left behind.

"This is it," Seph said, his voice hoarse from exhaustion.

The group made their way over to the concrete base of the tower.

"Do we have to climb up?" Tucker asked.

"No, there should be a door to get inside," Grace said.

They circled around and found a locked door.

"If your aunt was here, wouldn't she have made sure the door was open?" Emma said.

Seph shook the door and felt along the edges to see if there was a way to grip it.

"Maybe she left a key nearby?" Seph said.

"I'm starting to feel weird," Grace said, sitting down.

Seph looked at his friends and realized they were all exhausted, but there was something else in their eyes. "I think James's medicine is starting to wear off."

"We need to get these chips out, now," Emma said, looking at Grace.

"No, we have to call for help first," Grace said. "If not, and my equipment sets off an alarm, they will bring us right back into the city and put new nano chips on, and wherever Ava is, is where we will end up."

"Okay, everybody focus, breath deep and slow, think logically, and without relying on your emotions. We want to leave the city. We need to find the key into this tower," Seph instructed.

"Hey, why don't you guys rest for a minute? I can run around and look for the key," Tucker said. "Remember, I don't have that junk in my arm, so I'm still feeling myself."

"Hurry, Tuck," Emma said as she ate a protein bar. "I don't want to turn into a mindless drone."

Seph watched as Tucker lifted up rocks and pulled at the brush around the tower. Every moment that passed, Seph cared a little less if he actually found the key.

"Hey!" Tucker shouted.

The group all looked up.

"It looks like there is a rusty window over here I can crawl through if you give me a boost."

The group got up, looking around.

"You guys all feel it too?" Grace said.

"Yeah, I'm starting to feel okay if we don't make it out,"

Emma said.

"Girls, stay here and keep hydrating. Callum let's give Tucker a boost," Seph said, walking over to the other side of the tower. He knew he just had to think logically. He could get through this.

"How did we miss this?" Callum said, looking at the clear opening above his head.

"Well, it's not like we are in our right minds." Seph laughed and Callum joined him.

"Let's go, give me a lift," Tucker urged.

Callum and Seph each bent down, allowing Tucker to stand on their knees. Then they grabbed his legs and hoisted him up. He reached his hands on the opening.

"A little more…"

They lifted a few more inches and he was able to pull his body up. They heard him fall on the other side.

"Open the door if you can!" Seph shouted.

A few seconds later they heard the metal from the door scraping open and Tucker's head popped out with a smile. "That was fun!" he said.

Seph and Callum walked inside. Seph turned his flashlight on and right there to the side of a desk was a radio that looked just like the one he'd used at The Refuge.

"Is that it?" Emma asked.

"It's gotta be," Seph said.

"Do we really need to use it?" Grace said.

"Clearly we do," Emma said.

"I think I need to take a nap." Grace sat down in the corner.

"I wonder why it is affecting people differently?" Callum asked.

"It's because they're sending a blanket signal to everyone,"

Grace explained. "One level to all, but they didn't have time to realize that each person would be affected at different levels."

Seph was busy turning on the radio and setting it to the channel he remembered using with James. "Hello, June, can you hear me?"

Static.

He adjusted the volume dial, his fingers trembling. "Duke, Riley—this is Seph. We made it to the tower. Please respond."

More static.

Seph wasn't sure what they would do if they were out of radio distance. Then, through the crackling static, a voice broke through:

"Seph? It's Riley. We're an hour out from that location. Stay put. Keep quiet. We're coming."

The line went dead, but the relief in the room was palpable. Seph sagged against the desk, his breath leaving him in a shaky exhale. He just hoped they could all hold on for an hour. They needed Grace for this next part.

Emma held Tucker close, her chin resting on the top of his head. Grace sat cross-legged, her head resting against the wall. Callum stood at the door, watching out for any sign of life.

Seph closed his eyes briefly, exhaustion pulling at every muscle in his body.

They were almost free.

38

Seph

The room felt impossibly still, there was a thickness to the air that felt heavy, as though the world itself was holding its breath. Seph sat near the doorway at the base of the relay tower, his back pressed against the cold concrete wall, his eyes trained on the distant horizon. Every creak of the rusted tower above them, every faint sound of wind through the trees, pulled his eyes' attention.

Then, faintly at first, Seph heard it—the low growl of an engine cutting through the stillness. He scrambled to his feet, his breath catching in his throat.

Callum turned sharply, his silhouette framed by the pale light outside. "They're here," Callum said.

The distant glow of headlights appeared over the crest of the hill, two bright beams cutting through the gloom. The rumble of the truck's engine grew louder, vibrating through the concrete floor beneath them. For a single, terrible moment,

Seph wondered if it was a NexTech patrol, if this was how it ended. But then he saw it—the unmistakable shape of Duke's cargo van.

The vehicle skidded to a stop just outside the building, gravel spraying in all directions. The passenger door flung open, and Riley jumped out, his hair wild, his face etched with exhaustion. "Move!" Riley barked. "Let's go!"

They spilled out of the station in a tangle of limbs and bags, the weight of their exhaustion threatening to drag them down. Duke was in the driver's seat, his weathered face illuminated by the faint glow of the dashboard lights. His sharp eyes scanned each of them as they climbed into the empty space in the back of the van, one after another.

"Get in, we want to move away from this outpost as quickly as possible," Duke said, his voice firm.

Seph helped Tucker climb in first, his small backpack clutched tightly against his chest. Emma followed, her hand trembling as she gripped the metal edge of the van door. Grace and Callum jumped in after, and finally, Seph hoisted himself up and pulled the door shut.

The van lurched forward, gravel crunching under the tires as Duke gunned the engine. They jerked with the movements of the road, the city shrinking in the distance behind them.

"Now?" Seph turned to Grace.

"Now." Grace nodded, her face pale but resolute.

From her bag, she pulled out a small metal device—a crude, handheld tool with wires and blinking lights. She met each person's gaze, her voice steady but trembling slightly. "This is going to hurt. A lot."

Seph nodded and rolled up his sleeve, exposing the small, faint scar where his nano chip had been implanted. Grace leaned in, her fingers trembling slightly as she positioned the device over his arm.

There was a sharp hiss, followed by searing pain. Seph bit down on his lip, his vision blurring as he felt something being pulled—extracted—from deep within his arm. For a split second, he swore he could feel the chip fighting back, resisting.

And then it was gone. A tiny, metallic fragment dropped into Grace's hand, still faintly glowing with residual energy. Seph sagged back against the side of the truck, his breath coming in ragged gasps.

"Who's next?" Grace asked.

"Me…" Emma said, sticking out her arm.

A moment later the same sharp hiss was made followed by a gasp from Emma.

"Are you ok?" Tucker said, comforting his sister.

"Much better now," Emma said.

Callum stuck out his arm and Grace repeated the process. Each extraction left them pale and trembling, but lighter somehow—like a weight they hadn't realized they'd been carrying had been lifted.

Finally, Callum took the device from Grace's shaking hands. "Your turn," he said.

Grace hesitated, her lips pressed into a thin line, before rolling up her sleeve. Callum worked carefully, his brow furrowed in concentration. When Grace's chip was finally removed, she collapsed against the back of Duke's seat, her head resting on her knees.

"So they didn't detect anything, right, Grace?" Seph said as he looked out the back window.

"No, they would have already been here if they did," Grace

said, still breathing heavily.

* * *

The wind howled around them as the tower disappeared entirely, swallowed by the dense forest ahead. The van bounced and jolted over uneven roads, the sound of branches scraping against the sides filling the air. Seph sat with his knees pulled to his chest, his eyes locked on the horizon. Emma was beside him, her hand wrapped tightly around Tucker's. Grace sat with her head bowed, her breathing shallow, while Callum kept watch over the rear of the truck, his silhouette rigid as he watched.

No one spoke. The roar of the engine and the rhythmic bouncing of the truck filled the silence.

After what felt like hours, Duke pulled the truck over into a clearing, killing the engine. The sudden silence was deafening, broken only by the faint chirping of birds somewhere in the trees.

"Stretch your legs, go to the bathroom," Duke said gruffly. "We'll head out again in ten."

Seph climbed out of the truck bed, his knees aching from the hours of sitting. The others followed, moving slowly, their exhaustion evident in every step.

Tucker, Callum and Grace were talking by the van when Seph noticed Emma, standing twenty yards away scanning the trees. He approached her, his voice low, "You okay?"

"I keep thinking about them. My parents. All those people who… who can't leave. Who won't leave." She shook her head, her eyes welling with tears.

Seph placed a hand on her shoulder, his voice calm. "We

could only save those who wanted to be saved. We got out and maybe someday, we'll be able to free others."

* * *

The faint outline of white smoke emerged from the tree line as the van moved into an open clearing. Ahead, Duke's camp, The Refuge, sprawled against the base of a mountain, smoke curling lazily from chimneys, the faint glow of lanterns casting warm light against wooden cabins.

As the van rolled to a stop, figures began emerging from the cabins—tired faces etched with worry, brightening with relief as they spotted the newcomers.

"*We made it*," Emma whispered beside Seph, her voice trembling with disbelief.

Seph stared at the camp. The weight on his chest eased slightly, replaced by something fragile but undeniable: *hope*.

But deep in his chest, Seph knew this wasn't the end. It was only the beginning.

"*We made it,*" Emma whispered again, interlacing her fingers in Seph's.

Seph nodded, his voice low and steady: "Yeah. We did." He closed his eyes and let the familiar tingly feeling wash up his arm from her palm.

Before he stepped toward what lay ahead, he let himself soak in the feeling of her hand in his, her choice.

About the Author

Anders Edwards grew up in Seattle but now calls Colorado home, where he lives with his spouse and three children. A lifelong daydreamer and lover of stories, Anders was captivated by tales of alternate worlds from an early age, with *The Giver* by Lois Lowry remaining his favorite book and a source of inspiration.

Now, with his debut novel *Erased*, Anders explores the "what-ifs" of the future, blending his love for dystopian fiction with thought-provoking questions about society, technology, and human resilience.

Join the reader list to stay up-to-date on future releases.

You can connect with me on:
🌐 https://andersedwards.com